SWEETHEART BRAVES

CROOKED ROCK URBAN INDIAN CENTER BOOK 3

PAMELA SANDERSON

Cover design by Holly Heisey (www.hollyheiseydesign.com)

Editor: Lorelei Logsdon, (www.loreleilogsdon.com)

Visit the author's website at www.pamelasanderson.com.

❀ Created with Vellum

Tommy led with the pink box, but the three Ind'n women who made up the rest of the staff were having none of it.

"You're late," Rayanne said, barely glancing up from her computer. She was the Crooked Rock employee most likely to volunteer for extra projects.

"I'm here now," he said.

Linda took the box. As the boss, she was as dedicated as Rayanne, but ten years into the job, her enthusiasm had worn down and she was frayed around the edges. She broke the tape and popped the box open. "What's your excuse?" she asked.

He could tell them about the funny shimmy his aging car had developed along with new sounds—a series of melodic chirps that Margie said sounded like someone practicing elk calls. Life was toast if the car died.

He could tell them about his roomie-cousin Angie, the practicing alcoholic he was supposed to help sober up, only she'd gone out the day before and hadn't returned.

If he really wanted to get personal, he could tell them he was tired and lonely, and living a life that consisted solely of working and maintaining his own sobriety, and the whole thing was a sad, monotonous hamster wheel that he couldn't exit.

He stuck with the truth. "I took Margie and her gang of elders to bingo. The ball blower malfunctioned, resulting in threats of a brawl. Margie gave me money to get pastries to calm them but it went long and I still had to take everyone home."

The final member of the staff, Ester, hovered close by. Her eyes widened when she looked in the box. "Is that an apple fritter?" She grabbed it and took a big bite and then swirled her hips a few times. *You're my favorite*, she mouthed at him. Ester's stated job duties involved health programs, but she fixed their computers, managed the center's social media, and could be counted on to cheer them up, as needed.

Rayanne got up and proceeded to cut a giant cinnamon roll in half with a plastic knife. "Excuse accepted."

He helped himself to a muffin and went to pour himself a cup of coffee.

Ester drifted over and caught his eye. In a low voice, she said, "Everything okay?"

Tommy flicked his eyes to the ceiling and barely shrugged.

"I worry about you," she said.

Tommy put a finger to his lips. She was the only one who knew about Angie. The fewer people who knew, the easier it was for him.

"Your secret is safe," she reassured him.

Linda finished chewing and thumped a fat file that was wrapped with big rubber bands. "We all need to get out of here so come sit down. We'll fill you in on what you missed. Today we finalize the Chief Building purchase so we can get on with our lives."

She talked him through her list. Rayanne had an important meeting, too, and Ester updated the funding situation. The three of them traded remarks in the foreign dialect of non-profits: soft dollars, cost sharing, indirect rates, set-aside funds. He formed what he hoped was an attentive expression, the whole time thinking about what he should do to find Angie.

The office phone rang and Rayanne grabbed it. She listened for a moment, then made some distressed sounds and did something at her computer.

Linda said, "New business. Tommy, I want you to go to the intake coordinator training with Ester."

"Me?" What did an intake coordinator do?

Linda nodded with special meaning. "Once we're in the new building, we're going to have to get this operation up to speed. When Ester goes to her film workshop, we'll have a big gap to fill."

"I don't know if I'll be accepted," Ester said.

Linda shot her a tired look. Ester was crazy talented. There was no way she wasn't getting accepted.

"I can do more," he said, hearing the lack of conviction in his own voice. Way back when Linda gave him the job, conveniently downplaying his shortcomings, they'd intended that he'd take on more responsibility.

Rayanne got off the phone. "That tribal youth meeting changed their agenda. They need our statement this afternoon."

Linda dropped her head into her hands and muttered a string of bad words.

"He has to," Ester said. "I can't ditch the budget talk."

Tommy had grown accustomed to them talking about him like he wasn't there.

"Can you do it?" Linda asked him.

"Sure," he said.

"You know your actual title is Youth Program Director," Rayanne said.

"I'm aware." Apparently he was unsuccessful at hiding his discomfort.

Linda faced him. "It is critical that we have someone there." Her voice had become strained like it did when she was overwhelmed. "If you can't do it, tell me now, and I'll invent cloning or something."

Out of sight, he could sense Rayanne reacting and Ester shutting her down.

"Don't say you can do it if you're not certain," Linda said.

"Do I have to do a talk?" he asked.

3

Linda smiled patiently. "You need to read a prepared statement. If anyone asks a question, write it down and tell them we'll get back to them. Is that okay?"

It did not sound okay but reading from a piece of paper was the least he could do. "Do I write the statement?"

"Already written," Linda said, handing over a packet. "Look it over and ask if you have questions."

"Take notes at the meeting," Rayanne said. "You can listen and take notes, right? It's literally the least you could do."

He was already doing literally the least he could do. He drove elders to appointments and organized afternoon basketball for native kids. He picked up supplies and dropped off packages that had to be shipped overnight. He was not the staff member who experienced joy when an agenda was put in his hands.

"I can help if you need it," Ester said.

Tommy gestured vaguely and flipped through the file.

Linda said, "Last item: Native Professionals is tomorrow night. We're all going together."

Tommy groaned. Networking event. He'd end up standing against the wall wearing a *Hello My Name Is* sticker and clutching a sweating plastic bottle of water while he watched the clock.

He mustered his most tragic look.

Linda sighed. "No one is forcing you."

He dipped one shoulder as if he would think about it but there was no way he was getting stuck at a networking event.

Rayanne and Ester packed up and zoomed out. Instead of following them, Linda pulled a chair next to him. "I worry about you."

"Did Ester say something?"

"She said you had a lot going on and she was concerned."

Tommy scraped a hand across his face. "Everything's fine."

"Okay. I trust you, and I want to keep trusting you, but you aren't acting like you right now." If there was anyone in his life he could confide in, Linda was it, but he didn't know where to start.

"You don't have to worry about me," he said.

2

*E*lizabeth sat in the truck, knuckles white on the wheel. The engine hummed reassuring and familiar. She'd ridden in that truck as a little girl on trips with Granny and Leo. Now it was supposed to be hers. One lap around the orchard and it was time to pull out to the highway.

"You can do it," Granny said, a hint of impatience in her voice.

Elizabeth took her time with a slow calming inhale and exhale. The gesture did nothing. If anything, it made her tingling nerves and heavy heartbeat more pronounced.

"I can, I just don't want to," she whispered.

The key was still attached to the lumpy keychain she'd made for her great-grandparents at culture camp, a cylinder of woven beargrass with leather fringe.

"You gonna be stuck here if you can't do it," Granny said.

"I know," she muttered. The rez was the easiest possible place to drive, the narrow roads familiar, none of those terrifying intersections or multi-lane freeways to navigate. But she still couldn't bring herself to move forward.

A loud engine, like a lawn mower on steroids, thundered up the driveway and George's red truck bounced into view. He'd bought it so everyone in town would notice him coming and going. Everyone knew when he came to see her.

"That one helping?" Granny asked.

"He thinks so," Elizabeth said.

They'd tried once, George in the passenger seat, coaching, only he never stopped talking: "You can go faster. No need to stomp on the brake. It's too early to signal." The rest of his attention he directed to his phone, laughing at texts he didn't share with her.

"He made me nervous," she said.

"That's what he's like," Granny said.

George leapt out of the truck, his arms spread wide, like he wanted to hug the whole world. "Thought you were waiting for me."

Elizabeth leaned out the window. "We've been waiting. Granny and I need to get to work."

"You haven't gotten far." He gave her a cocky smile.

"Let's go with him," Elizabeth said, shutting off the engine.

George took Granny's arm and led her to his truck. She wore a droopy yellow sweatshirt that said: *Don't mess with me, I'm an Elder* and white pants that emphasized her skinny stick legs. A fanny pack hung off her hip and she had on a pair of giant wraparound dark glasses.

Elizabeth rushed after her and held out her cane.

"People see my cane, they think I'm old," Granny complained. She struggled for a grip to pull herself up into the truck.

"Secret is out," Elizabeth said, while George gave her a boost.

Once they got going, George said, "I told you before, I can take you where you need to go."

"I'm going to drive eventually," she said, her voice salty.

"Me too," Granny said. She was ninety-two, had shrunk to less than five feet, with her eyes so weak she couldn't read the numbers on the remote control. She hadn't driven in years but Elizabeth's recent onset phobia made her threaten to try.

"The casino isn't far," Elizabeth said.

"Casino is no job for you," Granny said.

She'd just finished college and Granny acted like taking that job was a tragic blunder.

"It's marketing. Promoting the casino. You should love me in this job."

"You should go see something," Granny said, pointing at the world outside the vehicle.

"I like being home," Elizabeth said. The whole time she was away she was homesick for the rez. She almost quit college when Leo died but Granny made her promise to finish.

Their tribal casino was a small operation but it had plenty of machines and the restaurant served Granny's favorite hamburger. As soon they got her out of the truck, she made a speedy track to the entrance, hanging on to her fanny pack with her free hand so it wouldn't slide off her narrow hips.

George grabbed Elizabeth's wrist. "I meant that. You don't have to worry about driving."

She had history with George, the on-again, off-again boyfriend during high school. He'd made his interest clear once she'd come home but already she had clues of how it would go. While she was away he'd gone from job to job: construction, handyman, fishing boat. Sometimes a delivery job that sounded sketchy.

She slipped out of his grip. "I'll keep that in mind."

Inside, she found Granny busy 'at work' parked in front of a nickel machine, her players club card attached to a neon pink cord that spiraled out and linked her to the machine. The sunglasses had disappeared and she stared at the flashing lights. An incomprehensible series of images and bright lines flashed and the machine chimed. Granny expertly pressed a few buttons, and the whole thing started again.

Elizabeth went to the back office to finish her new employee orientation. When she returned, her cousin Kora showed off her tattoos for Granny. Kora smiled when she saw Elizabeth.

"You're home!"

"It's true." Elizabeth held up the fat envelope holding the paperwork that represented her future: personnel manual, benefits, schedule, retirement. "I'm a real grown-up now."

"Awesome. What did they say about the driving?"

"No one said anything about driving." A cold finger of nerves touched Elizabeth's insides.

"The marketing assistant drives up and down the river going to businesses and, I don't know, places along the coast."

The back of her neck grew damp and she put her hand there. She blinked her eyes a few times and said, "I'll figure it out." She might have to lean on George after all.

Kora gave her a hug that wasn't a tiny bit comforting. "Come on, I want to show you two something."

Granny refused to look at anything until they found her a booth at the casino restaurant and got her a coffee and hamburger.

"We're making bets," Kora said while she ate. "Before the end of the year, most people think."

"Before the end of the year, what?" Elizabeth asked.

"You and George."

Elizabeth shrugged. "I don't think George is the one."

Kora laughed. "That's not what you used to say."

Granny made an unhappy sound. "George is a leaky boat. Nice for now but eventually you gotta get out of that thing." She stuffed another French fry in her mouth.

Kora laughed. "He's ready to settle down." She said it as if it were her job to convince them.

"No rush," Granny said.

"I'm not in a rush," Elizabeth said. She didn't add that in a small town, there weren't many options. "What's this thing you're going to show us?"

"Historical exhibit we put together," Kora said. "Granny is in it."

After dinner Kora took them to a long hallway lined with photographs. The exhibit consisted of split photos, one historical next to a similar, but contemporary photo. Fishermen now and then, a tribal house next to a plank house, a collection of baskets together with young people gathering today. Granny paused over each set. She came to a blurry photo that showed three girls in dance regalia, their arms hooked together.

"That's me," Granny said, tapping the photo.

"Really?" Kora said, studying the photo more closely. "If that's true, we need to document it."

"*Pffffffffft,*" Granny said. "You don't know nothing."

The three girls had braided hair and loops of dentalium shells around their necks. They all smiled, two of them with their eyes on the camera and the third staring off at something else. Elizabeth squinted at the image and tapped on the third.

"That's you."

Granny nodded. It was hard to imagine Granny as a girl. When that picture was taken she had her whole life ahead of her, no clue what it would bring.

George found them again, stood too close, looked down at Elizabeth and winked.

Granny pointed to the modern photo, a dance skirt fixed in a display.

"I want to see it," she said.

"What?"

"The skirt. From the picture."

"The label says it's at a historical research center up north," Elizabeth said. "How would we get there?"

"We got Leo's truck."

Elizabeth dropped her hand to the churning nerves that leapt up in her belly.

"I can take you," George said.

Elizabeth cringed inside. "Granny, are you going to be comfortable sitting in a car all day?"

"I sit around at home. I can sit around in a car," Granny said.

"It's a great idea," Kora said. "You could interview her and take photos."

Elizabeth calculated what it would take to pull off such a trip, several days at least. She needed to report to work before then. "We don't have time. Too bad this didn't come up a week ago."

"We can do it in two days," George said. "Travel tomorrow. See the thing. Home by the weekend."

No one was talking sense.

Kora said, "I'll call them, so they know to expect you. Linda's up there. She can show you around."

They were going on a road trip.

*L*inda waited with Audra in the lobby of City Hall. The center's attorney wore one of her professional lady suits with properly hemmed slacks and matching jacket, plus shoes with real heels complemented by a stylish trench coat with wide lapels and big round buttons.

Linda slid a hand into the pocket of her raincoat. The ad had said the garment would travel well but after spending the winter floating around in her back seat, it looked like something dug out of a trash can. She carried the pocketknife Arnie left in the longhouse months ago, expecting to hand it back but never managing to do so. Now she was used to having it.

Audra pulled a compact from her bag and checked her lipstick. "You good?"

"My makeup or my life?"

Audra glanced back at her with a half-smile before snapping the compact shut. "Your situation."

She meant Arnie and their disastrous—what would you call it—disagreement? Misunderstanding?

"I'm anxious to get this thing over with and get on with my plans."

"You two are okay," Audra said, more as a confirmation than a question.

Linda shrugged with as much indifference as she could muster. They'd seen each other once since the unpleasantness at the big tribal leader conference a month earlier. They'd sat on either side of Audra at the first city action committee meeting and exchanged notes with complete civility.

"Define okay," Linda said.

"You haven't spoken to him again?"

"We traded emails. We're getting the work done." The situation was more complicated than that, but no sense in rehashing it right now when they were so close to securing the center's future.

In truth, Linda never stopped fretting about Arnie. Not so much concerns about being fired, at least not yet, but she couldn't bear the idea that he didn't trust her any longer. When he'd joined the executive board of the center, the two of them agreed to become a team. Now they were like people who were civil for the sake of the children.

"He's here," Audra said.

Linda's stomach flipped as he headed toward them. He wore a charcoal gray suit with a white shirt and a bolo tie. His face was expressionless, his hands empty. He had his fingers in tribal projects all over the place, yet he never carried anything. She did her best to ignore the fiery flash of unease, a reminder of a long history of charged interactions and jumbled feelings.

No smile. No greeting. "Just you two?" he asked.

"Did you want me to bring the staff?" He always seemed to expect her to guess what he wanted.

"No, this is fine," Arnie said, turning more agreeable. "We prepared?"

Audra pointed to the packet in Linda's arms. "UIC staff went over everything. I went over everything else. We're ready to be done with this thing. By the end of this meeting, we should have a solid timeline."

"Great," he said. "Just to be clear, I want to lead on this."

"Lead?" Linda said, trying to keep up with the shift.

"I don't want to dilute our message."

"Dilute it from what?" Linda said, annoyance creeping into her voice. "The deal is done. We don't need a firm hand. It's paperwork and formalities at this stage. Don't you trust me?"

As soon as she said it, she wanted to snatch it back. That word. Trust. Like she was daring him to talk about it.

Arnie exhaled audibly. He glanced at the ceiling, his lips barely moving, as if praying for patience. "I know you can handle it but I would like to take the lead." He put his hand on his chest and raised his eyebrows as if to say: *You want to challenge me on this?*

She did not.

She said, "If I may, my most critical item is the move-in date. Fall is a lot to hope for, but even if it's after the first of the year, I need to be able to map out my plans to increase the staff and budget for equipment and furniture. All these tribal leader talks I've been doing, I've been emphasizing how soon we will be functioning."

"I've heard your talks. We're on the same page, don't worry," he said, his tone friendly but the flash in his eyes said he still hadn't forgiven her.

A clerk brought them visitor badges and took them through the security station to a meeting room. Instead of the group they'd been working with, they were introduced to a city attorney and a blank-faced older guy with thinning hair who described himself as a facilities manager.

After an endless amount of routine chit chat, Arnie cleared his throat and said, "Shall we get down to business?" He nodded at Linda's stack of paper. "How shall we proceed?"

The older man steepled his fingers and tilted his head to the side as if he were hearing all this for the first time.

The attorney was about Arnie's age, with a rust-colored beard and a way of punctuating every remark with an over-loud chuckle. He leaned over his laptop and tapped with enthusiasm. "We're up to speed on the important points. Let's do this."

Arnie nudged Linda's paperwork and gave her a look.

"Did you want me to start?" she asked, injecting false warmth into her voice.

He tapped the corner of the documents again and gave her a conspiratorial smile as if they'd carefully plotted the course of this meeting and now he was counting on her to deliver. She smiled with her mouth but the look she shot him was pure acid.

At least she was prepared.

They worked through the list, checking off funding, inspections, title report, and the endless fine print. Audra was a saint for reviewing all that for them.

They got through everything, everyone in agreement as hoped. "The last piece is the timeline," Linda said. "Any chance we get in there by September?"

The city attorney kept his eyes on his computer, his index finger swiping across the trackpad. "Not sure about that. That's one item we haven't hit on yet. The city wants to hold off on the transfer for three years."

Linda couldn't help it, she gasped. She slapped her hand over her mouth. Audra patted her shoulder, not for comfort but as an order: *Keep your mouth shut.*

From the look on Arnie's face, Audra should have been patting him. A slow-boil fury seeped into his face.

"Why three years?" Arnie asked, carefully measuring out his words.

The older guy held up his hands as if their protests were unreasonable already. "Unavoidable. Plans for the building changed at the same time our people were negotiating with your group. We apologize for the inconvenience."

The non-apology was followed by an exaggerated shrug of innocence. *Nothing personal, just doing our jobs.*

Next to her, Arnie adjusted in his seat, every exhale an audible huff. Before the NATG blowout, she would have grabbed his arm, but with everything between them so uncertain she kept her hands folded in front of her.

The delay would doom them. She'd been sweet-talking funding out of tribal leaders and tribal organizations with the promise of what they could do. They couldn't do anything without a location.

The attorney tapped his computer a few more times before leaning back in his chair. "We're willing to make some concessions."

"Such as?" Linda asked.

"We could show you some alternate sites that would be available sooner."

"To buy or to lease?" They'd endured months of paperwork, inspections, and funding conferences to secure the Chief Building. Starting all over would be soul-crushing, but if the city could give them something decent to lease in the interim she could salvage this.

"Leasing would be less likely," the attorney said. His tone said he didn't know.

She reordered the documents to hide her disappointment and distress. If they had no place to go, they were back to dismantling the organization.

"May I say something?" Audra said, looking at Arnie. He nodded. "We weren't prepared for such a huge setback. We'll have to meet with the staff and board members and get back to you."

ARNIE HELD TOGETHER his professional demeanor by force of will, but he wanted to punch his fist through a wall. The city's indifference to this transaction was stunning, and this was one more disaster in an endless list of frustrations he was juggling at the moment.

The three of them returned their security badges in silence. Outside, the rain had stopped but the pavement was wet and the breeze cold and damp.

"What are we going to do?" Linda's voice had that wavering quality it got when she was upset. He had to find a way to avoid this conversation right now. He was wound too tight, and he couldn't risk whatever fragile collegial connection that remained between them.

"Three years," she continued. "No one is going to wait for us to scramble around for another three years. How do we get back to where we were?"

"I'm not happy either," he said.

"We need to respond to the situation we're in and give up trying to get back to a state that is long gone," Audra said. "They brought up concessions. Why don't we see what we can get for this inconvenience?"

That's what an attorney would hear: they could get something for their trouble. But all of Linda's hard work drumming up tribal partners was for nothing if she couldn't get her programs running.

"I share the concerns about losing supporters," Arnie said.

"Yes, that worries me," Linda said. "Our goal with the Chief Building was to expand. That's what I've been bargaining with to get tribes to increase their support."

"We're going to have to recalibrate," he said. "I'll try to come up with some ideas and send them to you later. I gotta get going."

"What about looking at the alternate sites?" Linda said.

Audra laughed. "If the city is getting rid of property, it's not because there's anything great about it. I wouldn't get my hopes up. You two talk it out and let me know what to do." She gave Linda a quick hug and took off, leaving them alone together, exactly what he'd hoped to avoid.

He'd tried and failed to sort out his feelings since their dust-up. His anger had lost its bite, but he wasn't ready to forgive either. Mostly he was perplexed by how he took the deception more personally than he should.

"My rig's over a few blocks. We'll be in touch," he said.

"I'm that way, too," Linda said, falling into step with him.

Innocuous small talk was one of his superpowers but with her at his side, his mind had gone maddeningly blank. If she spoke first, it would be something probing and heavy because she was the kind of person who insisted every rift had to be smoothed over, every disagreement needed closure. For half a block the only sound was their feet on the sidewalk, and if possible, the sound of her brain churning for a way into the conversation he was trying to escape.

Her steps slowed, and she said in a quiet voice, "Are we going to talk about what happened?"

"Which thing?" he said, his tone light. His rig was still a block away.

"The thing that happened, not *intentionally*," she said, drawing out that word. "I tried to tell you we swapped the film. You didn't respond."

They stopped at the corner for a red light. Traffic was heavy through downtown and he had to get to the east side for another meeting. Too many responsibilities stacked on top of each other.

He said, "I know you tried. The conference was busier than I expected. Regardless, it was disrespectful. We brought in someone to help and then blew off her work without warning."

That someone was Katie but he avoided her name.

The light changed, and Linda picked up the pace again. "I'm sorry it worked out the way it did. Everything happened so quickly. But, uh, what about the other thing?"

The letter. She'd sent the intent to sue letter, knowing he didn't approve. Going behind his back bothered him more than anything. "The city talked to us. You got what you wanted."

"What we all wanted."

"And look how that's turned out. Don't do it again." He could hear how he sounded, but he had too much on his mind to be apologetic.

"You want me to sit by the phone until you have time to tell me what to do?" she said.

"We agreed we weren't going to threaten to sue."

"*We* did not agree. That was a decision you made."

Here was the Linda he'd known for so long. She could take the tiniest disagreement and chew on it forever like there was always one last point she needed to make.

"I don't see any reason in arguing about it," he said. "Please. No more surprises."

"Agreed. No more surprises," she said. "New topic. What do you think about getting me in front of your council again? They are our biggest supporters. If we can get them in front of this possible three-year thing, we could leverage their support to keep everyone in."

He bit back his instinct to shoot the idea down. "You're not wrong."

"I'm not wrong?" She elbowed him in the side. "Those are generous words from you. I remember when we...shit."

"We shit?"

She pointed to her car, one corner of it tilted down.

"That is one flat tire." He wanted to make a joke of it, but not only did he have no time to change a tire, he'd have to do it on wet pavement.

"How does that even happen?" she said, more crushed than a person should be about a tire.

"You know how to do it?" he asked.

"Do I know how to change a tire?" she said.

Arnie took off his suit jacket, eyeing the ground. He'd changed tires in worse.

"You don't have to do this," she said. "I have one of those roadside services."

"You should know how to change a tire."

"Gee, I thought Dad was in California."

He held out his hand for the keys. "You have a spare, don't you?"

"Of course, I have a spare," Linda said. She didn't go for her keys.

"Even if you call a service they have to get out the spare. I don't mind doing it." He didn't know why he was arguing with her; she told him she didn't need help, but his mama hadn't raised him to walk away if a friend needed help with a flat tire.

Linda dug through her bag and handed him the keys.

He opened the trunk and let out a long whistle, finding himself strangely charmed by the woman's steady predictability. Linda had always been this curious juxtaposition of polished presentation in the front, complete disorganization in the back. Her trunk was loaded with...what? He pushed around the giant plastic bags and assorted boxes and set aside a plastic pouch of never-used chains that he was willing to bet didn't fit the tires. She had one, two, three laptop bags that bulged with a computer inside. "I don't even know what to say about this."

"I need to get to Donation Hut," she said, her mouth curled into a defensive scowl, "and I like to be prepared."

"That's what you're known for," he said with a sigh. He unlocked the car door and folded his jacket on the front seat. He went back and pulled a box out of the trunk and set it in the back seat. "Old musty files?"

Linda's eyes grew stormy. "Forget it." She grabbed her keys back. "I'm serious. Leave it. I'll deal with it."

"I don't mind changing a tire," he said. "You should at least have an idea how to do it in case of emergency."

He pushed items around in the trunk, hoping to avoid clearing out everything to reach the tire. There was a box of books, a bunch of shoes, a workout bag, towels. His look of dismay must have been evident because she shoved him aside and slammed the trunk shut.

"I said, I'll take care of it myself. I don't need you to fix *everything*." The last word twisted off bitterly.

He'd misread the situation, but where did he go wrong? "Sorry, Lulu. I—"

"Don't call me that." She held her hand up and gave him a look that would slay a grizzly. It wouldn't be a successful day if he didn't make a woman angry with him. He left her alone as she asked.

4

***

ommy printed a fresh copy of the statement and reread it. He practically had it memorized. Ester or Rayanne wouldn't have thought twice about accomplishing such a generic task, but the sweat made his hands slick and the place behind his knees damp. All just to read a statement. His path to sobriety had been going to meetings, so after all these years he had plenty of experience talking in front of people, but his nerves knew the difference between that and a work meeting. He'd carefully cultivated a career that didn't involve getting up and doing talks for people.

Ester had suggested he practice reading it aloud, but he felt stupid every time he tried. He stood up.

"Good afternoon. The Crooked Rock Urban Indian Center is a growing non-profit dedicated to developing programs for urban Indian youth."

He tried again, speaking more slowly, pausing at the end of each paragraph. He read it again, adding a bit of television newscaster inflection. By the fifth repetition, the words came easily.

He checked the meeting address once more and realized there was barely enough time to get there. He scooped up Linda's folder and hurried to his car. Another burst of rain had come through and the sidewalks were wet and puddled. The busy campus pathways thronged with students and bicycles. He sometimes picked out a random individual and tried to guess how long he or she would take to get a two-year degree. He'd taken three years and one quarter to get his AA since the transition from drinking to not drinking had taken place during that time.

His aging Toyota had been renamed the Crunch after an unfortunate bumper remodel. One corner dented in enough so that the trunk wouldn't stay shut without duct tape. An elder in a big pickup truck had backed into him at one of the youth basketball tournaments. The man had offered Tommy cash rather than make an insurance claim, and Tommy took it. He used some to pay his friend Cody, the mechanic, for non-body repairs. Another wad was rolled up and hidden in a flashlight next to his bed. Someday he was taking a road trip on mountain highway TBD. Cody kept trying to convince him to do enough bodywork to make the trunk operational, but the car ran so poorly Tommy didn't want to bother.

That morning, the car had huffed and rattled and didn't start until the third try. He was relieved when it started right up. He tended to see the quality of his life reflected in the worthiness of his vehicles. The center's Drivemaster, a 15-passenger bus, ran great, and his car kept going, patched together but able to get the job done. That meant he was doing okay. He needed the Crunch now more than ever. It was a place he could be alone, and he needed to feel like there was always an option.

An endless line of cars rolled through the parking lot, searching for parking. Someone spotted him and waited for him to pull out. The car shuddered and for a breath-taking moment went silent before catching again. He backed out and put the car in drive and tapped the gas. There was a long pause before the engine coughed. He hit the gas again and the car made a mournful sigh and sputtered out. "Let's go, Crunch," he whispered in his most reassuring voice. He tried to start it again.

The car didn't respond.

Someone honked.

He tilted his head to the side, listening for any signs of life. He twisted the key again, imagining that the repeated motion was warming the car up and he'd be on his way soon. No luck. For now, the Crunch was dead.

The waiting vehicle had already whipped into the spot he'd vacated. His dead car blocked traffic in the narrow row.

It wasn't like he was unfamiliar with this type of humiliation. He put the car in neutral and got out and pushed. The car wouldn't budge and it didn't take long for someone to be moved by the sorry sight. A couple of guys from a waiting car jumped out to help. The Crunch lurched forward. He kept a hand on the wheel.

"Where to?" one of them called.

There was no place to go. Every available inch of blacktop was either filled with a car or part of the narrow aisle that snaked through the lot. They kept pushing and he gamely steered forward. There was a white striped area next to a handicapped space.

"How about there?"

"Not going to work," Tommy said, but the car's momentum was headed straight for that spot. The guys gave one last push and then ran back to their car.

He jumped in the driver's seat and guided the vehicle as best he could, but it blocked part of the no parking zone and the walkway from campus to the parking lot. He got out and propped the hood open and thought through his options. Campus had an automotive program but the only person he'd ever spoken to was the guy who'd agreed to let him park the Drivemaster behind their main building. Perhaps they could help him with this emergency.

Then he checked the time. There was no way he could wait around for that. He'd promised Linda that he would get to the meeting. The Drivemaster was a pain to park. He'd have to take the bus. He grabbed the paperwork from the car and hurried back to the office, slotting this development into his long list of troubles. He'd expected to drive this car into the ground, but he didn't think it would happen this soon.

As he headed back to the office, he left Cody a voice message.

"Hate to bug you, but the Crunch died. I'm on campus. Can you get me a tow? I'll owe you one. Another one."

Linda had a stash of public transportation passes in her desk and he dug around until he found one. He got on the computer to make a transit plan. He was typing in the destination address when the phone rang.

"Crooked Rock," he said, his eyes never leaving the computer screen.

"I'm looking for Linda Bird?" someone asked.

"Not here. She'll be in tomorrow," Tommy said.

"Do you know where she is?" The caller had a sexy rasp to her voice and he pictured a woman with flowing hair driving near the beach in a commercial for a luxury car. He might have enjoyed the sound if he weren't so distracted by all the knives he was juggling.

"Meeting."

"Do you know how I can find her?"

Tommy opened another tab to search for a map detailing bus stops near campus. "Who is this?"

"I'm her niece."

"I've known Linda for a long time. She's never mentioned a niece." According to the trip planner, there was a bus stop on the other side of campus and he had ten minutes to get there. If the bus was early, he'd be stuck with the Drivemaster.

"She's my cousin. My mom and her mom are cousins."

"Ah, Indian country," he said.

"Rez life forever," she responded, then laughed. "Who's this?"

"One of her lackeys. I'll tell her you called," he said. "I gotta go. I'm on my way out the door."

"Tell her we're going to be there tomorrow. Me and Aunt Dotty."

"Your aunt is dotty?"

"Dorothy Scott," she said like he should know the name.

"Great. Who are you?"

"Elizabeth. We need a place to stay. I want her to expect us."

Tommy stood up. "She will be informed. Drive safely." He hung up the phone before Elizabeth with the sexy voice could ask any more questions.

He dashed out the door, back across campus and up the hill to the bus stop. A half-dozen other students waited, wearing backpacks or carrying books. Too late he realized he'd left the paperwork on the desk. He couldn't risk going back. He took an enormous head-clearing breath. The statement was barely three pages, he could remember that, right? He tried to picture the first few lines but his mind became a panicked blur.

The document had to be accessible from his phone. He scrolled through his email, hoping Linda or Ester had sent it to him.

The phone chirped, and a text message displayed.

U take me 2 meeting?

Angie.

After all the hassles and worries, *this* was the moment she chose to reappear. He wanted to yell at her or lecture her or say something about how uncool it was that she'd run off. But here she was and finally asking to go to a meeting.

You okay? I'm at work.

Take a break? I want to go to the native one.

Tommy ran a hand through his hair. The deep rumble of a bus engine sounded and his bus approached the stop. Since Angie had arrived, he'd managed to drag her to barely a handful of meetings. She had a long list of special requirements, disliking meetings that were too big, or located in church basements. She preferred not to speak. It was hard to be optimistic about her success.

The bus came to a stop and passengers filed off.

Yes or no, what to decide. Employment fail, or cousin's life?

Linda would be furious but if he went to her meeting, he wouldn't get home until after five. Any number of troubling things could happen to Angie in that time. If he blew off the tribal youth thing, he could use the Drivemaster and have Angie at the native meeting in an hour. Ditch one meeting for another meeting. She wanted to go. She was asking to go.

He texted her back: *On my way.*

5

_E_lizabeth should have predicted it. George didn't show and instead sent an apologetic text about being out on a boat, leaving her to scramble around for another ride. Kora came to the rescue and took them to the train station. The train ride had been uneventful, they made it to the city, and now they were in a rideshare headed for campus.

"We need the Indian Center," she told the driver.

"I don't know what that is," he said. "They have maps on campus. Someone will help you when you get there."

The rain came down in big gray drops that drummed across the windshield. Granny gazed out the window, her expression unreadable.

"We gonna stop for lunch?" she asked.

"We'll eat as soon as we find Linda," Elizabeth said.

"I'm hungry," she said.

"I heard you." Being in the car on the busy city streets had reanimated Elizabeth's nerves and shrunk her appetite to nothing.

There was another long stretch of quiet, other than the plinking rain and the dull drone of the tires on the wet road.

"What time did you tell Linda we would get here?" Granny asked.

"I didn't talk to Linda," Elizabeth said.

"She don't know we're coming?" Granny said, giving her a comic look of dismay.

"I talked to some guy on her staff," Elizabeth said.

"You didn't call her?"

"The cell number I had was wrong so I called her office. Okay?"

Granny made a disagreeable grunt and let it drop.

The rain remained steady. Muddy pools dotted the roadway. A sign with big block letters announced they'd arrived at the campus.

"Let me figure out where to go," Elizabeth said, trying to read the map on her phone.

The driver waited to turn into a parking lot jammed with cars as if someone used advanced calculations to fit as many vehicles as possible. Up ahead, a line of cars crawled forward, each one in the futile business of finding an open spot. For the longest time, nobody moved.

The driver grumbled to himself before saying, "Everything is messed up. A banged-up car is getting towed. You gotta get out here."

"I'm not sure," she said, trying to get her bearings.

The guy pulled the car into a pedestrian thruway and somebody yelled. Elizabeth turned in time to see a bicyclist lean over and slap the side of the car.

The driver swore to himself.

Elizabeth's heart pounded in her chest. "Bags," she managed to say.

The driver popped the hatch and got out.

Elizabeth opened the car door. "Give us a sec to get our rain gear, too."

The guy set their matching backpacks on the wet ground. She jumped out and pulled the rain ponchos out. The guy watched, his impatience adding to her anxiety.

Elizabeth had bought identical leopard-print rain ponchos at an outdoor market before she left school. She yanked hers over her head. A car horn bellowed behind them and she jumped.

"How do people live like this?" she muttered.

The driver helped Granny out of the car, so she stood there in the rain until Elizabeth could get the poncho on her.

The driver took off before she could get Granny's cane.

"I don't know about that one," Granny said. The hood of the poncho left a circle that exposed her face and a wedge of gray hair. She looked like a ghost dressed as a bright yellow leopard. The rain ran down her hood and dripped into her face. "I need something to eat," she said.

"I know. Hang on to me while we find Linda." Elizabeth heaved a pack over each shoulder and helped Granny up the path. The rain was driving into their faces and she tried not to worry about the rain worthiness of their bags. She searched for a sign or a map or maybe a building that could be a student center. Anything to give them a clue.

People streamed by, each one focused on a destination, no individual lingering in the downpour. Granny grabbed someone's arm.

"We're lost."

The guy had no rain gear, only sweatpants and a hoodie, all of it growing wetter by the second. His dark hair was plastered around his face. If she had to bet, Elizabeth would guess he was Native, but his face was worn with fatigue, and he moved like a man on his way to his final battle.

He gave their bright raingear the once-over. "How is that possible? I'm pretty sure there are people three time zones away who can see you right now."

Granny grinned at him. She still had a grip on his sleeve. "We need the Ind'n Center."

"Longhouse is that way," he said, gesturing to a walkway.

Elizabeth met his eye, and they held eye contact for a couple of extra heartbeats.

"I'd show you, but I'm in the middle of a...crisis." He nodded toward the parking lot, his face grim.

"That's okay," Elizabeth said, her eyes still glued to his. "We can find it."

"Good luck," he said, and he trotted off into the rain.

Tommy would never have left an elder wandering around in a downpour if he had any other choice.

The rain had been going on and off all day, but it was back on now, and he couldn't remember where he left his rain shell. He hurried to the parking lot and back to the dead Crunch, hoping to get there before Cody.

He was *this* close to having one problem solved.

Meanwhile, he kept up with Angie by sending a text every half hour and for now she wasn't responding. She was troubled but she was trying.

When they were teenagers back home, they'd spent many a weekend siphoning cheap vodka or gin out of big jugs that they knew they would find hidden in the backs of cupboards, or in outdoor sheds. They'd sneak off to a picnic site by the lake and get drunk while plotting how to get more. There was never enough.

He wished his sobriety was something he could siphon off and share with her. She'd asked him to take her to the meeting and then insisted they leave before it finished because someone made her uncomfortable. She'd kept him up half the night, weeping about the unfairness of life and how everything was against her. One minute she begged him to forgive her for being so messed up and the next minute she blamed him for being gone during the day. She'd finally dropped off to sleep, and he had tiptoed to bed and locked his door, hoping she would still be there in the morning.

She was.

The woman needed to go to rehab. If she was going to succeed she needed more than he could offer, but every time he brought it up she freaked out and promised she was trying. The family counted on him and he hated to give up on Angie when she hadn't given up on herself.

He found the spot where he'd left the Crunch.

It was gone.

His lunch roiled in his belly. He called Cody. "Any chance you already picked up the car?"

"Nope, on our way. Something happen?"

"Yeah." He should have known better than to leave it overnight, except he'd been trying to save Angie. Didn't he deserve a break for that?

Cody said, "Sorry, bud. Find out where it's impounded and we can tow it from there."

"Car is gone. Forget it," Tommy said, envisioning his future with public transportation. He couldn't afford the impound, and the car didn't work anyway. Problem solved.

"Terrible idea," Cody said. "Get me an address. You can pay me back later."

People being kind made it worse. Like he was always going to be the guy who leaned on his friends. "Thanks. I'll get back to you."

He walked back to the office, soaked through and damp to his bones, shivering all the way to his toes.

Now on top of everything else, he had to figure out how to get by without a car. The Crunch wasn't just transportation, it was sanity. When the world felt uncertain and he craved a drink or needed to think quietly to himself without interruption, he relied on the Crunch and its crappy radio playing classic country music to keep him company while he drove along the backroads, clearing his mind, recharging his spirit and preparing to deal with life again.

He took a deep breath and went into the office. Ester would have a snack stashed somewhere. All he needed was a cup of coffee and some food and he could get through the rest of the day.

The ladies were crowded around Linda's desk, coffees in hand, sandwiches and cookies spread out in front of them. The coffee pot was empty.

"Coffee?" he said.

"You drink it, you make it," Rayanne said.

Ester jumped up.

"There's nothing wrong with him making his own coffee," Rayanne said.

Ester said something he couldn't hear and all three of them gave him a concerned look. Great.

"Do you have dry clothes you can change into?" Linda asked.

"I'll dry off in a second," he said.

Ester moved her space heater to his desk before coming over and emptying the coffee grounds into the trash. "Everything okay?" she asked, preparing the filter for a new pot.

He could never shake the feeling this was the kind of kindness extended to a loser.

"Compared to what?" he said, faking a lighthearted tone.

"How did it go yesterday?" Linda asked cheerfully. "Not as bad as you thought, I bet."

Tommy froze. That feeling of dread and remorse that he'd been suppressing all morning during the other distractions returned. His body sagged. The coffee maker made a gurgling sound. He kept his eyes on the orange light.

Ester blinked several times. "You didn't go?" she whispered.

He didn't say anything. He grabbed a cardboard cup. The coffee hadn't even started trickling out yet. As soon as it did, everything would be okay.

He was aware of Ester at his side gesturing or something, Rayanne's sharp intake of breath, Linda's frustrated sigh.

"Tommy?" Linda said.

"Sorry," he said. "I had a situation." That was as much as he wanted to share. A tremor started in his hands.

"Go sit down," Ester said. "Warm up. I'll bring it to you when it's ready."

"I'm fine," he told her. He didn't want to sit next to Linda. She had her head buried in her hands. Rayanne shot him a look of pure thunder.

"What does that mean—a situation?" Linda said, enunciating each syllable.

"Long story," he said.

"We asked you to do one thing." Linda's voice rose. Whatever attempt she'd made not to get angry was failing.

He wasn't even sure which excuse to make. The coffee finally came sputtering out of the machine. Ester took his cup and pulled the pot out so that the first drops went directly into his cup. When it was mostly full, she handed it back to him. "It's okay not to be fine, Tommy."

He understood where she was coming from, but the kindness only made him feel worse. "Not now," he said.

Linda finally sat up and shook her head. He was alarmed to discover that her eyes were half-filled with tears.

"I need to be able to count on you," she said. "Especially now. You know what the city told us yesterday? We can have the space. In three years." She barked out the last three words. "We need to make a plan and I need you, if you're going to be here, to be reliable. Do you understand this?"

Tommy nodded and sat down. Ester took half of her sandwich and put it on a napkin and gave it to him.

"You must fix it. Phone them. Apologize. Tell them you need to submit a written statement. Ask about coming to a different meeting. I don't care what it is. Failure is not an option."

Kinda late for that now.

Rayanne sputtered out a few words, but Linda shut her down.

"Sorry," he repeated, keeping his eye on the sandwich. Life would be so much easier if Linda would just fire him.

The office door opened a crack, and someone peeked in. "Linda?"

"Yeah?" Linda said, squinting at the door.

The visitor pulled the door fully open and urged a companion in, both of them dripping rain.

"Finally. We tried the longhouse first. They said you were here."

"Aunt Dotty?" Linda said. "Elizabeth?"

It was the elder and her friend in the blinding yellow rain ponchos who had been looking for the Indian center. This Indian center.

"We couldn't move fast because the rideshare guy took off with her cane." The elder tottered carefully, lurching to the first table and gripping it. Tommy jumped up and helped get her out of the rain gear before giving her his chair.

He turned Ester's heater so the warm air blew toward her.

Elizabeth wore an identical poncho. "It's gruesome out there." She let Tommy take the two backpacks she carried, and when she met his eyes, his heart stuttered with a complicated reaction that he'd forgotten he was capable of. She grinned at him for a long moment before peeling her poncho off.

He moved in slow motion, carefully laying out paper towels and setting the dripping backpacks down. Every time he snuck a look, her dark brown eyes were already on him. His breath caught in his chest. He was so unnerved by the intensity of his reaction. Rayanne never missed anything so he became self-conscious of his movements, trying to remain casual as he rejoined them, inching as close to Elizabeth as he dared, his blood humming in his ears.

Elizabeth shook out her damp hair and gave him a smile that was half sweetness, half danger. She wore snug jeans and a purple fleece pullover with yellow flowers so bright they probably glowed in the dark. He wanted to say something but he'd lost the ability to speak. While the rest of them traded getting-to-know-you small talk, he adopted a posture of casual interest as if he were hanging around only to be polite. But his eyes never strayed too far from Linda's cousin, all the shame and misery of the morning forgotten as long as he was in her orbit.

Linda's cousin and auntie had arrived.

Oh. Oops.

The realization was like a splash of freezing water. On top of everything else, he'd forgotten to tell Linda that sexy voice and a dotty aunt were coming to visit.

"What a surprise," Linda said.

---

6

*E*lizabeth had expected a more enthusiastic greeting. Besides Linda, there were two other women about her age and the too-cool-for-raingear guy who had directed them to the longhouse. He looked to be around the same age, too. The rain had left him damp and disheveled although on him it was kind-of cute. She kept expecting him to say something but he stood close by, silent and attentive. Every time she looked over, his puppy-dog eyes darted away. When they'd walked through the door, he had the shell-shocked expression of a man in the middle of the worst day of his life. The entire group looked like they could use a vacation.

"Something bad going on?" Elizabeth asked.

"No worse than usual," Linda said, looking around the room as if seeing it for the first time herself. "What in the world are you doing here?"

"Long story," Elizabeth said.

"Will law enforcement be involved?" Linda laughed. She got up and dug around a box until she found what she was looking for. She tossed over a towel. Elizabeth patted her face dry and handed it to Granny.

Elizabeth's gaze kept drifting back to the guy. He suddenly crossed the room and fiddled with something out of sight in the corner. "What kind of cane does Auntie use?" he asked, his voice low and warm.

"Kind?" Elizabeth repeated.

"Like a walking stick?" He lifted an expandable walking stick with a looped strap at the top. "I've also got your more traditional cane." He waved a light wood stick with a curved handle. He shifted his attention to Granny. "Do you like one with a grip handle? Or did yours have the little feet at the bottom?"

Elizabeth would have been charmed if it weren't so weird. "Why do you have so many canes?"

"I've always had an interest in mobility devices," he said, giving her a half-smile.

Granny finished drying her face. "Little feet," she said.

"Yours didn't have little feet," Elizabeth said.

Granny gave her a sharp look.

"I only have one, so you don't get to pick the color." He brought over a shiny silver cane and adjusted the height. Elizabeth could only stare in amazement.

"I like it," Granny said, using it to stand up. She went to hug Linda. "Miss you, girl. You in charge of all this?"

Granny had asked the question Elizabeth wanted to ask but couldn't figure out how to without sounding disappointed. Back home everyone talked like Linda was saving the world for Indians. But the so-called urban Indian center was more storage room than office. Tall stacks of boxes lined the walls. Clusters of mismatched desks and tables were pushed together for their workstations. A chair with a broken wheel had been pushed to one side. There was apparently a diverse supply of canes in the corner.

"Amazing, isn't it?" Linda said with fake enthusiasm. She had a weary smile and slumped shoulders like she never slept or heard good news. "What are you doing in town?"

"We came looking for my dance dress," Granny said.

"Family regalia," Elizabeth said, pulling up the photo on her phone. She passed it to Linda, who showed the others.

"Where is it?" Linda asked.

"A historical research center? I have the address."

"I bet that's over at the university. Should be interesting," Linda said, handing the phone back. "Who are you staying with?"

Granny pointed at Elizabeth. "This one was supposed to call you."

Elizabeth would have explained that she had called, but the miserable guy managed to look even more pitiful. He had to be the one she'd left the message with. She cleared her throat. "We were hoping to stay with you."

"I would have insisted anyway," Linda said with unconvincing enthusiasm.

One of the women on the staff came over and took Granny's hand. "I'm Rayanne. I'm Karuk. That's Ester, and that's Tommy. We're Linda's crack team of urban warriors."

Linda laughed at that.

"I like it," Granny said.

Tommy forced a smile and did a funny little wave. His eyes, dark brown and ridiculously expressive—both sweet and mournful, flicked to the ground and then back at her. It was hard to resist the urge to find a blanket to put around his shoulders and shove a hot cup of cocoa into his hands.

"You're all Natives?" Elizabeth asked.

"That's the idea," Linda said.

"I've never seen so many Ind'ns outside the rez except maybe the student group at school," Elizabeth said.

"You should come to one of our events," Rayanne said.

From looking around, it wasn't clear what kind of events she was talking about. Tall stacks of books and files covered their desks. Every workstation had a computer. Linda had a pile of documents in front of her, notes flagged throughout. Elizabeth tried to envision doing a project that involved that much effort.

"Dorothy and her husband, Leo, were big-time activists," Rayanne told them. "I wrote about her for one of my school papers."

It was always weird to hear people talking about Granny like she was a study project.

"When are we getting something to eat?" Granny said.

"Sorry," Elizabeth said, surprised the elder had waited this long to complain again. "We came from the train station. Took longer than expected to find you."

"I can grab you something," Tommy said. He pulled a chair next to Granny. "What are you up for? A sandwich? A burrito? Kung pao chicken?"

Elizabeth was accustomed to dealing with Granny's picky eating habits. "She usually likes—"

"Tell me about the chicken," Granny said, doing what Elizabeth called her elder cute-face. Granny could charm a charging elk herd.

"Chicken, vegetables, lots of flavors but not spicy. You'll like it," he said.

Elizabeth said, "I don't think—"

Tommy gave her a half-smile that said he had it under control. "You want something?" He turned the full blast of his handsome face to her. He had cheekbones for miles, and his dark hair was shaggy and almost to his shoulders. He was like the guys at home, except different. Not all self-satisfied BS. Something mysterious she wanted to unravel.

"I'll go with you," Elizabeth said, suddenly self-conscious that everyone knew what she had on her mind.

"It's drier in here," he said.

Elizabeth pulled her poncho back on. "I'm used to the rain."

"Tommy?" Linda said, her voice hard. "The minute you get back here you have problems to solve."

"Always," he agreed. He held the door open for Elizabeth and ushered her back into the rain.

"What kind of problems?" she asked when they got outside.

"I don't know where to start." He headed across the open green but the rain had left a wide patch of mud, so he changed course. He pointed to a concrete path. "Student center is this way."

"That was a cute bit with the canes," she said.

"Elders leave them on the bus all the time," he said, as if that explained it.

"Rain isn't as bad as it was earlier," she said, "and we can move faster without Granny."

"Elders can move fast if they want to. You ever lose one in the grocery store?"

"I lose that one at the casino."

"I can picture that." He was older than she thought when they first walked in. There was a weariness around his eyes. "How come you didn't tell Linda you called yesterday?"

"You look like you're having a bad day."

"And here I thought I was hiding it so well," he said without humor.

The path through campus was jammed with students and bikes. Elizabeth had gone to a smaller school, but the feeling was the same. She experienced a brief pang of memory, always homesick and longing to be back home with the familiar views of trees, river, and ocean.

"You from upriver?" she asked.

"From where?"

"Upriver? Rayanne said she was Karuk."

"No." He tilted his head, and they turned down a different path that led to a crosswalk. They stopped and waited for the light.

"This is a weird campus," Elizabeth said, "in the middle of the city. Where I went was more self-contained."

Tommy nodded and remained silent. The light changed and they crossed. A group of bicycles came up and around them, not regular students but like a team in training. They had matching helmets, with bright-colored jerseys and fingerless gloves. The group shot down the path and disappeared.

Tommy said, "I am from upriver but not what you meant. I grew up around Klamath Falls."

"You're Klamath?"

He nodded.

"I've never been up there," Elizabeth said, now trying to picture Tommy traipsing through his homeland.

"You're not missing much," he said. "This is the student center."

It looked as expected, a big box of a building with rows of bikes parked out front. Inside, the main entry had high ceilings and huge light fixtures, like the courtyard of a mall. A variety of couches lined one wall and a cluster of lunch tables filled another corner. A chorus of loud voices echoed throughout the room.

"This way," Tommy said with a gentle tap on her shoulder.

"I wasn't expecting this," she said, attempting to stay close to his side.

"You went to a small school?"

"It didn't seem like it while I was there," she said.

When they got to the food court, he showed her the different vendors. "That place has good pizza and there are perfectly respectable deli sandwiches there. That place has a salad bar if that's your thing." He went to the Chinese food counter and got in line.

She wasn't ready to venture too far by herself, so she followed him. "I'm a rez girl. I don't eat salad."

Tommy laughed. "That's what Linda says." He got two orders of kung pao chicken and they took it back to the office.

The minute they hit the door, Linda handed Tommy a square of white paper and he made a grim face and then took his cellphone and went outside.

Granny dug into the chicken. Linda came to sit with them.

"We've got a Native professionals mixer thing tonight," Linda said. "I don't have to stay long, but I need to show my face for a few minutes."

Elizabeth grimaced, but Granny sat up. "I want to go to that."

"You won't know anyone," Elizabeth said, filled with dread at the thought of standing around a crowded room making small talk with strangers.

"I can't meet them if I go home," Granny said.

"It's not that bad," Linda said. "You already have something in common with most of them."

Tommy returned. "She said we can email the statement and she'll try to sneak it in as if we'd attended."

Linda sighed. "Close enough."

"You going to that mixer thing tonight?" Elizabeth asked him.

"Of course," he said. "Wouldn't miss it."

Behind him, Rayanne made a strange hiccup and covered her mouth. Linda stared at him with her mouth open but didn't comment.

"I guess we could go," Elizabeth said. "Do you need a nap first?"

Granny nodded.

"You can use my car, I'll take the bus home." Linda picked up her keys from her desk and held them out.

A chilly buzz traveled down her spine. The sound of the keys and the thought of all the cars and the bikes in the parking lot and around campus brought up terrible memories. She didn't reach for them.

"I'll put the address in your phone. It's easy to find," Linda said.

"She don't drive," Granny said. "She don't like it."

"Oh," Linda said, "I know what's going on. I forgot about that."

Elizabeth was happy to skip the explanation. "Tell us where to go. We can take the bus."

"Don't be ridiculous," Linda said. "It's too much walking."

"I can take them," Tommy said.

THE WORDS SPILLED out without thinking. As soon as he'd said it, his mind flashed to Angie, at home by herself. If he drove them around and went to the mixer, she'd be alone all evening. But Elizabeth's smile was like the first warm day after a long winter, and that sunny expression managed to distract him from his growing collection of catastrophes. Besides, it was Linda's family. Angie could handle a few hours by herself.

Linda held the keys back to her chest.

"This is the part of this job I excel at," Tommy reminded her.

Linda nodded in agreement. "Okay, but use your car. No need to haul my family around in that creaky bus. I'll give you money for gas."

His car. No need to confess that problem right now.

"But I love the Drivemaster," he said.

Linda sighed. "They're tribal members. They're family. Please take good care of them. Aunt Dotty is a national treasure."

"The bus conforms with all state and federal safety standards," Tommy said. "It's comfortable, the environmental controls are in fair-to-good working condition, and I am happy to report that after a good airing out, it barely smells like hot dogs inside."

"That's quite a recommendation," Linda said. "I trust you on this."

He told Elizabeth where the access road was and then brought the bus around to pick them up, his mood buoyed at the thought of spending the afternoon with her.

He set Granny in one seat and Elizabeth took the spot behind him and leaned forward so they could talk.

When they got going, he said, "You don't like to drive?"

She shook her head. "Makes me anxious."

"Really? I relax driving. I can give you some tips if you want."

Elizabeth studied the dashboard as if seeing one for the first time. "I don't need any tips. What exactly do you do for Linda?"

There was no way to make driving elders and organizing basket-ball sound vital. "You know, this and that," he said.

"You like working for her?"

"I like all of them. Linda tries to do too many things but she's insanely dedicated. Rayanne is so focused and wants to learn every-thing. Ester is super clever at problem-solving."

Elizabeth leaned close like there was a vacuum cleaner running and she needed the proximity to maintain the conversation. His atten-tion was divided between the road and her presence, the sexy edge to her voice, the sweep of her hair at his elbow, the way she paused after he responded, as if everything he said required her careful consid-eration.

"Linda any good at this?" she asked.

"She's great." He almost added that she saved his life, but that would demand explanations he needed to avoid.

"I thought there would be more to it," Elizabeth said. "Urban Indian center. It sounds like a hub of activity. People coming and going. Instead, it's you guys in a room. You could be doing anything. What exactly do you guys do?"

It was a good question but the explanation complex. "We've had setbacks, so a lot of what we're doing now is preparation. We still coordinate health appointments and do after-school activities for kids. Rayanne brings meals to elders. Ester collects health data. Linda does lots of talks so we can get more funding. It takes time to develop programs."

"How much time? Hasn't Linda been working there for years?"

Granny cleared her throat. "Why you pick on Linda?"

Tommy shot a quick look over his shoulder. "Yeah. You were in there for ten minutes and you're an expert on our accomplishments? Linda works night and day and helps so many people, and she's always trying to do more."

"Guess that came out wrong. Sorry. It's just that when we were younger, she was always Miss Career-Focused and acted all mature like she knew what she was doing. First, college, and then moving up here being involved in all this." Elizabeth swept her hand in a circle.

"It's good what she did," Granny said. "I'm proud of her."

On the freeway, traffic backed up and slowed to a crawl.

"This is what I don't like," Elizabeth said.

"Traffic?"

"That, and it feels like everyone is angry and wants me to get out of their way. At home, there's no traffic but it still feels like something bad is going to happen."

"When I get worked up, I get in the car and drive. Usually, I head out of town, but sometimes I cruise around the surface streets. I'm having some trouble with my car and I can't wait to get it back. Some people have an emotional support animal. I have an emotional support vehicle."

"You're serious," Elizabeth said.

"I am."

"That's crazy."

Even though she sat behind him, he could sense her every movement. She leaned toward him, close, almost touching when she asked a question, and she kept an eye on Granny. He knew he was supposed to do more to carry on the conversation, but he had trouble forming coherent thoughts.

She leaned forward again, this time brushing his arm. "Why was Linda mad at you?"

He cleared his throat. "Not sure she's finished being mad at me." He could see part of Elizabeth's face in the rearview mirror, her eyes on him like there was something more interesting to look at than there was. She wasn't shy about being in his space. "What about you? What's waiting for you when you get back to the rez?"

"Casino," Granny puffed, not hiding her disapproval.

Elizabeth said, "Don't start. It's a great job. It's economic development for the Tribe. I get to be on the rez and take care of you."

Granny made another sound but didn't comment further.

"I start next week," Elizabeth said.

"When did you graduate?"

"Last month," Elizabeth said. "Took me an extra year to get through school. I had—" She paused, searching for words.

"She quit two times," Granny said, holding up two fingers.

"There were no Ind'ns there. A couple of overachievers formed a club but I had nothing in common with them." Elizabeth sat back in her seat and stared out the window.

He skipped sharing his story, the one where he also struggled with school, because that tale was tough to tell without mentioning the sobriety part, which would be the moment he became 1000 times less attractive to her. Someone like Elizabeth would not be interested in the living wreck that he was at the moment.

"How about you, Granny? How do you stay out of trouble?" He glanced over to see her give him a sly grin.

"I like the casino," she said.

"She always has visitors, family and friends or researchers who want an interview or to take her picture," Elizabeth said. "Leo, my great-grandpa, died a couple of years ago, but until then she was still cooking giant meals to feed anyone who stopped by. Washing dishes is one of my strongest memories of being at her house."

"Who does it now?"

"Not me. I hate cooking. No more giant meals," Elizabeth said. "Do you like cooking?"

Tommy laughed. "I collect cookbooks, but I never cook. Seems like a stupid thing to do when you're by yourself."

Elizabeth didn't respond to that. When he arrived at Linda's, Elizabeth asked, "You coming in?"

He wanted to. He wanted nothing more than to breathe the same air that Elizabeth was breathing, but he had to check on Angie before he took them to the mixer.

"Nah. I have an errand to take care of," he said, trying to sound like a person who didn't have a giant problem waiting for him in his apartment. "I'll be back to pick you up in a couple of hours."

---

7

*T*he twinge of regret grew stronger the closer they got to the event. Linda winced every time she replayed the scene, her bellowing at Arnie when he was trying to help and the look of surprise on his face when he left.

"Bets on whether Tommy shows?" Rayanne asked.

"He's bringing Aunt Dotty and Lizzie," Linda reminded her. She pointed out the high-rise where the mixer was taking place.

"I mean, will he come inside and talk to people?" Rayanne said.

"He said he wanted to," Ester said.

"He was making cow eyes at Linda's cousin," Rayanne said. "Wager? If he shows up, he will miraculously have clothing other than sweatpants."

Ester giggled. "I'm torn. You're probably right but he needs someone to stick up for him."

Linda said, "I always talk about looking professional. If he shows up in decent clothes maybe he heard me."

"Sure, sounds like Tommy," Rayanne said.

In their short history together, he'd never been particularly expressive, but these last few months he'd grown more out of it, always quick with an excuse and an apology.

"Does he talk to you guys? He's so secretive and...miserable, like every minute he's braced for terrible news. I never know what to think about him." Linda hadn't noticed any cow eyes but then having her family drop-in unexpectantly had created a whole new category of worries for her about things like clean sheets and her dismal pantry with nothing but soup and macaroni dinner.

"He tells me nothing, good or bad," Rayanne said.

Ester looked away and shrugged. "Does Arnie come to these things?"

"Who cares?" Linda said, too quickly. They arrived at the giant glass doors that led to the lobby. "What I meant was, I'm tired of him lurking over my shoulder."

"That's a weird thing to say," Rayanne said.

"I wish you guys would be friends again," Ester said.

"We can work together. We don't have to be friends." It hurt her heart to say those words out loud.

"What if he quits?" Ester said.

"No one is quitting," Linda said. "Especially not now. Remember: networking event. Talk to someone besides each other. I'll introduce you."

"I like networking events," Rayanne said.

"She's nuts, but she prepared me with the equivalent of three things," Ester said. "All of them end up with me talking about supporting urban Indians."

"Good," Linda said, pushing the heavy door open. "See if you can pass any of that to Tommy."

The lobby had a polished marble floor and imposing slabs of abstract art hanging on the walls. The mixer was underway. Linda scanned the group. No sign of Arnie. In case he showed up, she would try Ester's trick and be ready with three things: Nice day, nice tie, and, how did things get so blucked up between us? Maybe not. Two things would work.

They went to the temporary bar where Audra passed out name tags.

"Greetings, fellow professionals," she said, giving them all a hug. "Glad to see you. No Tommy?"

"My relatives came to town this afternoon," Linda said. "He's bringing them over."

"He's smitten," Rayanne said.

"Good for him," Audra said, handing over a marker. "Your name and tribal affiliation. You and Arnie strategize on your next move?"

"No," Linda said. "The ladies and I think we should look at the other sites and see what they offer. I hope to bring him to our way of thinking."

"The trick is to make him think it's his idea," Rayanne said.

"You are going to do well in this business," Audra told her. "The bar's got beer, wine, and a dismal selection of canned soda left from another meeting." She nodded at the people already gathered. "There was a tribal fisheries meeting today, so most of these folks are from that."

"I see someone I know from college," Rayanne said, dragging Ester with her.

Audra handed Linda a glass of wine. "I guess Arnie is still seeing the filmmaker."

Something uncomfortable squeezed behind Linda's ribs. She followed Audra's gaze. Tall tinted windows enclosed the building lobby. From outside, passersby would see their reflections, but from inside they had a clear view of what was going on out there.

Arnie, looking sharp as ever, stood near the lobby doors with Katie Stone, the woman who had made the film that the center had blown off, his words.

Katie stood with arms crossed, posture ramrod straight, her face puckered with annoyance. Arnie must be used to seeing that face on the women he knew.

"I hadn't heard otherwise," Linda said, unable to tear her eyes away. Arnie stood close but didn't touch. Linda recognized the look: pleading, conciliatory. He would be making promises, guessing what she wanted to hear, anything so they could get into the event. Katie's head moved back and forth: no. Whatever was going on, she wasn't letting up.

"Doesn't look like a pleasant conversation," Audra said, turning away.

"No," Linda agreed. She took a gulp of wine and hoped she wouldn't have to talk to the woman.

"Did something happen yesterday?" Audra asked.

A fresh wave of Arnie annoyance curled her upper lip. "I had a flat and he tried to help me." Her eyes were glued to Arnie. He put a hand on Katie's elbow and tried to steer her to the door. She shook him off, tossed her hands up, and took off with quick strides. Linda felt a tiny pop of relief. She turned her attention back to Audra.

"That was a problem?" Audra said.

"He was being all pushy and making fun of the stuff in my car, so I got mad and told him to get lost."

Audra took a thoughtful sip of her wine. "Maybe you two need couples' counseling."

"Not funny," Linda said.

Audra dropped her voice. "Sorry. He's here." She pulled out another name tag. "Good evening, Councilman Jackson."

Linda had missed it when he came in. Katie wasn't with him. He glanced at Linda before filling out his badge.

"Hello," she finally said, trying and failing to muster a breezy tone.

"Hey." He peeled the back off the sticker and put it on. To Audra, he said, "What's the beer today?"

"IPA or IPA." Audra flicked the cap off a bottle and handed it to him. "I have a law clerk who is supposed to be handing out drinks. I'd better go find him."

Linda shot her a pleading look but she slipped away. Arnie's red-rimmed eyes traveled around the room and his jaw worked as if he was still deciding whether to talk to her. Her two things faded on her lips.

He took a pull off his beer. "Everything work out okay yesterday?"

"After two hours, some kid from the service showed up. I had to take everything out of the trunk so he could get to the spare," she said.

Arnie smiled into his beer.

She'd promised herself she wouldn't apologize, but the words tumbled out. "Sorry about that—"

"Forget it." His gaze stopped at the lobby doors and the clear view to outside. Recognition flicked across his face; anyone watching would have seen the tiff with Katie.

Linda tried again. "What I mean is—"

"I'm serious," he said sharply. "I don't want to talk about this right now. We need to figure out how to do this together. We have the same goal. We'll work it out, but not right now."

"Sure," Linda said. She spotted Rayanne and Ester watching, but they both turned away when she caught them.

Arnie said, "After we met yesterday, I made a phone call. There's an informal Council planning meeting on Saturday. They said they would be happy to chat with you." He did his best to smile.

"You liked that idea?"

"That's why I arranged for you to meet with them."

"What are you thinking? A formal presentation, or a short-and-sweet pleading session with a Q&A?" Linda's head spun with possibilities. Arnie's Council participated in lots of regional activities, so she could pitch ideas for collaborative projects that might keep other tribes committed.

"It's a long trip for short and sweet, don't you think?" Arnie said.

"I wish we knew what kind of space we're going to have," Linda said. "What about the city's alternatives?"

"I thought we'd decided on that," he said.

"Right, and *we* decided what?"

A hint of a smile twitched at the corner of his mouth. "We should look."

"That's what I was thinking," Linda said.

Mission accomplished.

She went on. "If there's something decent, we'll ask about leasing. As long as we—"

Arnie's expression changed. Abruptly, he said, "Send me the info when you get an appointment. I gotta work the room." Then he was gone.

Next thing she knew, Virgil was there, waving from the door.

Somewhere in the room, Rayanne and Ester would be nudging each other, their eyes on this greeting, hoping to decode this funny relationship. If they had any insights, she would love to hear them.

Her friend-but-not-boyfriend, at least not yet, crossed the room, a friendly smile on his face. Virgil was tall and built for endurance athletics. When he wasn't on work travel he was always training to bike across the state or heading out for a trail run. There was an awkward pause while they decided how to greet each other, which ended in an inelegant half-embrace, half-back pat.

"Looks like you two smoothed everything over," he said, indicating Arnie.

"More or less," Linda said. "You're back from which trip?"

The relationship remained at an undefined simmer while they both used the excuse of busy schedules. They'd shared a few dinners but never managed to string something together even over consecutive weekends. Every time they saw each other, it played like a second date. She couldn't put her finger on it but they were never at ease, an odd formality coloring every interaction.

He offered a brilliant smile. "I went to Denver. Great trip. Next time we go out I want to tell you about it."

"Sounds intriguing," she said, trying to gauge how she felt. Did she want more? A laid-back guy would probably be a good match for her.

She spotted Tommy guiding Aunt Dotty to the door. "Come meet my cousin and my Aunt Dotty."

8

𝓔lizabeth pulled the heavy door open and waited for Granny and Tommy to go inside. During the time he'd been away, Tommy had ditched the soggy sweats, and he now wore unhemmed gray pants, the edges ragged under his feet, and a pilled black knit shirt, V-neck, her eyes drawn to the triangle of golden skin at his throat, imagining she could see his pulse there. He caught her staring, and she held his gaze until he was the one who looked away.

Linda rushed over as soon as she spotted them, dragging some man whom she introduced as Virgil without any relationship appellation.

Elizabeth shook his hand. While he spoke to Granny, she whispered to Tommy, "Is that Linda's boyfriend?"

"I think they're friends."

"Does she have a boyfriend?"

Tommy shrugged indifferently. His face said: *Don't know, don't care.* She'd have to corner Rayanne or Ester to get the scoop.

Elizabeth was well acquainted with her own dislike of social events like this, so she didn't miss Tommy tense up and shift his weight from foot to foot like he couldn't get comfortable.

From across the room, Ester made crazy eyes at Tommy and indicated her clothes, then his, and then did some sort of waving body dance steps that he acknowledged by pointing his chin at her.

Linda handed Elizabeth a marker and sticker.

"I have to have a name tag? This is awful," she muttered, printing her name and sticking her badge to her chest.

"We can leave whenever you want," Tommy said, filling out one for himself.

Elizabeth eyed Granny, grinning ear-to-ear, no doubt telling one of her stories. She loved a new audience. Linda's not-boyfriend stood next to her, completely engrossed.

Granny lived for this kind of attention. "We're at Granny's mercy," she told Tommy. "We won't go anywhere until she's ready." She spotted someone pouring a glass of wine. "I see drinks. That'll help. I'll be right back." She talked the guy into letting her take two beers and returned to Tommy's side and shoved one in his hand. She took a long pull. "This is all they had. At least they're cold."

Tommy held the bottle like he was holding a hand grenade. She was about to ask him if he'd rather have something else when Ester came over and stopped in front of him. "Trade you," she said with a playful gleam in her eye. "Nice outfit, by the way." She took the open beer and shoved a water bottle into his hand before going back to join Rayanne.

He let out a long exhale. A private joke between them, evidently.

"Did she walk off with your beer?" Elizabeth said, not sure whether to be annoyed.

Tommy shrugged. *What can you do?* "I'm not supposed to drink when I'm operating the Drivemaster."

"That makes sense, I guess," Elizabeth said. "How mom-like of her."

"I don't mind," Tommy said. He took a sip of water. "There was a long time where I went without a reliable Ind'n woman in my life, and now I have three. It's like working with your sisters. They love you, but they give you hell all the time."

"Do you have sisters?"

"Two. Older. Different Dad. I don't see them."

"How delightfully rez," Elizabeth said. "Your dad have any kids with a different mom?"

Tommy held up one finger. "Brother. Also older. Only met him once." Every bit Tommy revealed about himself had a hint of sadness. His eyes kept traveling back to the door as if he was working on an escape plan.

"Your errand go okay?" she asked.

"Which errand?"

"When you dropped me and Granny off you said you had an errand."

He picked at the label on the water bottle. "It went fine." She expected him to elaborate, but he kept his attention focused on the label.

"Do you have a girlfriend?" she asked, picturing him running home to tell someone he had to work late. Dropping off something for her to eat. This person asking when he would be home.

Tommy chewed that over, laughing to himself like the answer was too complex to address properly. "No. I don't have a girlfriend. You?"

"I don't have a girlfriend." Her smile widened.

She held his gaze for one long breath, then another. They were sharing something but she wasn't sure if it was the same thing.

"Do you want to get out of here?" he said. The words fell out in a jumble. She must have misheard him.

She followed his eyes to the door, wondering what he had in mind. The suggestion sent a flare of heat through her.

"Lizzie!" Granny's voice cut across the room.

"Duty calls," she said with genuine regret.

He shook his head and smiled: *It was a crazy idea.*

She grabbed his sleeve and pulled him with her as she went to see what Granny wanted. She waited for Granny to insist on something to eat or ask her some obscure question, but instead she pulled her next to her and said, "I didn't want you to miss this."

Linda's friend Audra was a sharply-dressed attorney with excellent taste in shoes—suede pumps in a color some would call dusty rose—if only she had a place to wear shoes like that. Audra explained how one of her clients put together a program to bring a cultural perspective into their tribe's legal system.

Granny said, "White man court always wants to punish. Our tradition wants to heal with the community. You understand the difference?" Granny looked at her as if they hadn't had a hundred versions of this conversation over the years. Granny was always advocating to use cultural traditions to address problems.

"You've taught me well," Elizabeth told her.

Most of Linda's staff had gathered around Granny for this conversation. Everyone had ideas about programs for Indians in the city and what they could do to keep tribal people connected. Rayanne wanted to have a place to serve elders regular hot meals. Linda had so many ideas it was hard to keep up: classes, cultural events, music, art. Even Tommy chimed in with something about basketball and traditional games. Granny was at the center, her favorite spot, a smile on her face and quick to comment when she had something to add and turning to tap Elizabeth's arm like she might miss a detail.

The tension eased out of her shoulders and she relaxed in spite of herself, enjoying the easy camaraderie of this group, trading jokes and teasing back and forth. Even Tommy, who struck her as the type who had mastered the art of avoiding attention, was at ease in the mix, elaborating on the comments of his co-workers. They'd created a caring rez family away from the rez.

The event gradually wound down. Another over-achieving professional dude in a suit came by to say goodnight, his body language stiff and overly formal.

"Have you met my Aunt Dotty?" Linda asked.

He adjusted his tie before he leaned over to shake Granny's hand. "You're related to Dorothy Scott? How come I didn't know about this?"

"And my cousin, Elizabeth," Linda said.

"You must be an activist, too," Arnie said. It sounded like a command.

"I always support Granny." Elizabeth leaned back and whispered to

Tommy, "See what it's like being related to a famous activist?" She feigned a tired sigh.

"Better than not being related to a famous activist," he said.

Elizabeth laughed.

"You all need to get busy," Granny said. "I'm not going to live forever."

"Don't say that," Elizabeth said.

"We're working on it, Auntie," Arnie said. He asked her a couple of boring questions about timber resources but somehow managed to make it sound like flirting. Elizabeth did her best to suppress a yawn.

Everyone was clearing out. A native guy built like a barn door came in and searched the room. Ester waved, and when his eyes landed on her, he broke into a smile. They hugged like people reunited at the airport after being apart for ages.

"Who is that?" she asked Tommy.

"Ester's boyfriend," he said. "They're really good together." The guy was a head taller than Ester, with ridiculous muscles.

"I'd want him on my side in a bar fight," she said.

"He would be if you hang out with us," Tommy said.

Ester brought him over and introduced him as Theo. He bestowed just the right amount of attention on Granny before chatting with the group. He was in school and Arnie had helped him. They were like one big weird family.

With the event wrapping up she hoped she could sneak off with Tommy and have a drink after he dropped them off. She was about to ask him when Linda said, "We gotta get out of here. I need to get some sleep. I'll take you guys." She hugged Tommy. "Thanks for bringing them over. See you tomorrow."

"Oh, okay," Tommy said. He held Elizabeth's eye. "See you."

"Tomorrow," she said.

9

There were plenty of clouds in the sky, but the sun poked through, slanting beams glimmering off the river below. The road that led to the lookout was one of Tommy's favorite places to drive when he needed to de-stress, either stopping here to gaze at the view or to continue the scenic drive along the river.

Granny had one hand on the railing and the other gripped her cane. The wind whipped up again, hard enough to make her wobble, but her face was pure delight. "Never thought I'd see this again," she said.

Elizabeth wore a long-sleeved pink dress that showed off a significant segment of bronze leg with every gust of wind, and a pink sweater. She wore ankle-high black boots with a heel that brought her almost eye-to-eye with him. Her hair tangled around her face.

"This is like where we live, only gigantic," she said. "It's so pretty, it's like a painting. If I lived here, this would be my favorite place."

Tommy stood next to her, resting his arm alongside hers on the railing. "It's my favorite place," he agreed.

Elizabeth had stayed at the front of his mind all night. When Tommy heard that sexy voice was Linda's cousin, he envisioned a junior version of Linda, serious, reserved, someone who enjoyed problem-solving and meant it when she made comments like, 'completed paperwork relaxes me.' The cousin was smoky-eyed and full-lipped, all curves and raw intensity.

"A couple of weeks ago I had that bus filled with elders and I took them to the first salmon ceremony at the longhouse upriver. It rained and there was a misunderstanding about where the elder table was located. You know how a group of elders gets when they think they're being wronged?"

Granny did a funny fist-pump and said, "You bet."

The wind whipped up again. Elizabeth inched closer, her arm aligned next to his, her hip bumping against him. He couldn't keep his eyes off her, the deep V of her neckline, the curve of her neck, her hands gesturing when she spoke.

"I'm a little worried about Granny blowing away," she said for his ears only.

"I can catch her," he said. He could feel the heat of her, even with the wind.

There were a thousand reasons why this was a terrible idea. She was Linda's family, only in town for a short time, and he had nothing to offer. She was precisely the kind of out-of-his-league woman that he'd chased after when he was drinking. They found him interesting at first because he wasn't threatening and he was a good listener, but as time went on it became clear that he would never be more than a friend.

But as long as Elizabeth was around, he wanted to spend as much time with her as he could.

His phone vibrated in his pocket, and he checked the ID. Angie.

"I need to grab this," he said, reluctantly stepping away from Elizabeth.

"Everything okay?" he said when he answered.

A half-sob on the other end. "Not really. Can you come?"

His eyes flicked to Elizabeth. She pulled her flimsy sweater more tightly around her. She leaned over to say something to Granny.

"I'm working," he said.

"Can you get away?"

Elizabeth's dress flapped up again, and he got a glimpse of pink panties before she yanked it back down, the skirt fisted in her hand. He could only see her in profile, but her smile was sneaky.

He cleared his throat. "You did good yesterday. Can't you find a meeting on your own?"

"I'm having a hard time." Angie made a dramatic sniffle.

"I'm in the middle of an errand. I can't get away this minute. What have you done to take care of yourself?"

He could picture Angie wandering around the house, still in pajamas, ignoring the coffee-making supplies he'd left out.

"Angie?"

"There's nothing here."

"You need to take initiative. Take a shower. Get dressed. There's a twenty-dollar bill in the recovery book in the kitchen. Go get coffee and a sandwich. Read the book while you're eating."

"Then you'll come?"

Elizabeth turned around and gave him a radiant smile. He'd waited his entire life for someone to give him a smile like that. She held up her phone and pointed to the bus and helped Granny away from the rail.

"If I can," he said.

Angie sniffled again.

"I'll stop by," he said. "It will have to be quick. Do you want me to bring you anything?" He braced himself because she always managed to come up with some inconvenient errand for him.

"No. I don't want to be a bother." She disconnected the call.

Almost immediately his phone went off again. At least Angie was talking to him. But when he checked, it was Cody.

Elizabeth and Granny were on the bus, smoothing their wind-tossed hair and laughing about something. Their easy rapport made his chest tight. He got Elizabeth's attention and pointed at his phone and held up one finger before he took the call.

He needed good news, something, anything to keep from falling into a hole. Whenever he needed car repairs, he told himself it would cost eight hundred dollars. That way, if it was expensive, at least he was prepared, and anything less meant he'd gotten away with something.

"How bad is it?" Tommy asked.

"The Crunch isn't worth saving," Cody said.

And like that, he was back on the precipice and teetering at the edge. The wind gusted again with the damp scent of coming rain. Out on the water, a tugboat pushed an empty barge upriver.

"Sounds like my life," Tommy muttered.

"Something going on?" Cody asked. Tommy realized what his words sounded like to Cody.

"The usual. What do I owe you?"

"How about I take whatever I get from the junkman and call it even."

Tommy should have been relieved, but even this small kindness, this one additional problem off his plate, created a heavy futile feeling in his belly.

"I'll get over there and clean it out. There are basketballs in the back."

"No worries. We'll find something you can drive," Cody said. "An old junker that has a few miles left in it."

Tommy didn't want to talk about money, so he left it at that. Now he had no car.

He returned to the bus. "You both good?"

Granny ran a hand over her hair. "Wild out there. Do I still look pretty?"

Tommy couldn't help chuckling. "You look great. Should I stop for coffee or take you to the historical people?"

"I'm okay," Granny said.

"I'm good too," Elizabeth said with a smile of pure joy that lifted his mood from the depths.

~

ELIZABETH DIDN'T MISS the shift. The good-natured guy showing them the pretty view had gone gloomy. He'd started the morning loose-limbed and easy confidence and now his shoulders rolled in and his chin dipped down.

Back home, there were no surprises from the native guys she knew. They'd seen each other at every rez event, every school dance, and every weekend at the beach their entire lives.

Tommy was a mystery, quiet but a lot going on beneath the surface.

Today he wore black pants and a rain shell. No matter how heavy the rain fell, he never pulled up the hood. He acted like a man who had no idea how hot he was. He steered the bus back through town with calm authority.

She wanted to know everything about him, but he divulged information in aggravating tiny bits.

"Bad news?" she asked.

"If I didn't get bad news I wouldn't get any news at all," he said, unsuccessfully playing it for a joke. He didn't say much for the rest of the drive, letting her feed him the directions from the phone.

Once they arrived, Tommy helped Granny out. "I've got to take care of something. I'll be back to pick you up."

"You're leaving us here?" Elizabeth said.

Granny set off, fast like she could be if she wanted. She gestured that they should come along.

Tommy touched Elizabeth's elbow. "I promise I'll be right back. I have to do this. Put me in your cellphone."

Elizabeth tapped the number into her phone. "Our appointment won't take long. We can help you with your errand after." She'd seen the name Angie on his phone, the tortured look in his eyes. She wanted to know more. "Don't you want to see Granny's ceremonial dress?"

Granny cruised onward, passing a prominent sign that warned visitors they'd have to check in. Tommy stared at the sign; she imagined she could see the thoughts turning in his head. She struggled for a good reason other than she wanted to hang out with him.

"Sure, I guess," he said. "Let me park that thing and I'll meet you in there."

The historical research center was a located in a two-story gray brick building with small windows. The reception area had creaky wood floors and a couple of glass display cases. A young man sorted sleeves of yellowed newspaper clippings at a small desk, the only other furniture. He told them someone would be out in a minute.

There was no place to sit so they checked out the displays. One case contained antique dishes and utensils, a child's shoe, and a moldy book opened to a page with an indecipherable scribble of black ink. A display on the wall had a tribal hand drum and several woven baskets.

Tommy stayed glued to Elizabeth's side.

"Granny has tons of baskets at home," Elizabeth told him.

"Different tradition," Granny said, her tone suggesting that she wasn't impressed with this collection. "Ours is prettier."

A hand-drawn map of the area covered one wall, every swell of land and body of water with a name carefully lettered over it.

Granny made a dismissive sound. "White men like to name every-thing after themselves."

Tommy traced a path along the river to the viewpoint they'd visited earlier and then rested his finger on a spot farther up river. "That's the longhouse," he said. He had working hands, stained in the creases as if he worked on cars, the knuckles scraped. She wanted to know those hands.

"Too bad we don't have more time," he said.

"Me too," she said. They would be on their way home soon, and she would leave Mr. Sweet Eyes behind.

"Mrs. Scott?" An older lady with ruddy cheeks and a mop of frizzy gray hair came out to greet them, breathless, as if she'd run from some other corner of the building. "What a terrific surprise. I'm Dr. Murray. Welcome."

"Kora—someone from our tribe—did she call to tell you why we were coming?" Elizabeth said.

"Yes. We're thrilled," Dr. Murray said. "You came from the reservation when? How was the trip? You must be tired, we can make this quick." The woman fired off one cheerful question or comment after the other, without waiting for a response.

She took them back to a bright room filled with work tables and rows of tall shelves. The shelves sagged with books and organizer boxes stuffed with documents. Some of the tables were stacked with storage boxes and plastic bins of various sizes. The room smelled pleasantly dusty like old books and dried grass. A trio of students worked with plant samples and a giant book of illustrations.

"This okay? We don't have a lot of time," Dr. Murray said. "Sorry everything is such a mess. We've got a lot going on right now." She waved at the students. "Can one of you go grab us a chair?" No one moved until Dr. Murray nudged one of them and he disappeared from the room.

"Identification," Dr. Murray said, her hands waving over the table like she was performing a magic trick. "People, places, things. So much here, it's hard to know where to start." She went to a cabinet with wide, flat drawers and whipped them open and shut, choosing and setting aside items sealed in clear sleeves. She found something she wanted and cleared away a spot on the table. It was a picture identical to the one at the casino.

"This is what you're here to see," Dr. Murray said, her finger tracing the dance dress. "I didn't know that was you in the photo. I've updated our records. What can you tell me about this? Can you identify the other girls?"

Granny moved around to take a closer look.

Elizabeth sidled closer to Tommy. "I'm not convinced that's her," she whispered. "She likes to mess with researchers."

"She wouldn't be the first," Tommy whispered back. He'd finally taken off his rain jacket. Underneath he wore one of those supposedly wrinkle-free shirts that always look rumpled. She reached up to fix the collar.

His whole body stiffened, but he leaned to her, to make it easier to reach. When she removed her hands, she said, "Sorry. Too familiar?"

He kept his eyes on Granny but gave the smallest shake of his head.

Granny carefully studied the photo, before saying, "I need my glasses." Then she laughed.

The others laughed, too, but Elizabeth had heard that joke before. Granny dug around her fanny pack and pulled out her glasses and took another look at the photo. She tapped on one of the dancers. "I might know this one. Give me a minute."

Dr. Murray brought another plastic bin to the table. She pulled on a pair of plastic gloves and took out a carved spoon and set it down.

Granny leaned against the work table to get a closer look before she picked it up. The students' eyes grew wide, but no one stopped her.

"Not ours," Granny said, turning it over in her hands.

"Are you sure?" Dr. Murray asked.

Granny gave her a stony glare and Dr. Murray picked the object up with both hands and put it away.

"This always happens," Elizabeth whispered. "Researchers. Academics. They think Granny has nothing better to do than answer their research questions."

"What happened to that chair?" Tommy said, using the loudest voice she'd heard since she met him.

"Hang on," Dr. Murray said. The student arrived with a desk chair.

Granny settled into it with a huff. "I thought you were in a hurry. You got my dress?"

Dr. Murray's friendly demeanor became apologetic. "I'm sorry for the miscommunication. The ceremonial dress isn't here. I was so pleased to have you, I wanted to show you what we have."

Elizabeth stared, a mixture of disbelief and frustration stirring in her belly. "Where's the dress?"

We shipped it to a museum down south for a cataloging project. We're identifying regalia from up and down the coast. It's on loan for a temporary display. It's coming back here. It's our piece."

Granny snorted at that.

Dr. Murray tried again. "Sorry. My point was that you could come back here to see it. Meanwhile, we have a couple of other ceremonial dresses if you'd like to see those."

"Glad you folks are taking care of our dance regalia while it does not fulfill its intended purpose," Elizabeth said, not hiding her annoyance.

Granny did the tiniest shake of her head: *That's enough.* Elizabeth couldn't match Granny's heroic patience with interviewers.

"What if they went to the other museum, could they see it there?" Tommy asked.

"I don't see why not. I'm heading down there this afternoon. That's why the rush." Dr. Murray wrote something on a card and handed it to Tommy. "Sorry we don't have more time." She rushed them out so she could finish getting ready for her trip.

Back outside, Granny walked more slowly, her head drooping as they headed back to the bus.

"Box after box of our stuff. Why don't we take care of it ourselves?" Elizabeth said.

"You should," Granny said.

"I'm not smart enough. I barely made it through school as it is. That lady has a doctorate," Elizabeth said.

"It's your tribe," Tommy said, handing her the card Dr. Murray had given him. "You don't get that in school."

The museum was in California. There was no way to get there. Back on the bus, Granny groaned as she eased into her seat. A silly road trip had turned into something bigger, and Elizabeth couldn't bear to let her down.

"Could you take us?" she asked Tommy.

"I wish. Even if I could get away, I don't have any wheels," he said. "Sorry to let you down, Auntie."

"When do you get your car back?" she asked.

After a long pause he said, "Never. It died. That was the call earlier."

Maybe his mechanic was Angie.

"Let's ask to borrow Linda's," she said.

"I can't leave town," he said without further explanation.

"At least we tried, Granny. We can come back here someday."

Granny muttered to herself.

Tommy got the bus going again. "You two have to go home?"

Elizabeth said, "Yeah. I have to start work. It's my last night in town. Do you want to do something fun?"

"I'm not fun," he said with an adorable nervous ring to his laugh.

"Let me be the judge of that," she said, hoping he had a favorite spot, a fun bar with live music, or a little cafe with desserts she couldn't get at home.

"Unfortunately, I can't."

She couldn't tell if he was genuinely regretful or if she'd misread their interactions.

"I have a situation I can't ignore," he said. "Drop you off at Linda's?"

She and Granny had to pack up and figure out how they were getting home. "Hope we see you before we go."

LINDA WOULD NOT APPROVE of him using the UIC bus as his main wheels but he could keep that a secret for now. One problem at a time. He'd told Angie he'd come by and he failed. She was bound to stir up some drama to punish him.

He picked up a couple of cartons of Pad Thai and walked back to the apartment regretful that he wasn't having dinner with Elizabeth. He pretended he had a different sort of life, where he was free for spontaneous plans and could date an incredible woman.

Tommy could hear voices as he walked up to his apartment. The front door was ajar. He clung to the hope that she had gone to a meeting. Maybe she found a friend and they decided to brew up some coffee and talk about their plan for staying sober. Then a man's bellow of laughter followed by the clunk of a bottle falling and rolling across the floor. Tommy pushed the door open.

Angie's upper body was draped over the kitchen table, her face buried in her arm, her body shaking with laughter. The guy was college-age, his backpack leaning against the wall. He was a head taller and probably had fifty pounds on him, but there was nothing menacing about the visitor.

"What's going on?" Tommy said.

Angie sat up and pushed her hair back from her face. She wore stained sweatpants and one of his T-shirts that was too big for her. She gave him a comic look of surprise. "You're home early."

"Have you been drinking?" Tommy asked, even though it was obvious. They each had a beer in front of them and the empties lined up on the table.

"Have you been drinking?" she repeated in a high-pitched voice. "This is my friend Jason." The real surprise was that she hadn't brought home more Jasons. She was still too young to buy. She leaned over and kissed her Jason.

"You can't have friends here, Ange."

"You can't stop me," she said.

"I can. This is my place. Jason has to leave."

Jason studied the beer bottle. He had the bearing of a drunk man ready to make poor decisions.

"No trouble, bud."

"I'm not your bud," Jason said.

"He bought the beer," Angie said.

Tommy was overcome with competing urges. One, to grab them by their shirt fronts and kick them out. The other, to hand over the apartment keys and run away. There had to be someplace he could go that was easier than this.

Something in Angie's face wavered like already she had regrets, but it was too late. She'd jumped off the cliff, and if she was in free fall, she was going to get the most out of it.

Tommy took a deep breath to push down the burning resentment and tried to see the person who needed his help. His eyes stopped at the four unopened beers on the table.

If they'd been sitting out, the beer wouldn't be as cold as he liked.

Nothing beat the first sip of a frosty beer on a warm day. How long had it been?

Angie followed his gaze and gave him a sneaky grin. She pushed a bottle toward him. His eyes traveled from it to her, and the glassy look in her eye and the tilt of her head.

He'd promised to help her.

To Jason, he said, "Pack up the beers and get out of here."

"No!" Angie sounded like a small child getting her favorite toy taken away.

Jason struggled with the command. He stared at the beer while he made up his mind. Tommy's hands were shaking. He set the bag with their dinner down on the counter. He didn't want to even pretend that he would fight. That guy and his beers needed to go.

"Please," he said. "Take it and leave."

Jason grabbed his backpack and shoved the beers inside.

"Can I go with you?" Angie said.

"I don't care," Jason said. He zipped up his backpack and held out his hand.

"Not a good idea, Ange," Tommy said.

"Shut up. Like you think you're my dad or something," Angie said. She got up and grabbed Jason to steady herself.

"You're a grown-up, you can do what you like," Tommy said. He couldn't stop her, but if anything happened, he'd carry it with him forever. "I'd like for you to stay. I brought dinner."

Jason put his arm around her. "I'm not a bad guy," he said. Angie gave a knowing smile. Everyone is your friend when you're drinking.

"I don't want dinner," she said. They left without closing the door. He weighed the idea of going after them before deciding it was best to leave them alone.

Tommy put one of the food containers in the refrigerator and took the other to the couch. By then, it was cool and hard to swallow, but he made himself eat.

He was halfway through it when his phone rang. *Elizabeth.* An unfamiliar jolt that he identified as happiness surged through him.

"Hey, something going on?" he said, picturing her on the phone, sweeping her hair over her shoulder, a half-smile on her face, a smile that said she had tricks that would surprise him.

"It's Elizabeth." Her voice was warm and sexy.

"I know. You're in my phone."

"I may have found a car for you," she said.

"You're looking for a car for me?" What was it about him that inspired people to help him all the time?

A throaty chuckle floated into his ear. She would duck her head, pretending to hide her smile. "I told Linda your car died. That guy Arnie has a car you can use. A loaner. She can drive you to the rez this weekend to get it."

"She talked to him?" Tommy said.

"I guess. They're doing a presentation or something."

Having a car to use would make life easier, but there was that kindness again. He couldn't escape the idea that he was everyone's special project, the guy that they all helped out of a mixture of pity and obligation.

"That'll help. Thanks."

"If you have a car maybe you could do a little getaway."

She was making an invitation. He tried to picture them taking off to go camping. He would take her on the long-awaited road trip. The mountains of Montana would be perfect. "Where do you want to go?"

"The museum in California?" she said, her voice still playful.

He deflated on that. She wasn't inviting him to run off with her. She needed a favor.

"I know it's crazy. I don't want to let Granny down. She's fixated on seeing this thing."

"I wish I could," he said.

"Linda won't let you take time off? For Aunt Dotty?"

For a moment he considered confessing. He could tell her about Angie and everything that came with it. For once he could share the burdens that he was keeping to himself.

"I can't. Family...work. Too many obligations."

"I can't change your mind?" Her soft velvet voice in his ear, so full of promise.

"You're the only one who could, but not the right time. You two figure out when you're leaving?"

"Back on the train tomorrow. We'll be home by dinner."

"I can take you to the train station," Tommy said. One more chance to see her.

"Keep thinking about that road trip. I'm going to change your mind," Elizabeth said.

ommy woke up to a loud pounding sound and a muffled but very distraught voice. It took a minute to shake off his sleepiness and figure out what was going on. Someone was banging on his front door. A mixture of hope and dread flooded through him. Ordinarily if she were on a bender, Angie would be gone for days, but maybe regret came quickly this time.

He pulled on a T-shirt. The knocking stopped. His phone on the nightstand sprang to life.

Linda.

He glanced at the time. He wasn't late. He picked up the phone.

"What's going on?"

"Where are you?" The words rushed out, clipped and breathless. He checked Angie's bedroom—empty—before he went to the front door.

"I'm at home. Hang on a sec." He pulled the door open.

There stood Linda, in sweatpants and a hoodie, hair pulled back, her face frantic. Her eyes widened, and she clutched him to her. "When they said the bus crashed I didn't know what to think."

"The Drivemaster crashed?"

All the air went out of him and he went weak in the knees. He turned to the kitchen counter. An open carton of Pad Thai sat there. His keys and wallet were gone. He'd gotten in the habit of taking them into his room with him, but with Angie out—for what he assumed was the night, he hadn't thought about it.

"I got a call about forty-five minutes ago. They said the bus was abandoned at the scene. That bus is your baby. I assumed the worst." Linda gave him the kind of troubled look that people give you to apologize when they've doubted you. "It must have been stolen from campus."

Tommy shook his head. He didn't want to tell the truth. He couldn't lie.

"I have a situation," he said, his voice unsteady.

"You said that yesterday when you missed the meeting." Linda was like a big sister. She had watched out for him way back when he was newly sober, staggering through the days, one at a time, all raw and uncertain. Her face was filled with concern, but her eyes were all business. There was no way he could avoid telling her.

"My cousin's been living here so she could sober up. She has not been successful."

"That's what you've been so mysterious about?" Linda said. She wiped a tear from her eye with a shaking hand. "What a terrible idea. Not yours, I bet."

He gave the slightest shake of his head.

The apartment had a balcony, narrow and dusty, big enough for two chairs. Angie sat out there sometimes, so the sagging curtain was pulled back enough to show a sliver of gray sky. Linda's eyes rested there. "Do you have coffee?"

"No," he said, overwhelmed by a wave of self-pity.

She nodded as if this was another in a long line of expected defeats. "How did your cousin get the bus?"

"My car died and then got towed. I used the bus to get back and forth from work."

The tears faded as she processed this. One hand rested on her hip, the other reached up to cover her face. When Linda was stressed, it took over her whole body. Words didn't come for either of them. He kept his eyes on the floor.

She huffed a few times before she said, "You are infuriating. You have us. You have all three of us—we love you—you know that, right?"

His throat had grown painfully tight and he tried unsuccessfully to clear it. He was the kind of person who could always hold everything in and at the moment he was failing. He wiped the back of one hand across his face.

"Why don't you let us help you?" She wasn't scolding. She was hurt.

"I'm doing fine," he said, barely croaking the words out.

"You are a recovering alcoholic with a practicing alcoholic in your home. The bus, which is supposed to be parked on campus, side-swiped three cars before it crashed into a trash dumpster. I don't think you understand what 'doing fine' means." The longer she spoke, the faster and louder the words came out.

"Is it drivable?" That's where his mind went. One last chance to see Elizabeth would be moot if he had nothing to drive.

"I don't know. We have to go see," Linda said.

"I can pay for it," he said, breaking out in a light sweat because there was no way he could pay for it.

"We have insurance," Linda said. She put her hands on his shoulders. "You know what we're dealing with at the center. I can't worry about you, too. You need to figure this out. Do you have a counselor or sponsor? Someone, anyone you can talk to?"

Tommy shrugged. "Maybe I don't want to talk."

"You can't do this alone. You can tell me it's none of my business. It's your life. But if you want to keep working with us, you need to get it together. There are lots of resources. I can call—"

"I'll do it myself," he said. He dreaded the idea of Linda getting involved. Calling people and sending him off to talk.

"People care about you," Linda said. "I want—"

"I get it," Tommy said.

Linda threw her hands up, the sisterly demeanor gone. Boss was back. "You need to deal with the police, the insurance, all of it. I don't want this to waste any of Rayanne or Ester's time. Understood? If you can't do it, tell me now, and I can start looking for someone who can."

The day had come and she'd finally had enough. They were having the conversation. If he was going to ask for help, now was the time, but dealing with insurance was easy compared to everything else he had to do.

"I can do everything, don't worry." He did his best to convey confidence but his mind was reeling. He needed to find Angie, and he needed to call his uncle. He needed to figure out how he was going to get around.

"Arnie has a car you can use. I'm going to the rez on Saturday. You can come along. Get dressed. We'll share my car today." She gave him a warm hug. "It's going to be okay."

"I know," Tommy said, doubting that was true.

ELIZABETH FINISHED SEARCHING the kitchen cupboards and moved to the shelves in the hallway that Linda referred to as the pantry annex. She found half-empty bags of pasta and rice stuffed into plastic bins, some with carefully printed labels, others lidless and a hopeless mess, an organizational project abandoned in the middle.

"There's no coffee," she called.

Granny poked through a drawer in the kitchen. "She got filters."

"I don't know what to tell you," Elizabeth said.

The front door opened, and Linda came in.

"Is he okay?" Elizabeth asked. Her heart had gone cold when she heard about the bus crash.

"He's coming in. You can ask him," Linda said, failing to hide her exasperation. "There's no more coffee. We drank it all, and I forgot to get some. I'm going to go get ready." She went back to her room and closed the door.

Tommy did not appear. Elizabeth opened the front door. The sky was gray and the air heavy with damp cold. Linda's car sat in the driveway with Tommy in the passenger seat, hunched over, eyes squeezed shut, like a person who had given up on the idea that he wasn't a disappointment.

"Hey!" She waited for him to look up and gave him a sunny smile.

He took his time getting out of the car.

"You're okay," she said, more relieved than she would have expected.

"Depends on what you mean by okay." He pretended to laugh and held up Linda's keys. "You two ready to go?"

"To the train station? We don't need to be there for a couple of hours." His hair was all bedhead like he was on his way home from an unexpected hook-up. He would be fun. It was a crime that they couldn't have fun. "You look like a man with a story to tell."

"You are mistaken," he said, forcing a smile.

"You coming in?"

"No. I'll come back," he said. "I gotta deal with..." He puffed out his cheeks.

"Work stuff?" she said.

"Exactly." He didn't leave, though. He stood in the driveway, hands limp at his sides.

"Granny needs coffee. We drank all of Linda's. Do you have time?"

Something sparked awake in him and his shoulders relaxed. "Not really."

"For Granny? She likes her doughnut and latte."

Tommy took his time like he couldn't make up his mind.

"She'll pay," Elizabeth mouthed.

Tommy smiled briefly and gestured to the car with his head. "Good, because I don't have a wallet. Don't ask."

"You're driving without a license? How rez."

"I have a license," he said. "Not on me."

"Never heard that one before," she said, her grin widening. She went to tell Granny what they were up to and ran back out before she could ask to come along.

"She's going to wait here," Elizabeth said when she got in the car.

"We're going to a fancy shop," he said as he pulled out. "Not a chain."

"Are you a doughnut expert?" she asked.

"I wouldn't say that," he said. "Are you? Is there a doughnut hot spot on the rez?"

"No." She studied him while he drove. He wasn't a big guy, but he had broad shoulders. His clothes looked like they'd been plucked from the dryer and balled up in the laundry basket until this morning when he put them on. But what would you expect from a guy who woke to the news that his bus had been driven into a dumpster?

The hangdog stoop was gone now that they were in motion, some confidence returning now that he was at the wheel. He waited for a trio of bicycles to pass before he made a right turn onto a busy street, a blur of storefronts and fast food. A few raindrops splashed against the windshield and he fiddled with the levers until he found the wipers.

"Where do you get Granny her doughnuts?" he asked.

"She likes those old-fashioned ones you get at the grocery store. It's like a sugar bomb glazed with more sugar. They're not good for her, but at her age, she should get what she wants."

"This place has the blueberry jam with lime curd and crusted salted caramel kind of doughnuts," he said.

"For real?"

"They're good. Granny won't complain. I have a way with elders." That smile again. If she were standing, she'd be weak in the knees. Tommy turned onto a two-lane street. "Here's the tricky part, parking." He slowed down and pointed to a shop with a line out the door.

"That good, huh?" Elizabeth said.

"You want to jump out and get in line?" He stopped the car.

"No," she said quickly, "I'll walk with you."

He was silent then, driving up a side street and then around again until she lost her bearings.

He parked the car. The air felt like rain coming. Neither of them had rain jackets. "Wait here. I'll see if Linda has an umbrella in the trunk."

"I don't mind the rain," she said.

"Humor me," he said. She waited while he dug around the trunk and slammed it shut. He came to her door and held out a gray-streaked wad that, shaken out, turned into a lightweight rain jacket that looked like it had been in a war. "That trunk is packed with everything under the sun except an umbrella."

"I don't need an umbrella." She put on the jacket. Tommy walked fast, always a half-step ahead of her.

Elizabeth skipped a few steps to get even with him. "You go back to your rez often?"

"Not really," he said.

"What's it like there?"

He shrugged. "Trees, river, lake. The usual. We're going this way." They turned the corner. "I rarely go back home."

"Why? Did you knock up the Chairman's daughter? Run over someone's dog? Did your pants fall off during the Horse and Cowpoke Days parade and you're too embarrassed to show your face in town?"

"Could be any of those," he said with humor. His phone rang and he checked the display. "Funny you should ask," he said, shaking the phone at her. When he answered, all he said was, "Where are you?"

There was a long pause while he listened to the person on the other end. His steps faltered, then he stopped walking.

"Tell me where and I'll come get you."

He gave Elizabeth a sheepish shrug as if to say: *What can you do?* But there was an edge to his voice.

He turned away and muttered something she couldn't hear. He nodded at whatever the person said. "Stay put. Promise me. I'll be right there."

Tommy put his phone in his pocket and took out the car keys. "I gotta take care of this. I'll come right back and pick you up in front of the store."

There was no way Elizabeth was getting left behind in this strange place. "I'll come with you."

"Not a good idea." He pointed out a bus stop, a half-block away. "I can give you the fare, and it's an easy bus ride to Linda's—"

"Where are you going? A strip club? A men's prison? Hot yoga? I can deal with it. Take me with you."

His hands fell to his side and clenched into fists. Every exhale was a frustrated sigh. His eyes turned back to the direction of the car.

Elizabeth couldn't figure out what was happening. "Why can't you tell me what's going on?"

He threw back his head and forced a laugh. "Let's go, then."

TOMMY DROVE to a diner not far from his apartment. Elizabeth sat next to him without saying a word. Today she wore purple skinny jeans and the purple fleece with yellow flowers. She smelled good, and on any other day of his life he would give anything to have her sitting next to him. But this was a disaster. Once she got a front-row view of his life at the moment, she would give him a kind look of pity and turn around, happy to be on her way out of town.

"You don't have to tell me if you don't want," she said.

"I don't want," he said.

"How bad could it be? Did you run over a box of kittens? Steal the donation bucket from a convent? Make an orphan cry? Whatever it is, you can tell me."

Holding it in was exhausting but he couldn't make the story come. He preferred to avoid these confessional moments, and by keeping the story private he avoided giving anyone an excuse to lecture him.

"What can I do?" Elizabeth said. She had her body turned to him, ready for anything.

The weariness was tearing him apart. He blurted out, "My cousin lives with me. She crashed the bus."

Elizabeth exhaled with an adorable little whistle between her teeth. "That was her that called?"

"She's a mess. She's a...she drinks."

"Oh." Elizabeth conveyed her complete understanding in that single word.

"I'm supposed to help her sober up and I'm failing." They arrived at the diner.

"Is this the first time you've dealt with this kind of thing?" Elizabeth asked, shaking her head like she couldn't believe what she was hearing.

"Not really," Tommy said.

"You already know this. If she doesn't want to get better, that has nothing to do with you. You can't tear your life apart because she has a drinking problem."

The accumulated weight of all the secrets and keeping up the illusion that everything was okay was yanking him down. There was a part of him that wanted to propose they find a brunch with Bloody Marys to help them get through this.

Elizabeth's eyes stayed on him, achingly understanding.

He spotted Angie through the window. He said, "People are counting on me."

"I get it." She tilted her head at the diner as if to say, *shall we?*

"Maybe you can get Granny something while I deal with this."

They walked in together. The diner was half full and smelled like bacon and coffee. Elizabeth went to the bakery case.

A disheveled Angie sat in a booth by herself, her eyes swollen from crying. Her trembling hands clutched a coffee cup, empty packets of sugar and cream scattered in front of her.

"You hurt?" Tommy asked when he sat down.

She shook her head.

"I need my wallet."

Angie gave him a look of disdain before throwing it on the table.

He resisted the urge to check the contents. He put it away. "What happened? Was Jason with you?"

Angie let out a sob. "He ditched me as soon as the beer was gone."

No loss there. A server came over and plunked a coffee mug in front of him and filled it without asking. She gave him a cheerful smile. "You need a menu?"

"Not sure yet," he said.

"How are you doing?" she said to Angie.

Angie pretended to smile and let the server top off her coffee. When she was gone, Angie nodded at Elizabeth. "I didn't know you had a girlfriend."

Elizabeth waited at the glass counter by the cash register, her dark eyes darting around the busy diner. Her bright clothes were the most colorful thing in there. She spotted him checking on her and flicked a teasing eyebrow at him before the counter clerk took her attention away. That tiny exchange gave him a surprising thrill.

Tommy returned his attention to Angie. "How could I have a girlfriend? I don't even have a life."

Her eyes welled up with tears. "Am I in trouble?"

"You stole a bus and crashed it and then ran away. What do you think?"

"I knew I shouldn't be driving so I was trying to park," Angie said as if explaining away a little misunderstanding.

"We're all in trouble. I'm in trouble," Tommy said. "You have to face this."

The server returned with a plate loaded with crispy potatoes and fried eggs and triangles of buttered toast. "Need anything else?"

Angie didn't say anything. Tommy wanted to make a joke about bail money, but instead, he said, "Another place setting?"

The server pulled a set of utensils wrapped in a paper napkin from her pocket and put it in front of him before she hurried away. In the short time since they arrived, two more booths had been seated and every chair at the counter filled. The diner was overly warm, even without a coat, and the booth felt crowded.

Angie used a mangled napkin to wipe at her eyes. She pushed the food at Tommy. "Do I have to go to jail?"

"I don't know...drunk driving...maybe?" Tommy leaned forward. "You need to call your dad. You need to go to the police. You need a lawyer. I don't know how to deal with this level of trouble."

Elizabeth left the counter. He fished for the keys, so she could wait in the car, but she scooted into the booth and reached across him to set the paper bag. Every time she brushed against him the air squeezed in his lungs.

"I'm Elizabeth," she said to Angie. She shot him a dazzling smile while she snuck the utensils from him. "Anyone plan to eat this?"

The tension at the table deflated a half-notch. Tommy pushed the salt and pepper to her.

"Like you're reading my mind," she said, holding his gaze.

His heart hurt with how much he wanted her. That smile.

"Whatever," Angie said in a voice heavy with scorn. After a moment's hesitation, she pulled herself to the edge of the booth. "I'm getting out of here."

The lightness in his heart extinguished just like that. "Don't move," he said.

Angie stayed where she was and wiped her sleeve across her eyes.

Elizabeth didn't acknowledge the unfolding drama. She took a couple of bites before she pushed the plate at him. "I love a greasy breakfast and this one meets and exceeds all expectations. Want to try?" She wiped the fork off with her napkin and handed it to him. She picked up his coffee cup and took a sip.

He took the fork from her, a spark of arousal startling him. He stared at the plate for a long moment before taking a bite. Tommy didn't realize how hungry he was until he tasted the eggs. Angie made a production of extracting another napkin from the dispenser and wiping her eyes. Elizabeth didn't say anything. She handed him his coffee and nudged her leg against his in their own silent conversation. They traded the fork back and forth until she pushed the plate over and said, "Finish it."

He shoveled the last couple of mouthfuls and drank the last of the coffee.

Angie hiccupped a few times and then said, "Could you say you did it?"

Elizabeth went rigid next to him but didn't say anything. Tommy shook his head. "I drive for my job, Ange. I can't do that."

"Not to mention, you're not the one who crashed the bus," Elizabeth said.

"Mind your own business," Angie said. She jumped up and stormed out of the diner.

She expected him to follow because that's what he'd done before. They would strike a bargain, and she would keep her part of the deal for a few weeks, and then the cycle would start again.

"How many second chances have you given her?" Elizabeth asked.

"Enough," he said. "I should call the police."

Elizabeth tilted her head toward his. "Sorry you have to deal with this." Her face was inches from his. He could feel her exhaled breath. He couldn't remember the last time someone's gaze had drilled through him like that. She said, "I'll take care of the bill and meet you outside."

He knew he should say something but he couldn't stop staring at her lips. They froze like that for the space of several heartbeats. He couldn't bear the idea of her leaving. He searched for an excuse, some reason to drag out their time together. Being around Elizabeth was the only thing he'd looked forward to in as long as he could remember. If he was going to drown, he wanted as much oxygen as possible before sinking below the surface.

The server stopped by the table again. "More coffee?"

The moment passed. Elizabeth pushed the cup away. The server put it on the empty plate and carried it away.

11

The car smelled like coffee and blueberry muffins. Elizabeth had given Linda her muffin and coffee when they dropped her off at the office. Granny still had hers. She sat in the back seat with the takeout cup on one knee, the paper bag open on the seat next to her.

"We gonna stop somewhere?" she asked.

"We're on our way to the train station," Elizabeth said.

"I don't like my food in my lap," Granny said. "The station gotta place to eat?"

"Does it?" Elizabeth waited for Tommy to answer. He'd barely said a word since they left the diner other than friendly banter with Granny as he loaded her into the car and exchanging some work-related planning with Linda before he dropped her off at the office.

"There are benches in the station," Tommy said.

"She likes to eat at a table," Elizabeth said.

"You'll be on the train soon. They have those little fold-down trays," he said. "You ready to go home, Auntie?"

Granny made a non-committal grunt at the back of her throat. "Didn't get to see my dress," she said.

"I'll get us to that museum, Granny. Not sure how but I'm working on it," Elizabeth said.

They drove through downtown. The clock tower of the train station loomed ahead. He pulled into a line of cars waiting to drop passengers off at the main doors.

Tommy took his eyes off the road long enough to shoot her a look. "I thought you were starting your job?"

"I might have to take a few days without pay. They won't mind. Everyone loves Aunt Dotty, and you know how it is on the rez."

The SUV in front of them stopped and the doors on either side popped open. A college-aged woman got out of the driver's side and went around to hug the guy from the passenger seat. They could hardly tear themselves apart. The driver waited until he had gone through the doors into the train station before she got back in and drove away.

Next, it was their turn. Tommy stopped the car and got out to help Granny. After this, they were unlikely to see each other again. Why couldn't a guy like this show up at home? Even in the midst of his problems, he had a steadiness about him. His life was in upheaval and he was here for them, reliable and grounded. Had George ever been this dependable?

Elizabeth got out and watched Tommy as he navigated Granny out of the back seat, letting her do as much as she could but hanging right there to make sure she didn't fall over. He said something she couldn't hear and Granny responded with a huffy laugh. As Granny pulled herself out of the seat, the muffin bag tangled in her clothes. It landed on the ground with a slap and the muffin rolled out and under the car.

"Fukoladola," Granny said.

"I owe you a muffin," Tommy said.

"Yeah, you do," Granny said, reaching up to thump his chest. He set her up with her cane and went around to pop open the trunk. He turned to study the cars and cabs lined up behind them. His eyes narrowed, staring into the distance. She'd never met anyone like this, his quiet competence was surprisingly sexy.

And she was never going to see him again.

A wave of disappointment washed over her and she forced herself to shake it off. She took out her backpack and unzipped the front pocket. She pulled out the tickets and slapped them against her hand. "Thanks for hauling us around," she said, hoping she didn't sound weepy.

Tommy grabbed the strap of Granny's backpack and then let it go. "I know another spot where we could get doughnuts," he said.

Granny opened up with the delighted grin of a little kid. "We got enough time?"

Elizabeth glanced up at the clock. "Sorry. We don't."

Tommy kept his attention locked on Granny. "I know a rest stop south of town that has nice picnic tables."

"What are you saying?" Elizabeth asked.

Tommy looked like he was doing complex equations in his head.

"We need to get in there and catch our train," she said.

"What if I take you?" Tommy said.

"You want to drive us to the rez?" Elizabeth asked, the ridiculousness of the plan overshadowed by the possibility that they didn't have to say goodbye.

"No. I'll take you to the museum," Tommy said.

"You know where it is, right?" she said, but she was ready to run with the idea, too.

"That lady gave me the name of the place," he said. Whatever stress and anxiety he'd been dealing with, he'd put it behind him now. He stood closer to her than he needed to, but the proximity thrilled her.

"What about—?" Elizabeth said, pointing over her shoulder at the imaginary manifestation of the problems Tommy was having.

"It'll all be there when I get back," he said. He eased the backpack off her shoulder and threw it in the trunk. He took the tickets from her hand and tossed those in too, and slammed it shut.

"Doesn't Linda need her car?"

"It's a day of driving. We get there tonight. Go to the museum in the morning. I'll drive you guys home and return Linda's car late tomorrow night. She'll understand." He helped Granny back in the car.

"You're delusional about how long the driving will take," Elizabeth said, but she didn't try to talk him out of it. They'd have to spend the night somewhere. Already she was thinking about what she wanted to do to him.

"Something being a terrible idea has never stopped me before," Tommy said. "Besides, we're doing it for Auntie."

Elizabeth stood next to the car, off balance by this sudden change in plans. Tommy shut Granny in and stood next to her, close enough for her to see a faint stubble around his chin. He was in her personal space, his feet inches from hers. "You coming?"

"Quick," she said, climbing in the car, "before you change your mind."

"I'm not changing my mind," he said.

TOMMY LEANED against a tree with his phone in his hand. He had the center's number on the screen, but he couldn't bring himself to press the call button.

The clouds had broken up and warm sunlight showed through. The tall trees made the rest stop like a park. Granny was set up at the picnic bench, a pink box full of doughnuts in front of her. She'd grimaced when he told her about the fancy ones, but she was polishing off doughnut number two without slowing down.

If this was a mistake, it wasn't too late to turn back. He could put Granny and Elizabeth on the train tomorrow. The Angie problem could be strung out another day—he didn't even know whether she was in jail or what—and he could deal with the wreck like he promised Linda.

Back at the table, Elizabeth caught his attention and nodded at Granny, who was digging through the pink box again. Then Elizabeth gave him a smile that he felt in his entire body. He wanted to hold her. She would be soft and smell sweet. Nothing could happen with Granny around, but with one night...even the remote possibility was enough to keep him moving forward.

He swiped through his contacts and called Ester instead.

"Yo! Are the rock stars on their way?" Ester asked.

"They sure are," Tommy said. "I need a favor."

"Anything for you, my brother from another mother."

"I need to keep Linda's car for a day. Can you tell her something?"

A group of Canada geese flew in a sloppy formation overhead. Their squawks drifted down like sounds of outrage.

"Ester?"

"I'm sorting through that request," she said carefully. They all expected him to implode. It wasn't a matter of if, but when.

"I'm still sober," he said.

"Of course...sorry. I'm sure it's terrible for you when we assume the worst but crashing the bus, and now driving off with Linda's car…. It's hard to know what to think."

"There might be a girl."

"You mean Angie?"

"No, a girl I like."

"Elizabeth? I thought you said they were on their way."

"They are. With me."

Ester sighed. "You're driving them home? What about the insurance stuff?"

Tommy's eyes stayed glued to Elizabeth. She leaned forward to make sure Granny could hear her, and the two of them made each other laugh. Her hair was tossed around in the breeze and she kept pushing it out of her face. She caught him looking and crushed him with that smile again.

He didn't know what to say next. "I need...something right now. One good thing."

"Did you tell her about your issue?"

She meant not drinking. Tommy didn't answer.

"It won't matter to her. She was falling for your sweet brown eyes the minute she stepped through the door."

Ester was right, though. He had to tell her. "I will," he said.

"Isn't she kind of vixeny for you?"

Elizabeth picked that moment to yank the fleece over her head.

The shirt she had on underneath rode up to show a slender band of brown skin at the waist. She shook the fleece out, and the neckline of her top gaped enough to reveal a pale pink bra strap.

"Or just vixeny enough," he said.

"Oh. Has anything happened?"

All this information gathering was to appease Rayanne, but he wasn't about to cooperate. "I'll fill you in later."

"I'm all for you, bud, but is this the best time?" He knew what she meant.

"I thought that part of me was dead and it's not. I want to, you know, help them out."

"Good for you. I'll cover for you. Now give me something. A nibble. A tiny hint."

"Gotta go," Tommy said.

"Wait! You have to talk to Linda after everything that's happened."

"I'll have the car back to her tomorrow night. I'll do it then. Tell her 'leave without pay' is fine. We've got Auntie with us. We're on a mission. Thanks, E."

He returned to the table.

"What did Linda say?" Elizabeth asked.

He shrugged, trying to convey a sense of mystery. "You ladies ready to go?"

"I'm missing my work," Granny said. The elder had slowed down. She still had half a doughnut on a napkin in front of her.

"Oh yeah?" Tommy said. "Where's work?"

"When she goes to the casino, she calls that work," Elizabeth said.

"It is my work," Granny said.

"I can take you to work," Tommy said, pulling out his phone. "There are casinos up and down this highway. You want to stop at lunch or do you want to stop for dinner?"

Granny tapped her finger at him. "I knew you was one of the good ones."

～

EVEN AS THEY were on the road, Elizabeth expected Tommy to reconsider this road trip. A couple of times she said, "You can still change your mind." But he shook his head.

The afternoon passed quickly. As they headed south, the sky was clear except for a few puffy white clouds. Tommy found a classic country station and Granny napped in the back as they sped down the highway.

"What did you study in college?" she asked.

"You know, the usual. This and that," he said.

She leaned over and playfully punched his arm. "We're road tripping now. Knock off that mysterious stuff."

He rubbed his arm, pretending he was in pain.

She tried again. "What kind of student were you?"

"Struggled." He took his time, carefully choosing his words. "I wasn't much of a student. Easily distracted, I guess. How about you? Were you a brainiac like Linda?"

"My issue was that I was homesick all the time. Then Leo died and I felt guilty because I wasn't there. I came home. The only reason I even finished was because Granny insisted. I didn't want to let her down." Elizabeth left out the part she didn't want to talk about.

"Did you ever think about grad school?" he asked.

"Ugh. No more school. I want to be home and with my family."

"I agree with you on the school. Linda sat me down one time. Since I like working with the kids, she thought I should be a teacher."

"What do you think?"

Tommy paused, trying and failing to picture it. "It took a platoon to get me through a two-year degree. Not sure I'm capable of more. We're about an hour away from the casino I had in mind. Granny can punch her time card, and we could get some dinner."

Elizabeth nodded. "At first, I wanted to discourage it but the casino is a good idea. We can stay there and get a decent room. Usually when we go somewhere, Granny wants someplace cheap. Like, the most terrible bargain lodge with torn curtains and flimsy towels you can see through and road construction outside so that jackhammers wake you up before the sun rises."

"Sounds like my apartment," Tommy said.

"Then we have to go to the horrible restaurant that's attached. Not a good greasy spoon like that place this morning. No, a terrible place where everything comes out of the same fryer. She orders the same thing–a patty melt with French fries. And she never complains no matter how terrible it is."

"Does she like those places because no one asks whether she has a reservation?"

"Hilarious," she said with a groan.

Granny snickered in the back.

Elizabeth turned around. "We're stopping in an hour, so you can make some money, that okay?"

Granny reached up and patted her arm. "Thanks, Lizzie."

1 2

*T*hey walked through the casino doors and into the tiled entry. Tommy was amused to see Granny a few steps ahead of them.

"You play? Elizabeth asked.

Tommy shook his head. "Never interested me."

"I think it's fun in small doses like a weekend out of town with the girls, but no more than that."

"So, it's not *your* job," Tommy said.

"Very funny," she said.

Granny elbowed her way past elders decades younger and straight to the machine she wanted. She plopped herself down in a chair and dug around her fanny pack for her wallet.

"You want me to hang out with Granny, so you can wander around?" Tommy asked.

"Go!" Granny said with a dismissive wave. "I don't like people watching me."

"She lives for this." Elizabeth glanced at her phone. "Granny, we'll come back and get you for dinner, is that okay?"

All of Granny's attention was on the screen.

"We'll come back in about forty-five minutes and take her to the buffet," Elizabeth said.

"That's precise," Tommy said.

"It's more like an hour, but it usually takes some time to find her," Elizabeth said. "Shall we get a drink?"

Tommy hesitated before he shook his head. "Why don't you school me on how these crazy machines work."

"Certainly." She wandered through the various banks of machines before deciding on one. "Sit."

Tommy did as instructed. The machine had an image of a wolf howling at the moon at the top. The screen in front of him was a grid that displayed a random assembly of symbols and shapes: a caldron, something that looked like a lumpy basket, a bow and arrow, numbers in multiples of one hundred.

"What is all this? Do I need a row of wolves to win?"

"All will become clear shortly," Elizabeth said. "Do you have money?"

Tommy pulled out his wallet to see if he had any cash. His secret wad of twenties would have come in handy on this trip. Too bad he hadn't planned this better. All he had on him was a twenty and two singles. At least Angie had left him something. He didn't have money to lose but he was the one who'd asked to see the machines. The demonstration would not last long. He pulled out the twenty and fed it into the machine. Elizabeth leaned over his shoulder and touched a finger to a round glowing button in a line of confusing buttons. He couldn't focus his attention with her chest pressed into his back.

"You want the maximum bet. Your credits show in the corner of the screen. That button makes the bet." She rested her hand on his shoulder.

He took a deep breath. The buttons were different sizes but the labels meant nothing. He hadn't heard a word. He pressed the round button in the middle, and the images on the screen moved around in a dazzling display of changing lights while the speakers played sounds that meant his money was being chewed up and taken away. The animation stopped and a series of neon lines crisscrossed the results.

"Great job," Elizabeth said.

"Did I win?"

"Yeah. You got some gold coins, what looks like a raccoon tail, a stack of barrels and a bunch of sharp silver rods. Spears?"

"How much?"

"Nothing monetary."

She leaned against him again. His body was responding predictably.

"Try again," she said in his ear.

Lust for a woman who gave him her complete attention. When was the last time that happened? His heart thumped in his chest. His eyes stared at the symbols without seeing them.

Tommy did as he was told and watched the symbols reassemble in front of him. Elizabeth remained pressed against him while she went through the results. "Even better. You got trolls, two kinds of owls, a box of jewels, and what looks like a pile of sticks, kindling perhaps."

"You have no idea how this works, do you?" Tommy said, twisting around to face her.

"I have an idea," she said, making it sound like she was talking about something else. She held his gaze until his groin went tight.

A wolf howl came out of the speakers. Tommy felt like he was panting. He returned his attention to the screen. "I press the button, and the money goes away."

"This is how our people make money. Stick with it," she said. "It takes the machine a while to warm up."

"I don't believe you," he said, but he pushed the button again. The same jangle of sounds and flashing lights. He identified a different sound, an owl hooting?

"See? You won credits that time." Elizabeth pointed to one corner of the screen where the credit count zipped upward.

A thrill surged through him. His luck was changing. "How much?"

Elizabeth squinted at the numbers. "Seventy-five cents."

He tried to hide his dismay. "I thought it would be more."

"Isn't that how it always is?"

He dutifully continued to play, watching his credits dwindle. He was down to his last play when Elizabeth stopped him.

"We need some magic voodoo," she said.

"I hope you've got some because I'm fresh out."

"Last one, together." Elizabeth hugged him from behind, grabbing his hands and threading her fingers with his. She held their hands above the button. "Sorry. Too familiar?" she said, her breath in his ear.

"I'm good," he said, but his hands would have been shaking if she wasn't holding on to them.

"Think good thoughts." She held him tight. He throbbed with longing. The thought that sprang into his head was of him spinning Elizabeth around and pushing her back against the machine, pulling her legs around his waist and using his hands to cup her ass and rock her hips against his. How about that for magic voodoo? An unintended gasp snuck out of him when she pushed their hands on the button. He hung on to her while the screen went through its pulsing lights and chirps and beeps.

Elizabeth pulled away from him and squealed. "We won!"

Tommy didn't see anything new on the screen but the credit count rolled up again.

"What now? A dollar? Five dollars?"

"One hundred bucks," Elizabeth said. She gave him a high-five.

"For real?" he said.

"For real," she said.

There was a brief moment when he was going to hug her from the front but he stopped himself. "Show me how to cash out."

"Are you sure?"

"I know everything I need to know about the slot machines," he said, surprised by his relief. A hundred bucks in his pocket, while they were on the road, would come in handy.

She pressed the button and held up the ticket once it had printed. "You want to try some table games?"

"Perhaps you've mistaken me for one of them rich Indians. You might have to shift your attention elsewhere if that's what you're looking for."

"My attention is fine where it is, thank you very much." She grabbed the front of his shirt and kissed him on the lips, like it was something they did every day, and then pulled away to gauge his reaction.

The noise and lights of the casino floor faded away until it was only Elizabeth in a warm glow in front of him. He leaned forward, and she kissed him again, this time with intent. She put her arms around his neck and gently bit his lower lip. He couldn't help the gasp of surprise, and she smiled and pulled him closer and dipped her tongue into his mouth, peppermint and good fortune.

His arms circled around her and she was exactly as soft and sweet-smelling as he imagined. He couldn't remember the last time anyone kissed him. Only a few times since he got sober.

"You taste like a mountain," she growled in his ear.

"That's good?" Tommy asked, suddenly self-conscious about everything.

"It's insane," she said and focused back on his mouth again.

It seemed obvious that this was what he was hoping for when he volunteered for this trip, but now that it was happening, it was a surprise the way she felt in his arms and the confidence with which she made this decision.

"We have to get out of here," Elizabeth said.

ELIZABETH SLID her hand down his arm and threaded her fingers into his. She pulled him along, not sure where she was taking him. She couldn't wait to get that shirt off of him. He wasn't a huge guy, but he was all tight muscle wherever her hands landed. Her eyes darted around the casino. She needed a plan. These situations where two people had a connection always managed to resolve themselves. They'd get a room.

"Elizabeth," Tommy said. He squeezed her hand. She squeezed back, understanding his impatience. Now that they knew they wanted the same thing, it couldn't happen fast enough. She stopped again.

Casinos were all the same–confusing mazes of machines and ugly carpet. She wanted the hotel lobby.

"Elizabeth," Tommy said again. He pulled her to a stop and faced her, those sweet, mournful eyes looking deep into hers. She leaned up to kiss him again. She was ready to climb onto him right there in the lobby.

He put a hand on her shoulder, not pushing her away, just enough pressure to hold her in place. "Granny?"

Granny.

"Right," she said, her desire not quelled in the least. She wiped the back of her hand across her mouth in a feeble attempt to change the course of her thoughts, but all her desire was balled up and focused on this one warm-blooded gorgeous man. Her head flipped through the possibilities. She'd planned extracurricular fun around Granny before. "Dinner first. I can sneak into your room after she goes to bed."

Tommy took a moment, as if he had to swallow a golf ball. He chuckled to himself, a private joke she didn't get. "I'm not going to have a room. I'm sleeping in the car."

"Why would you sleep in the car?" There was no way this guy was sleeping in the car.

"That hundred bucks is the majority of my wealth at the moment," he said. "I can't get a room here. I don't even have a toothbrush. I didn't think this through at all."

Elizabeth's lust waned with the uncertainty. "Are you sorry you're here?"

"No," he said unequivocally, "it's not that."

"Okay, we won't fool around." She hated the idea but they would figure something out. "Tonight, anyway," she added.

Tommy's body made a funny little tremor.

"You don't have to sleep in the car. We can get a room with two beds. I'll sleep with Granny." There was something unbearably sad about him thinking sleeping in the car was a possibility.

"Don't you think it's weird to all stay together?" They still stood face to face. He reached up to push her hair over her shoulder, his fingers brushing over her throat. A different, more uncertain feeling rose in her, a growing fondness. She wanted more than a tussle.

"It's not weird," she said. "It's part of our tradition."

"It's part of your tradition to invite the guy who works for your cousin to stay with you and your Granny? I've slept in a car lots of times."

"Linda's like your family, and now you're like our family," she said.

"If you think Granny won't mind. Shouldn't we get her for dinner?"

From somewhere across the casino there was a chorus of celebratory cheers. She grinned at him, as if the joy of strangers meant something good for them, too. She kept his gaze and kissed him one more time, with a promise of more to come.

By the time they found Granny, she'd secured a casino club card and sweet-talked someone into giving her coupons for the buffet and a discounted room.

"One of the advantages of traveling with a famous elder," Elizabeth told Tommy.

"What are the disadvantages?" he asked with a playful smile.

"As if you didn't know," she said, her hand grazing his ass.

She followed Tommy as he walked Granny through the buffet, two plates balanced on a tray. He never ran out of patience with her. And Granny hung on to him, too. He was worming his way into everyone's heart.

Granny schooled him on how to work a buffet. "Don't waste your time on those salads at the beginning. They take too much room and then you don't got a place for the good stuff." Tommy made sure she got both prime rib and salmon like she wanted.

After dinner, they dropped Granny off in the room and went back to the parking lot to get the bags.

"See, she doesn't care," Elizabeth said. The parking lot was huge, but Tommy led them right to the car.

"I think she wants me for herself," Tommy said. He handed her one backpack and threw the other over his shoulder.

"You might be right."

"I gotta figure out what I'm doing," he said. "No bags."

"You can wear one of my T-shirts," Elizabeth said.

Tommy gave her a leisurely once-over, pausing in all the right spots. "I don't think that's going to work. I'll check the gift shop."

"Good idea. You should get one of those T-shirts with the owl and the dream catcher with the moon in the night sky."

"Remind me not to let you pick my clothes," he said.

"I'm good at picking out clothes." She dug around Linda's trunk. "What is all this stuff even for? Linda's trunk is a mystery for the ages."

There were a variety of boxes and bags, workout stuff and a couple of blankets.

Tommy grabbed a blanket. "I could still sleep in the car."

Elizabeth snatched it from his hands and stuffed it back in. "You will not." She peeked in one of the garbage bags. "Check this out, there are clothes mixed in with the towels."

"Probably lady stuff," Tommy said, opening the other bag.

"Sweatshirt. Sweatpants. A T-shirt that says Beat Braves. These look sufficiently manly to me."

"Let me see that," Tommy said, examining the clothes.

Elizabeth pawed through the other things in the car to see if there was anything else he could use. She found a plastic zipper-top bag. She held it up to see it in the light of the parking lot.

"Why does Linda keep a giant bag of condoms in the back of her car?"

"The usual reasons? You know how she likes to be prepared," Tommy said with a snicker.

"This is taking being prepared to a whole new level." Elizabeth tossed them back in and shut the trunk. "If I'm not going to get the full meal deal, can I at least kiss you one more time before we go up?"

Tommy helped her jump up on the car and she wrapped her legs around his waist and dug her fingers into his hair and kissed him hard, her tongue flicking over his, her desire laid bare for him.

"You're making me crazy," he said when she finally let him up for air.

"I like you too," she said.

13

---

*L*inda took a deep breath before she climbed into Arnie's rig. The floor was free of take-out menus and there was no sign of clothes ready to be dropped off at Donation Hut. He was a different version of the self she was accustomed to, his hair still damp from the shower, and he smelled good, like soap and fresh clothes. No suit on a Saturday. He had on a well-worn, long-sleeved denim shirt, and a pair of jeans. She hadn't seen him in jeans since college.

"Surprised to hear from you," Arnie said as she buckled her seatbelt.

"That makes two of us," she said. "Thanks for taking me. I wasn't sure whether you were still in town." She settled her bag on the floor between her feet. There was no sign of an overnight bag. Maybe he had a drawer at her house. She didn't want to know.

He opened his mouth, then snapped it shut. Whatever he planned to say, he changed his mind. He touched something on his phone and then dropped it into the center console and took off.

The silence became unbearable. "In the spirit of no secrets..." she began.

"Oh, terrific," he said, making an exaggerated motion of settling back to hear.

She should have phoned him immediately, no way to change that now. "We had an incident. Tommy has my car."

"What kind of incident?"

Linda puffed out her cheeks, not sure where to begin.

"Is this going to make me mad?"

The man could be so aggravating. She made a quiet sound of agreement. "Should we stop for coffee?"

"I got you one," he said, gesturing with his chin. "Bottom cup. Milk and sugar?"

There were two take-out cups in the center console. He knew her coffee order. She tried to remember his, black? She took a tentative sip and it was cool enough to swallow. "Thanks." She took a big gulp and waited for the caffeine to do its magic. Traffic was light as they headed out of town. Arnie grabbed his coffee and took a sip. In the middle of the console he had a pair of sunglasses, a roll of breath mints, and a credit-card wallet.

He followed her gaze. "I have a new system to keep my personal cards separate from my government card. I've accidentally used the government card for personal more than once. The Finance Department is not amused."

For some reason this made her recall his pocketknife, which was currently in her purse. She'd bring it up later.

"You were saying?" he said.

There was no excuse for putting it off. "There was a crash involving the bus. Still don't know whether it's drivable."

"Crash? Did anyone get hurt? Is Tommy okay?"

Linda wasn't sure how to respond. "He's not injured. He wasn't driving. His alcoholic cousin has been living with him. Practicing alcoholic."

"Isn't he—?"

"Yeah. She got tanked up and took the keys and bashed it up."

"Where was it parked?"

"At Tommy's apartment."

She braced for Arnie's anger. Somehow this would be all her failing. The terrible way she managed her staff and her lack of authority.

He didn't say anything right away. Instead, he scratched his head and kept his eyes on the road. Linda waited, her body tense, both hands wrapped around her coffee.

"That guy can't catch a break," he finally said.

She almost laughed with relief. "True. But he's not a good decision maker. It's like he knows what he can handle, but he takes on too much anyway. I love him like family, but I also want to wring his neck."

"Sounds about right," Arnie agreed. "How did he end up with your car?"

"I should have seen this coming. Elizabeth has always been like that"—Linda made a sweeping gesture with her hand—"working some sorcery to get people to do things for her. There was a day when I envied her for it. There was always a guy who wanted to take her on a houseboat, or get her tickets to some concert she wanted to go to, or give her a kidney. She's a terrific human being but Tommy is in such a precarious place right now. He's taking her on a road trip." She'd gotten in the car determined to keep this ride as professional as possible, and now she was spilling her family business.

"He's a grown man. He'll be fine."

"He ran off with my car after promising me that he would deal with the bus and all his other screw ups. I don't think he's fine."

Arnie's mouth curved into a knowing smile. "Maybe he's going after what he wants, for a change. It'll be good for him."

Linda stared at him in amazement. "They have Granny with them. They're taking her to see ceremonial regalia."

Arnie laughed. "Who hasn't worked around an elder cock-block? I will be rooting for them."

Linda didn't even know what it meant to work around an elder cock-block. He never could let her forget how easy it was for him. She tried to share his humor. "The message is that he'll be back tonight, so I'll trade cars with him tomorrow, and you two can work out the car loan."

"I wouldn't loan it if I was worried about it," Arnie said. They drove a few miles in silence before he said, "To be clear, we want the same thing."

Was he telling her, or asking for reassurance? Either way, the remark annoyed her. "You mean we both want the center to succeed."

"And you, to be the one."

"Right," she said, a flush rising in her cheeks. *We're talking about work.* She continued, "What I'm talking about today, all the programs and events that I want to oversee. I can be the one who does it. I thought you had doubts." The words spilled out, pure honesty.

"The doubts I have aren't about you. I'm afraid with the way things are going they're going to want someone to be accountable. If it comes to that, I want you to make the decision."

Linda remained firm. "If it comes to that, we'll talk about it. Meanwhile, look what I deal with. People micromanaging my decisions. Everything needing to be discussed in committee."

"Nature of the beast, don' t you think?"

That's what the person micromanaging would think.

"For today, we need support for the delay. That facilities manager guy said they would take us to alternate sites in a week or two. We're actively working on the problem."

"I'm with you," he said.

She could hear the "but" about to follow but while he sorted out whatever he wanted to say next, his cellphone rang. He tapped an earpiece she hadn't noticed earlier.

"Sorry about this," he said to her. "When you're on Council, you're always at work."

"You don't have to explain to me," she said.

"Hey." Arnie's voice dropped. She glanced at the phone and saw the display: *Katie.*

Oh.

She shrank back in the seat pretending that would give him more privacy. She studied the dashboard and the button for the glove box. She guessed what was inside: breath mints, a heavy-duty flashlight, an ice scraper, maps.

She'd been in Virgil's car one time. He drove an older dark-green

SUV that had been used to transport runners on a weekend relay event. It was tidy but smelled like workout clothes. He'd taken her to a restaurant out of town by the river. Pretending not to listen to Arnie's call reminded her that she and Virgil had no firm next date on the books.

Arnie said, "Not a good time...I'm in the rig. I've got work people with me."

That's what she was to Katie, work people. There was a long pause. No doubt Katie wanted to know which work friends.

Arnie stammered, "No...yes...probably not. Can I call you this afternoon?"

Linda tried to determine from this side of the conversation whether he'd stayed with her the night before.

"Sure, sure. We'll plan something. I said I'd call you."

If she were betting, she would bet this was not the case. She was dismayed by how much this amused her.

Arnie disconnected the call. She caught his attention and pantomimed blowing her nose.

He popped the center console open and handed her a packet of tissues. She would never know what was in the glove box. She'd never looked in Virgil's glove box either. She removed a tissue and dabbed her nose and returned the pack. He threw it back where it came from.

The phone rang again, and Arnie made an annoyed sound at the back of his throat.

"Yeah?" There was a long pause. "How much later? Fine, we'll be there this afternoon." He clicked the phone off. "The meeting is running late. They want you to stop by late afternoon."

"That's fine. I can keep myself busy until it's my turn."

"And deny you our fine rez hospitality? I'll feed you lunch and take you over when it's time."

"*A*lways gotta be stairs," Elizabeth said, groaning inwardly at the steep staircase leading to the museum's main entrance.

The museum was located in the heart of downtown, surrounded by rectangles of brilliant green lawn, a peaceful oasis amid the busy streets. The building was constructed of white stone walls with pillars. Hanging banners advertised the featured exhibits.

Tommy stopped in front so Elizabeth could unload Granny. The car stuck behind them honked and Granny gave them a cheerful wave as she hobbled up onto the sidewalk.

"I'll meet you in there," Tommy said.

The sight of him driving away made her uneasy but she shook it off. He would never leave them but right now they were so dependent on him.

"I don't mind the stairs," Granny said, grabbing for the fat metal handrail and hoisting herself up the first step.

The sky was clear except for a few patchy clouds. Elizabeth had put on a bright orange sundress, and the sun felt good on her bare skin. She walked next to Granny, one step at a time. At the top, there was a small sign pointing out an entrance ramp that would avoid the stairs.

"That would have been helpful earlier," Elizabeth muttered.

There was a bronze statue out front of a doe and two fawns. Tommy made a silly face and stopped to pet the doe before running to join them.

"You came back," she said, sounding more desperate than she intended.

Tommy rewarded her with an uncharacteristically bright smile. "Linda told me I had to take care of her family. I can do that right." He held one of the big doors open for them. Elizabeth gave him a look heavy with meaning. She had some ideas for how he could take care of her.

The man was having an ever-growing searing effect on her. Ever since she'd kissed him, she couldn't stop thinking about touching him. Every move of that lean, lanky body, the careful way he spoke, each word delivered with great weight, and the way he looked at her, like she was the only one who mattered.

They had one more night together, and she was determined to make sure a good portion was spent groping and getting groped. Her eyes lingered on his hands.

Inside, the museum entry room was huge. Why didn't they use some of this space for the museum? It had a high ceiling and a polished floor. A group of middle-graders was gathered in one corner, their voices echoing across the room.

"Two courts," Tommy said, looking around.

"Two quarts?"

"Whenever I'm in a big room I try to figure out how many basketball games I could have going at the same time. I think I could do two in this room."

"It would be noisy," Elizabeth said.

"True," he said. "Now what?"

Granny shuffled over and got in the entrance line. She waved them over. "We go inside and look at everything."

"Shouldn't we tell them you're here?" Elizabeth asked. "We shouldn't have to pay to see our own stuff."

Granny shook her head. "We're gonna be looking at all the stuff."

She bought their tickets and took the museum map they handed her. The first wing took them through different geographical regions: forest, farmland, and desert. The museum was busy with families and kids. Granny moved slowly but showed no signs of being tired. When she set her mind to it, she was tough.

They stopped at some photos of early timber harvest. "Have you seen the coastal redwoods?" Elizabeth asked.

"Nope. Never been out where you guys are from," he said.

"It's amazing to walk through those trees." She put her hands over her heart. "I don't even have words for it. I can't wait to show them to you." She said the words knowing how unlikely the reality. Tomorrow she and Granny would be home, and he would be on his way back.

"Maybe before I leave," he said as if thinking the same thing. Her heart grew heavy hearing him say the words.

"Here's the Indian exhibit," he said as they entered a new hall.

Half the room was made up of dioramas and the rest of it was assorted artwork and glass cases filled with artifacts. Tribes from different areas were grouped together and shown hunting, food gathering, or basket weaving. California had so many tribes there was a lot crammed into the exhibits.

They found the display that showed Yurok, Karuk, and Hoopa in ceremonial regalia.

"The three tribes spoke different languages but shared certain cultural activities," Elizabeth explained.

"You remember who I work with," Tommy said.

"Linda and Rayanne have schooled you?" Elizabeth said.

"They are never not schooling me," he said.

Granny walked along the rail, studying the exhibit. Several of the models wore ceremonial regalia, each labeled with the materials and special meaning of the items.

"It's weird to look at mannequins dressed to represent your ancestors," Elizabeth commented.

Granny pointed at the girl with the ceremonial dress made of deer hide and decorated with abalone and bear grass. "That's not my dress."

"It might be in another exhibit," Elizabeth said.

"I'll go find someone to ask," Tommy said, going back the way they'd come.

They sat down on a bench with a good view of the display. There was a rough approximation of the wooden dance house, the dancers lined up unnaturally to show off the regalia.

"We're a museum exhibit," Elizabeth said.

"Better than invisible," Granny said.

LINDA WOULD BE WAITING for his call. But every time he got his phone out, he ended up putting it away again. He could already imagine the pitch of her voice rising as she used every iteration of words that meant: bitterly disappointed. If she would just fire him, he could stop dreading all of this. He left the phone in his pocket. No sense calling her until he knew when he'd have the car back.

At this point he'd lost it for Elizabeth. His priorities shifted a little further whenever she laughed or leaned into him to listen to whatever he had to say. He could hardly sleep the night before hearing her in the other bed, turning over, getting up to go into the bathroom. The sound of a toothbrush. Returning to the soft scratch of covers as she got back in bed. He'd spent the night afraid to even roll over and look at her bed in the dark.

I can sneak into your room after she goes to bed.

Every time he replayed those words he almost passed out. Someone like Elizabeth wanted him. He wanted her too. He wanted her teasing voice in his ear. The whole thing seemed manufactured to break his heart, but he was willing to deal with it if it meant these brief moments of happiness now.

He found a museum guard and asked about Dr. Murray, and the man said he would find someone to meet them at the exhibit.

When he found them again, Granny's head was low with a sad look of dejection.

"I don't like seeing our ceremony things in a museum," she said.

"What can we do?" Elizabeth said.

"*Poof* on those people," Granny said.

As a swear word, *poof* didn't sound like much, but it sounded terrible coming from Granny.

"These are ours," she said, wringing her elder hands together. A tear came from the corner of one eye. Elizabeth wrapped her arms around her. Granny said, "You kids have a lot to do. You don't like to hear it, but when I'm gone, someone needs to work on all this."

"We are, Granny," Elizabeth said.

In the short time Tommy had been with the center, he'd heard about any number of programs and procedures, but he didn't know anything that would help them now. He wanted to say something reassuring but what could he do?

"These research and museum people aren't our friends. They act friendly and interested, but they take our stories and then sell them back to us." Granny let out a long sigh. "Maybe it's time to go home."

Tommy checked the time. If they left now, he could have them home late, and if he drank enough coffee, he could have the car back by early tomorrow morning. Enough to minimize Linda's wrath. Elizabeth could report to her first day of work on time.

But he wasn't ready to say good-bye.

"Maybe it's not on display. Maybe they're cataloging it, whatever that means," Elizabeth said.

"Let's wait and see what they say," Tommy said.

While they waited, Granny told them a story about a trip to find someone's fern patch and they ran out of gas. All these ladies up in the mountains, having a great time, unconcerned about how they would get home. "Be camping there still if someone hadn't come found us," she said. "And happy to do it."

Tommy sat next to Elizabeth and she reached over to hold his hand. They were people who held hands now.

Time slowed until he could barely keep his eyes open. He couldn't imagine how the museum staff stayed awake inside there all day.

"Did you call Linda?" Elizabeth asked.

"I intend to," Tommy said.

She gave him a smile that promised many things. "When?"

"As soon as we know what's going on. Should I ask again?"

"I don't know," Elizabeth said. "Now that we've come this far I want Granny to see that dress. But does it matter?"

At last the museum guard returned. "Dr. Murray isn't here today. She's expected in tomorrow if you would like to return then."

Tommy squeezed Elizabeth's hand. One more day.

Granny made an unhappy sighing sound.

"I'll bring the car around," Tommy told them.

On his way out the door, he finally called Linda and was relieved when the call went straight to voicemail.

"Sorry. It's me. You wanted me to take care of your family, so I am. That sounds like a bad excuse. Your car is fine. We're on a mission. One more day. I will have it back to you tomorrow night. Promise. I'll call again."

*A*rnie pushed the door of his house open and peeked inside. The television was on.

"Hey, kids," he said.

The three teenagers on the couch looked up.

"This is my friend, Linda." He introduced each kid and family connection. In the back of his mind, all he could think about was how weird it was to have Linda in his house. When they'd first met, he'd always wanted to bring her to his home place and show her around. Now she was here and he felt strangely unsure of himself.

All three kids jumped up. They gave Linda a careful once-over. "Bye, Uncle Arnie," one of them called as they left.

"Welcome to my tiny house." He used the remote to turn off the TV and opened the curtains to bring in the daylight. The kids had left a bag of chips and some open cans of soda on the coffee table.

Arnie picked up the sodas, still half full, and took them to the sink.

"You trust them by themselves?" Linda took her time looking around the room. She paused to scan his bookshelf.

Arnie laughed. "They're family."

"Do you know how teen parents are made? You don't think about them bringing their boyfriends and girlfriends and calling this the make-out house?"

After a pause, Arnie said, "Now I do. I hope you're okay with meat and bread for lunch because that's what we're having."

"I'm starving. Anything is fine. Bathroom?"

Arnie pointed down the hall. As soon as she closed the door, he worried whether it was clean enough. He opened the fridge and pulled out the leftover meatloaf and gravy and set it to reheat.

Linda returned and didn't have a look of horror, so it must have been okay. She walked around the main room studying the old photos and heirlooms on the walls. Arnie opened a bag of dinner rolls and threw a few in foil and put them in the oven. He pulled the butter out of the refrigerator.

"How long have you lived here?" she asked.

"When I got home from college there was an ancient mobile home on this lot. I lived in that for a year and, after freezing my ass off all winter, convinced the family to help build this. I know it's small. I always figured if my situation changed, I could knock out a wall and build on." By situation change, he meant starting a family. He'd had a version of this conversation with Katie, at her instigation. That woman loved to seize on a project. She'd sketched out some ideas for rearranging the place—knock down that wall and put a master bed and bath on this side—like it was an undertaking for them together. They were not on the same page in the relationship, that was for sure.

Linda nodded. "Sounds about right. The house Granny lives in started out as a two-room cabin. They did two additions but not like they examined what they had to make a plan. They would add something on and then cut a door in the wall. It's a funny old house. I haven't been there in ages."

"Coffee?" he asked, surprised by a flare of nerves like he'd brought home a date and wasn't confident how to proceed.

"I can make coffee," Linda said.

Arnie pulled a filter out of a drawer, intending to toss it on the counter, but it fell to the floor. He grabbed another one. "Coffee beans in the freezer. Grinder on the counter. This is the extent of my hosting. If there's something you want, help yourself."

Everything he said sounded like it had two meanings.

Linda prepared the coffee with ease, more at home in his kitchen than he was at the moment.

She said, "Those photos, the historical ones. All family?"

"I come from a long line of leaders," he said.

"I've heard all about your family." She gave him a patient smile.

"Right," he said. He put plates and utensils on the counter. "Coffee cups are in that cupboard."

They each prepared a plate and carried it to the table.

"Not bad for sad bachelor food," Arnie said.

"Since when are you a sad bachelor?" Linda said, her lips turning up into a bemused smile.

Arnie didn't know why he'd said that. The joke fell flat. "I meant I eat like one."

There was the sound of tires in the driveway, and a familiar truck flashed by the window.

Terrific.

"That's my mom. The kids must have mentioned your name. I should have known she would want to meet you."

A strange look passed over Linda's face. "How does she know who I am?"

There was a knock on the door.

"You can come in, Mom," Arnie yelled.

Diane Jackson, professional busybody, charged into the room while dragging a bulky plastic bag. She had short hair that she dyed dark brown to hide the gray, and eyes that missed nothing. His entire life he couldn't get away with anything. He'd throw a rock at a car on one side of the rez and thirty seconds after he arrived home, Mom would know and punish him for it.

"Grandma replaced her comforter, but the old one was practically new. I thought you might—" She feigned surprise at seeing someone there as she gave Linda a careful look. "I'm not interrupting anything, am I?"

"Nothing that can't be interrupted by Grandma's blanket," Arnie said.

"It's a comforter," she said.

"Mom, this is my colleague, Linda. She's meeting with some folks after the budget and planning meeting."

"Why aren't you there?"

"Because I'm here." He got up and took the bag with the feeble-excuse-for-a-visit comforter and threw it in the guest room. "Thanks. Linda is borrowing the green car because...well, it's a long story. Linda, this is my mom, Diane."

"Nice to finally meet you," Linda said, wiping her mouth and standing up.

"The kids said you had someone here and I wanted to see what was going on," Diane said, her cover story already forgotten. "What about—?"

"She didn't come with me this weekend," Arnie said, not wanting to explain everything in front of Linda.

"Is everything—?"

"Mom, do you remember when I was young and complained about your nose in all of my business? You said when I grew up and paid my own bills then you would leave me alone. Remember that?"

Mom made a production of thinking it over. "Not really." She turned her attention back to Linda. "And you're lending her the green car? I thought you were friends."

"It's not that bad. She only needs it for one day." To Linda, he said, "You won't have any problem with it, promise. I'll be back in town next week if there is any trouble."

Arnie hoped this wouldn't be weird, but his hopes were quickly dashed. His mom pulled out a chair to sit with them. "I remember stories about Linda when you two were in college. I can't believe we never met before. I thought he'd bring you here eventually, but it never happened."

"If I had a chance to go home, I wanted mine," Linda said, clearly enjoying this bizarre interruption.

"Will you be staying for dinner?" His mom eyed their plates, no doubt preparing a lecture for later about how poorly he fed his guests.

"I can't today. I've been busy with company, and I need to get back home so I can get organized around the house," Linda said with complete seriousness.

Arnie stifled a laugh. Linda was a competent mastermind in many fields, but organization was not one of them.

"We'll try to change your mind. I know others in the family would love to meet you."

Arnie urged her to leave using the power of his glare. "Thanks, Mom. We have to work now."

She ignored him. "How late will the meeting go? You'll need dinner if it's late."

"Hard to say," Arnie said. He got up from the table and took his empty plate to the sink.

"You're welcome if you change your mind," Mom said.

Linda turned into the woman who knew how to bend people to her will as politely as possible. "I appreciate your generous offer," she said. "Another time, for sure."

"I will hold you to that," Mom said, with no doubt that she meant it. She gave Arnie a knowing look as she left.

Linda continued eating while failing to pretend she wasn't amused. When the truck was gone, she said, "Relax, Arnie, I know how moms are, and I can see where you get your stubborn streak."

"You have no idea," Arnie said. "If the discussion goes too late you can stay here." He didn't know why he said it or even thought it. The words had popped out, pure hospitality, and now the idea of Linda spending the night made his mouth go dry. He hoped it didn't come to that.

"I wouldn't want to trouble you," she said.

"It wouldn't be trouble," Arnie said, not wanting her to dismiss the terrible idea so easily. "We're colleagues. There's a guest room. It has a lock, clean sheets. Grandma's comforter." Why would she need a lock on a guest room door? Also, the sheets were probably dirty.

"It's not that far to drive," Linda said. There was a long pause before she added, "I think it would be awkward."

"What if Ester needed a place to stay? Would that be awkward?" Why was he still talking about this? Of course she would want to go back, she had her own thing going with ol' whatshisname.

Linda took her plate and coffee cup to the kitchen and put them in the sink. "I guess not, but I'm sure I'll have plenty of time to get home, so we don't have to worry about it."

1 6

They went through the business of finding a motel. Tommy thought Elizabeth was exaggerating, but Granny wasn't happy until they'd found the reassuringly named Sleep-Right Motel tucked between the freeway and a major thoroughfare. The bright red neon sign was missing the last "L," so they kept joking about their mote room.

They took her to a nearby diner where she skipped the patty melt in favor of an unappetizing looking open-faced turkey sandwich swimming in gravy and ate every French fry on her plate. Tommy and Elizabeth exchanged amused looks while they picked at their dinners.

"You want some of my fries?" Elizabeth asked, making it sound like she was offering something else. They sat across from each other in the booth. She had her feet on his.

"Sure," he said, "you want some of mine?"

Elizabeth leaned forward and took one.

He liked to think Granny was oblivious to the tension, but she'd been around long enough that she was probably enjoying being the obstacle. She took forever to finish her meal because she kept telling them stories about traveling with Leo. Like the time he got a speeding ticket trying to keep up with a freight train on tracks parallel to the highway. Another time he slid into a ditch to avoid hitting a cow in the middle of the road.

Tommy might have enjoyed the stories more if Elizabeth hadn't been caressing his shins with her toes, a simple gesture that made it nearly impossible to form complete thoughts.

At last, they took her to the motel and made sure she was settled. Tommy sat on the second bed, pretending to look at his phone, but really he was waiting to see what Elizabeth would do. After the dinner entertainment, there was no way they were going straight to bed.

"We're going out for a little while. Is that okay, Granny?"

"Set up my TV and be gone with you," Granny said. She wore a baggy T-shirt that said, *Elders Do It With A Trick Hip* and black stretchy pants.

Tommy set up her program and put the remote on the bed.

When he got out to the car, Elizabeth sat in the driver's seat, both hands on the wheel, staring intently at the imaginary road ahead. She hit the turn signal and looked over her shoulder.

"Did you want to drive?" he asked.

"Playing around." She turned the signal off and faced forward again.

"I can take you driving."

"I'll think about it."

"I would be right next to you," Tommy said.

"I'll keep that in mind."

Elizabeth crawled over the center console, her dress riding up so that he got a peek of lacy white panties. She took her time pulling the skirt back down.

He'd already forgotten what they were talking about.

"Let's get a six pack and go somewhere," Elizabeth said.

A six-pack.

She'd given the perfect opening to explain. He could have water. There was no reason to make a big deal about it. Except right at that moment, he didn't want to have a drinking problem. He wanted to drink a beer with a beautiful girl and pretend it was a date and not worry about Angie or his car or anything else.

"Maybe not tonight," Tommy said, doing his best to sound as if this was a great idea for another time.

"Probably right," Elizabeth said. She nudged his arm aside and popped opened the storage compartment of the center armrest and picked through it. "Tissues, sunglasses, coupons, gas rewards. Ah-ha." She pulled out a curled blister pack and held it up. "Gum. Want a piece?"

"I'm good," he said. She popped a piece from the wrapper and put it in her mouth. She waved it at him again.

Back in the day, he'd gone through buckets of gum, trying to hide his alcohol breath. Gum or sometimes coffee.

His breath.

Her eyes sparked with lust. She licked her bottom lip. The pangs of desire that had been building all day collected into a blaze of heat.

"I'll take some."

Elizabeth took her time pushing a piece out of the wrapper and slipping it into his mouth, her fingers grazing his lips. His brain sputtered at the contact. He could barely get his jaw to work on the gum.

"You have nice hands." She took one hand and turned it over in a business-like manner. The small gesture sent a spasm through him. She drew on his palm with her finger.

"I get that a lot," Tommy said, the mint blast and the shift between them clearing his head.

Elizabeth hung on to him as if considering whether to keep him in her pocket. "No, it's not. What are you known for?"

The only things that came to mind were uncomplimentary. Things you wouldn't say to a woman that you wanted to regard you with something other than pity or annoyance. "I'm not known for anything. What about you?"

"Granny. If I show up anywhere around the rez, that's the first thing people ask, 'Where's Auntie?' It could be midnight around a bonfire on the beach. Don't get me wrong, I love her like crazy. I'm taking care of her until she's gone."

She laced her fingers with his and squeezed. She had the look of a woman on a mission. She shifted in her seat, filling his senses with her. The minty scent of her gum and sweet girl smell, her eyes making clear she knew something that he didn't. She rustled around until she found what she was looking for. He couldn't see in the dim blue light. She wrapped the gum up and crammed it in the stuffed ashtray. Every move was deliberate. She knew he waited for what would happen next.

In a low voice, she said, "Would you want to get in the trunk?"

"What?" The warm fuzz of anticipation hiccupped.

She covered her mouth while she laughed. "The back seat. I meant the back seat." She grabbed his arm. "Get in the back seat with me." Warm again. Not a shy request. She knew he wanted it too.

"Here? In the parking lot of low-rent motel? They have surveillance cameras. They don't want people to get it on in their parking lot."

Elizabeth broke eye contact long enough to glance around the parking lot as if she needed to remember where they were. "Are we getting it on?"

"Or discuss the Dawes Act and the right-up-to-the-current-day impact it has on tribal communities. Or whatever you had in mind."

Elizabeth gave him a funny look.

"You hang out with Linda, the stuff rubs off on you," he explained.

"I approve. We're almost on the same page. Let's go," she said.

"What about?—" He pointed his chin at the motel door.

"She's an adult. She's probably happy I'm off with you rather than one of those miscreants. She likes that word, miscreants. It sounds hilarious when she says it. She also likes to call people bums or rotten cabbages."

"I'm honored Granny likes me more than a rotten cabbage." Tommy started the car, ideas reeling through his head. They could try a parking lot but a business would have cameras. "Ideas?"

"Are there any woods around here?" Elizabeth asked.

"Woods? Don't you watch horror movies? It's like we're begging to be murdered."

"Where I come from, everything is woods," Elizabeth said. "I haven't been murdered yet. How about a park?" She took out her phone and he followed the directions she gave him. The first park was small, only a brightly lit playground with a few benches and a half court.

"That won't work," she said as he drove past.

Back when he drank, there had been many nights like this. Him and who knows who else, driving around looking for parties, or people they knew who had money, or people like themselves, hammered and seeking kindred spirits, people who would be easy to talk to.

"Maybe this isn't such a great idea," he said.

"It's an amazing idea," Elizabeth said.

"I'm not sure we're rating the same idea," Tommy said.

"There's a bigger park not far from here. Want to try it?"

Tommy couldn't sort out the jangle of things going on in his body. Common sense was getting crushed out by desire.

"We can look," he said, confident he wanted this to happen but uncertain about the way they were going about accomplishing it.

The only sound in the car was the two of them adjusting in their seats, and the tires on the highway. The warm, sexy anticipation that thrummed through him when they'd left the motel cooled as they looked for the park.

"We can make this work," Elizabeth said when they found the entrance. There were clusters of green trees and shrubs and grassy open spaces on either side of the parking lot. Another car was parked in a one dark corner, so Tommy pulled into a spot on the opposite side.

There was a long pause while they considered the view, a pair of unlit tennis courts, and across the way, a pavilion where people could celebrate birthdays and graduations. The other car in the lot came to life and slowly drove out, leaving them alone.

"I can't believe we're doing this in Linda's car," Tommy said.

"She'll never know," Elizabeth said.

ELIZABETH EXITED and got back in the back seat. Tommy still hadn't moved. The keys were in the ignition. He did not have the bearing of a man fainting from lust. He acted more like a man who wanted to run away. Maybe she'd miscalculated.

"We won't do anything too crazy," she said, her words conveying the opposite of what she wanted.

"What's too crazy for you?" he asked, locking back at her.

"Come find out," she said, daring him with her eyes. She attempted to convey the magnitude of her desire by sliding her tongue along her lower lip.

Tommy removed the keys and got in the back with her. He adjusted and readjusted himself before settling next to her. He jumped when she dropped her hand to his knee.

"How is this even going to work?" he said.

"Figuring it out is part of the fun," she said.

"I associate fooling around in a car with making poor choices," he said.

"So it's not your first time." She lightly stroked the back of her hand over his zipper and was rewarded with a harsh exhale. "Too familiar?" she said into his ear.

"Come here," he said. "Keep your hands where I can see them." He moved over and pulled her legs over his lap and put his arms around her. She curled into him.

"Car cuddling is okay, too, I guess," she said, her desire still at a hard boil. She nuzzled his neck and then kissed along his jawline until he tilted his face to hers and kissed her hard. Harder than she expected. She thought she'd been coaxing him along, but instead, it was like he was waiting for the right time to slam into her. His mouth was on her, hungry and insistent. Her dress rode up her thighs. His hand stroked her legs politely. She growled in the back of her throat and shifted on his lap, rubbing the most important spot until he groaned and pulled back, panting.

She ran her fingers through his hair. "You're cute. Have you had a lot of girlfriends?"

"I've had a manageable amount," he said. His lips skated over her collar bone. "Lots of boyfriends?"

"Sometimes more than I can manage," she said and shifted her legs again until he held them in place.

She found his eyes and made her meaning clear. "I want you."

"I want you too. But I'm not taking my pants off in a car parked in the city, pretending a few trees around is private," Tommy said.

"No need to take them *off*. The entire existence of the zipper is for easy access."

"I disagree about entire existence, but I see what you're getting at." Tommy adjusted her in his lap, and she became aware of his hand sliding around to stroke the inside of her thigh. "Skirt is easy access, too." She jerked in his arms before letting out a gasp of surprise.

"Sorry," he said. "Too familiar?"

She couldn't help but smile. Her eyes slid closed and she adjusted her legs.

"I want to show you a little trick I learned in the war." His breath was warm, his voice teasing. His hand stroked farther into the crease.

"You were doing this in the war?"

"It was all talk back then." He stroked one knuckle lightly over the sweet spot.

She let out a sharp breath. Her head dipped down.

"During our down time, we'd talk about technique, possible outcomes, sustainable practices."

Her eyes opened long enough to give him a doubtful look. "What kind of war was this?"

"Does it matter?" Tommy said. His hand didn't stop moving.

Elizabeth shook her head and shifted in his lap. "Come on. I want the whole thing." She wiggled a hand free and worked it toward his waistband, fumbling with the opening.

He stopped her before she could get her hands on anything interesting. He draped her arm around his neck. "We're not doing that right now," he said in a faintly scolding voice. His hand returned to stroking. "Do you me want to stop this?"

The best she could do was a contrite whimper. He kissed her neck until she squirmed. He moved his hand to her belly and slid under the waistband of her panties.

Elizabeth exhaled a long, ragged breath. His fingers curled around, and one slid inside, then another. He stroked at a steady pace, all of her attention locked on the tension blazing inside. She shifted her hips slightly. With her mouth in his ear, she said, "Could you...?"

He made a clever adjustment, the heel of his hand rubbing across the right place while he changed the pressure and the angle of his fingers, she couldn't keep track. She fluttered her eyes open long enough to see him studying her. She expected him to be gloating over the going-over he was giving her, but the look he gave her could only be considered naked wonder.

"Never mind." She gnawed on his earlobe and tried to steady her breath. "You're good," she said, fighting to get the words out.

"Beginner's luck," he said.

"You're no beginner." She hid her face in the crook of his neck. He smelled like boy and something that reminded her of home. "If you keep it up like that I'm going be screaming my head off in about thirty seconds," she whispered.

"You want me to stop?" he said.

She shook her head.

"You have to scream on the inside."

She alternated between high-pitched gasps and throaty laughs, like the quiet laugh shared in a darkened theater. Tommy nudging her gently, a simple query, and her response a shuddering sigh. She threw her head back, and a loud moan slipped out. "It's always the quiet ones that surprise you," she exclaimed.

Tommy kept his hand moving but he used his free hand to turn her face to his, and he jammed his tongue in her mouth, which made her laugh again. Like it was that easy to quiet her. She caught it between her teeth, and he twitched against her, long enough to miss a beat.

He pulled back and whispered into her mouth, "You can't make noise like that out here."

"No one will hear me," she said, her voice unsteady, echoing through the car.

"Hold it in," he said in her ear.

"Nope." She pressed her lips together and rocked against his hand, her arms around his neck. Usually, at this moment she let her mind drift, but this time she was focused entirely on the control he had over her.

"You're beautiful. Kiss me again," he said. When she turned her face back to him, he licked her lower lip and then bit it, and she groaned again. "Not helping." He dipped his tongue in her mouth while she panted into him. She couldn't think straight any longer, she just kept grinding her hips, her face buried in his neck, holding in the screams that burst from inside. The heat built up and flashed through her and she was gulping and trembling in his arms.

Once she finished, she collapsed into him, tilting her head up and planting a dizzy kiss on his cheek. She untangled herself from him and fixed her skirt and curled up next to him on the seat, her head on his shoulder, her hand in his.

"Sleepy?" he asked. The vibration of his voice was warmly reassuring. She was surprised by the surge of feelings, much more complicated than pure satisfaction and more like she'd shared something she didn't expect.

"I'm recovering. No one's ever done me like that before."

Tommy kissed the side of her head. "Glad you liked it."

"As soon as I regain consciousness, I'm going to be liking you."

He exhaled sharply with what she hoped was lustful anticipation. "Looking forward to it," he said in a hoarse voice.

It was a perfect moment, even if they were in the back of Linda's car. The night was quiet except for the sound of traffic. She wanted to say something about them, but she wasn't sure what. One of Tommy's hands reached for her nape, and a finger drew lazy circles at her hairline.

Suddenly someone pounded on the roof of the car and a flashlight blazed through the window. A loud voice commanded them to get out of the car.

Tommy inhaled sharply and his body froze.

"Uh oh," she said, stifling a giggle, "busted. At least you don't have your hand up my dress."

"Don't joke around," he said. He climbed out of the car and helped her out.

"Park is closed," the officer said. He looked like every cop she'd ever seen, angry and humorless. A female officer stood back by the police car.

"Sorry," Elizabeth said. "I wanted to park here. He tried to talk me out of it. He said this was a bad idea."

"He was right. You talk to Officer Duran while I talk to this guy."

Elizabeth let go of Tommy's hand.

"You been drinking?" the officer said to Tommy.

"Not for five years," Tommy said.

"Drugs?"

"Not for five years."

Before she could hear what else he said, Officer Duran was interrogating her with the same questions about alcohol and drugs and confirming she was safe. It didn't take long, and they were back in the car and on their way back to the motel, neither of them saying a word.

BACK IN THE MOTEL ROOM, Tommy went into the bathroom to change into his sweatpants and brush his teeth. When he came out, Elizabeth went in, the two of them still quiet.

Every time he replayed the sound of the police officer pounding on the car roof, he went cold again. He couldn't calm the tremor in his hands.

They had a tiny room almost precisely the size of two queen beds. A small gap separated them. Granny was bundled up in one of them, lightly snoring. He crawled into the other bed, the sheets scratchy and the flimsy coverlet smelling vaguely of unwashed human.

Elizabeth finished in the bathroom and crawled into bed, leaning her warm body into his. How was he supposed to return to his old life without the endless thrill of Elizabeth? Every minute it was something new, the endless amusement in her voice, and her serious eyes when she listened to him. Right now, the sense of her next to him, more than lust, a tightness in his chest.

"What about Granny?" he said when she wrapped an arm over him.

"She won't care. She'd be more surprised to find me in the same bed with her in the morning."

He wasn't about to argue. He gathered her into his arms, their bodies pressed tight down to their toes, overwhelmed with a feeling of contentment that had previously eluded him.

"I heard what you said to the cop," she said. "Why didn't you tell me?"

His heart sank again. Drinking. Not drinking. It always had to be part of the conversation. He should have told her at the beginning.

"Normally I don't hide it. I guess I was afraid of what you would think. You know, rez life."

"You got your act together."

"I'm not fun anymore," he said.

"You are plenty fun, Mr. Magic Fingers."

The motel room was dark except for the light from the parking lot that leaked around the curtains. She propped up her head with her hand. "Does it bother you to be around people drinking?"

"If they keep asking me if I'm sure I don't want a drink—like most of my family and friends back home—then yes. But otherwise, no."

"How do you feel about it?"

Tommy searched for the answer she would expect. "Honestly, I wish I wasn't. It's exhausting navigating people and social events. Managing a mask."

"What mask?" Elizabeth said. "The mask that you're keeping it together? Can it be okay not to keep it together and still be sober?"

"I think that's what I'm doing," Tommy said.

Her index finger stroked up and down the inside of his arm, a careless gesture of affection that made him realize how much he was missing, keeping himself closed off for so long. His heart wanted to crack open, even this little bit.

"What's the worst thing you did while drinking?" she asked.

That's where people went. Always wanting to know about the worst moments. "I never hit a woman, if that's what you're asking."

"I wasn't. I don't imagine you're the hitting type," Elizabeth said.

"There is no hitting type," he said, the words bitter in the back of his throat.

She cupped his face with her hand, brushing his lower lip with her thumb. He couldn't remember wanting anyone like he wanted this woman.

"I wasn't a violent or mean drunk. I was a make-terrible-choices drunk."

She smiled in a way that made his heart squeeze tight. "I've made some terrible choices sober." She sat up and plumped the flimsy pillows together before settling in again. Fitting her body carefully into his, their faces inches apart. He'd never been like this with anyone.

She asked, "What's one terrible choice?"

"Why do you want to hear terrible things?" After a brief hesitation, he reached up to brush her hair back.

"I'm getting to know you," she said. "Maybe I have terrible things, too."

"Maybe. I had a general poor exercise of judgment. Driving. I always promised myself I would never be the drunk that got behind the wheel, and then it would happen again. How about this? One night I was out driving around town with some people I barely knew, they might have been selling drugs. They had a pistol that we took turns shooting out of the car window."

"That's pretty bad."

"At the time it was exciting. I wasn't one of those dull zombies shuffling through life more dead than alive. I was wild and fun."

"I understand the impulse," she said.

"I kept telling myself I wasn't that bad. Nothing wrong with waking up hungover every day, staying in bed until three in the afternoon."

Even now he cringed at the memory of suppressing the daily

shame. Begging, stealing, or mooching to get that next bottle. Finding new friends to party with. Waking up in strange places, next to strangers. "I'm terrified of becoming that person, again."

He was aware of every shift of her body, always finding a way to close the spaces between them, to touch in a different place. Every part of him sang in terror and delight.

Elizabeth kissed his chin. "What is your plan?"

"Do what I'm doing. Get through the day."

"Right, but what is your long-term plan? Where do you want to end up?"

He hadn't grown up in a goal-oriented household. Nobody had ever asked him that except Linda, and she hadn't asked in a long time.

"I'm not good at future plans. My goal is to keep it together." Saying the words gave him a sense of futility, like that was all that he had to look forward to: day after day of simply getting by. "At the moment I need to deal with Angie."

She didn't say anything, but he felt every inhale and exhale she made. A cool hand reached up to stroke his hair, slide along his brow before her fingers traced around his ear. "Why do you have to deal with Angie?" The words came out light and judgment-free.

The same question he'd asked himself a hundred times, whenever Angie kept him awake or forced him to abandon his plans. Every time she cried or yelled or asked for money. But what did it say about him if he abandoned her now when she was trying so hard to change?

"I'm getting sleepy," he said, even though he didn't want to miss a second of this night with Elizabeth.

She kissed him gently on the lips. "Turn around."

He rolled over, and she spooned him from behind, one arm slung around his chest, pulling herself into him and fitting in snugly, and for the first time, he felt like he was in the right place.

17

Tommy left Granny on one of the hard, stone benches, the only seats in the museum entrance, and then went to the Lost and Found.

"This will sound weird, but an elder in my group left her rolling walker here. I don't suppose you have it?" He already knew it wasn't weird because he'd gone back to search for every kind of lost cane, crutch, walker, even portable oxygen cylinders, numerous times in his career.

The young woman at the counter had her curly hair pinned back from her face. "Happens more than you might think," she said. "Black or red?"

Tommy let out an exaggerated sigh of relief. "You have it? Great. The red one." She brought out a dinged-up cart with a canvas bag fixed to the front. "She'll be so grateful," he added. He wheeled it back to the museum entry hall.

Elizabeth rushed over as soon as she spotted the walker. "She will take your head off if you bring that to her."

Tommy shook his head and gave her a lazy smile. "She likes me."

"She's not the only one." Elizabeth managed to covertly touch him in a private place, her expression innocent, the touch quick and light to remind him his turn would come.

He jumped back, unable to hide his grin. His mind kept flashing back to Elizabeth shuddering and panting under his touch. He refused to imagine all the things that would have happened later if Granny weren't with them.

"You'll see," he said.

Granny gave the device a hostile once-over, but she let him adjust the handles and then sat down on the padded seat. "Not bad." She opened the canvas bag and inspected the contents. "Cough drops. Wet wipes. Fruit snacks." She closed it with exaggerated defeat and said, "Better than nothing."

"You're the only one who has ever gotten away with that," Elizabeth said into his ear.

All he heard was *the only one*. That's what he wanted, to be the only one.

"They said Dr. Murray would come out and see us," Elizabeth said. She sighed and put her cold hand into his warm one and leaned against him. "I guess there's one good thing about going home tonight. You need clothes."

"Do I stink?"

Elizabeth leaned closer and sniffed. "No. But your look hints at an extended walk of shame." She gave him a playful smile. She didn't know his signature look was rumpled sweatpants and previously worn T-shirts.

Elizabeth had on another dress, one with tiny pink flowers and a plunging neckline that gaped when she moved her shoulders a certain way. She managed to move her shoulders that way a lot when she was around him.

There was a huge clock at one end of the entrance hall. A half hour went by and still they waited. Granny stared at the ground.

He said, "Do you still have that phone number for Dr. Murray?"

"It's in the car," Elizabeth said. "You okay, Granny?" The elder groaned unhappily.

Tommy went to the information desk to find out how much longer.

"Someone is on the way," the volunteer told him.

"That's what you said when we got here," Tommy said. "That is a ninety-two-year-old elder who has worked her whole life on behalf of Indian people, and you are making her wait to see her family heirlooms. In our culture, we take care of our elders."

"I'm just a volunteer," the young man said, but he brought out a couple of bottles of water. "I'll call back there again."

Tommy gave a bottle to Granny and opened the other for Elizabeth.

"That was sweet," she said.

"I hate seeing elders being ignored like this," he said.

Another half hour passed. The visitor line grew longer and then shorter again. The museum cafe opened, and Elizabeth went to inspect the menu. She came back with a cookie for Granny.

"If you want to spend fifteen bucks on a ham-and-Swiss panini with field greens, this is your spot."

"Grilled cheese? I like that," Granny said. She took a bite of her cookie.

"This is taking longer than we thought," Elizabeth said.

He had been thinking the same thing. At this rate he'd be up half the night driving home.

"Maybe too late for you to go back?" It was a statement. He wanted to stay too.

A hopeful feeling bloomed in his heart. Tommy pressed his leg against hers. "I don't know. I've got people expecting me."

"I'd make it worth your while," Elizabeth said.

Tommy laughed, his entire body throbbing with desire. "It's already been worth my while."

"We gotta get Granny home. The family will give me so much grief, dragging her all over the place," Elizabeth said.

Granny brushed the crumbs off her front in slow motion.

"Maybe we should talk her into going. We'll set up a time to come back," Elizabeth said.

Dr. Murray appeared at the museum entrance, and the volunteer pointed to them.

"There she is," Tommy said.

Dr. Murray hurried over, the words rushing out. "The trip down took longer than we thought and the accommodations were screwed up. I wish I'd known you would be here." She lowered her voice. "The item is not on display."

"We know," Elizabeth said. "We toured the exhibits yesterday."

"If it were just me, I'd haul you back there. I'd love to hear you talk about it as part of our documentation. But I'm not staff, I'm a guest, and I can't convince anyone to my way of thinking."

Granny wilted in her seat. "They won't let me see my dance dress?"

Dr. Murray held up her hands in surrender. "According to the collections manager, the museum's position is, if there were a formal process initiated by the Tribe, the artifact could be viewed, but as it is, the museum can't open its collection archive to any visitor that asks. Especially for a loaned item."

"I thought you was someone fancy," Granny said.

Dr. Murray forced a laugh. "You and my mother both."

"You explained it was her family item?" Elizabeth said.

"I'm sure it sounds petty to you," Dr. Murray said. "It's not like they can open a box and pull it out. They have archival procedures, so we would need to process it."

"How do we set up a formal process?" Tommy asked.

"Go back to the Tribe, provide official notice. Not something that can happen in a day," Dr. Murray said. "I haven't given up, but I can't do anything today."

"Always how it is. We'll fix it later," Granny grumbled. Tommy expected her to say more, but the fight was leaking out of her.

"Should we come back?" Elizabeth said.

"I don't know what to tell you," Dr. Murray said. "I can keep trying but no guarantees. It will be on display eventually. I could contact you then."

"We could make another trip," Tommy said, ideas for a plan forming quickly. "I could visit and bring you out here."

Granny reached over and patted his arm. "You're a good one, but these people..." She grumbled unhappily to herself.

Dr. Murray apologized again before heading back into the museum.

"That was a big pile of nothing," Granny said. "Don't let me see my own dress."

"Sorry, Granny. I'm disappointed, too," Elizabeth said. "Let's get out of here."

ELIZABETH COULDN'T HELP FEELING RELIEVED. They were headed home and Tommy had volunteered to bring them back. Another visit. This wasn't over yet.

Granny gave them both a cross dismissal when they tried to help her down the ramp. Elizabeth hung back with Tommy, her heart twisting with every careful step the weary elder took. The sun was up in the afternoon sky, and a breeze stirred the leaves on the trees, bringing the scent of freshly mowed grass. A group of kids ran around the deer statue, posing for selfies while a woman tried to coax them into a family photo.

Granny stopped and tugged at her sweater. Tommy set the brakes on the walker and helped her shrug out of it, one shoulder at a time. She wore a gray T-shirt with a black and white photo of a fishing weir and a fisherman. The text said: *Lands and Sea Protector*. She had light green pants on that had a splash of grease from when she dropped a piece of her breakfast sandwich. They hadn't expected to be away this long and had no clean clothes left. And after all that, they'd fallen short of their goal.

Granny let Tommy walk with her, holding the sweater over his arm, his attention focused on her like another member of the family. They had a few more hours together, on the road. Elizabeth would see him react to the place she called home.

Granny's step hitched. She stopped and braced herself against the handrail, her breath labored.

Elizabeth tried to sound cheerful. "We know Dr. Murray now. We'll come back when it's on display."

Granny gave her a disgusted look. "What if I'm not around?"

Elizabeth blinked a few times, afraid she was about to lose it. It was one thing to know she wouldn't be around forever but another thing to be talking about it. Granny hugged an arm against her chest, and the walker rolled out of reach. Tommy pushed it back and set the brake. Granny set her shaking hands back on the handles, her eyes glued to the ground.

"We'll be in the car in a minute," Tommy said.

When Elizabeth was little and Granny in her seventies, they liked to hike into the woods and look for mushrooms. They would go up steep mountainsides slippery with leaves and damp earth. Granny had worn a netted bag draped across her chest as she pointed out little humps in the dirt and they'd fall to their knees and dig with their hands to see what they'd found. Watching Granny struggle on a gentle concrete ramp made her throat ache. She couldn't imagine a world without Granny.

"You'll outlive us all." Elizabeth intended to tease, but her voice was uneven.

Granny waggled a scolding finger, something Elizabeth had endured thousands of times. "All these things going on,"—she gestured at the museum like it was a mess that needed to be cleaned up—"I can't do it no more."

The tears pressed behind her eyes. Elizabeth cleared her throat. "We need to get you home so you can sleep in your own bed and park on your couch without so much running around."

Granny grew more agitated. "Our things are dead in there. Those people aren't our people. They call themselves doctors and call our things objects. Put 'em away in a cupboard where nobody sees them. For what? We bring those things into being for a purpose. Not for a closet."

"I don't know what we can do," Elizabeth said, renewing her frustration with the museum and their rules. "Could you show us how to make a ceremonial dress?" She could picture them gathering the materials and working on it together when she came home from work. Her mom and some of the cousins might like to make something, too. Kora could document it for one of her tribal projects.

"Then one of these people wants to take that one, too," Granny said. "We need our own people handling these things."

"We said we'd look into it when we get home," Elizabeth said.

Granny leveled an angry look at her. "We know it's in there."

Tommy gave her a sly look. "You want to break in and search the back rooms until we find it?"

Granny's face brightened at the idea. "You two. I don't move fast enough."

"You'll bail us out of jail?" Tommy asked.

"It's my dress," Granny said.

"Was your dress," Elizabeth said. "We can't make them show it to us. It's time to go home. I start work tomorrow. Tommy is already in trouble."

Granny grabbed the walker and fumbled with the brake before she slowly turned around, so she was facing the museum again. She shuffled back up the ramp, an inch at a time, pushing the walker with small steps.

"We're going home," Elizabeth said.

"Go ahead. I'm sitting there until they show it to me." Granny kept moving, each step more labored than the previous, every exhale a wheeze of defeat.

Tommy watched Granny move past him, an amused smile on his face.

"This isn't funny," Elizabeth hissed.

He circled an arm around her waist. "I like a sassy elder." His calm, steady gaze helped quiet the uncertainty.

"We need to get her home," she whispered. His body pressed warm and firm against hers, one hand stroking her back, in no hurry to do anything. The gesture was supposed to be comforting but it reminded her she wanted to get her hands all over him.

The walker clanged against the handrail. Granny had let go of it again, and she sagged against the rail.

Elizabeth's heart dropped to her feet, but before she could move, Tommy was at Granny's side, keeping her on her feet and wrangling the wheeled walker all in a split second.

Granny propped herself up. "You two go back to Linda. Find out about the process."

Tommy put his arm around her shoulder, holding her steady. "Auntie, we've done everything we can. We did our best, but we all need to get back. I wish we could have done more."

"Things never get better when we give up," Granny said. "That's why we lose everything."

Elizabeth sighed. She wanted the decision to be Granny's. She didn't think they could force her into the car.

Tommy said, "Let's get lunch and make a plan. Maybe there's someone at your Tribe who can make some calls. We'll come back."

Elizabeth tried to picture George being this patient with Granny. He'd have pressured her until she relented and she would have punished them with a poor temper.

Granny knees bent as if she wanted to sit on the ground. If she went down, they might never get her up. Tommy swiveled the walker around, but she refused to sit down.

"Fine. We'll go back inside," Elizabeth said. "You can get your fifteen-dollar grilled cheese."

She waited for Granny's response—a chuckle, happy that she got her way, but the grumpy face remained.

Tommy offered Granny his arm. "I want to help you because I'm worried."

Granny ignored it. "You worry about the wrong things."

"Want me to borrow a wheelchair to get you back inside?" Tommy asked, unable to keep a straight face. Granny swatted his arm before grabbing onto it, her strength miraculously restored.

18

---

*A*fter lunch, Granny parked herself on one of the stone benches. Tommy pulled Elizabeth aside, and she surprised him by putting her arms around him and hugging him tight, fitting comfortably in his arms, like she was meant to be there.

"Now what?" he said. All the abandoned responsibilities weighed on his mind. He'd missed another call from his uncle, and there was the insurance adjuster appointment. Linda would never forgive him for not being there.

Elizabeth adjusted her arms around him, her cheek on his shoulder, showing no signs of letting go. This was the part he wasn't prepared to leave. Both soft and substantial against him, her breath in his ear, the sweet smell of her hair, and the distressed look in her eyes every time Granny faltered.

She said, "Is this thing that's happening here temporary?"

"Has this risen to the level of a thing?" Tommy said, trying to keep his tone light. She loosened her hold on him and held his gaze with a look of tender affection. "I don't want it to be," he said.

The activity of the museum receded and it was just the two of them. He wanted to declare himself, whatever that meant. Whatever fragile thing they could keep together, over the long distance, even with only a vague plan for the future in mind, he was willing to try. He needed to know that, somewhere in the world, Elizabeth was thinking of him and they were working toward something together.

But thinking about her and the future only reminded him of the family counting on him at home. Angie needed family support after her screw up. Arnie had a car for him now but how long would his goodwill last? The unanswered questions churned through his head.

He studied Elizabeth's face as she went through a set of complex emotions he couldn't guess. She said, "When I agreed to take Granny on this trip, I thought it was nostalgia. Now I understand. It's not just a ceremony dress. It's like her family. I can't ask her to leave."

"The museum can, beloved elder or not," Tommy said. Over at the information desk, a couple of people in security uniforms joined the volunteer. They were deep in discussion, periodically looking over at them.

"When you get back, you can ask Linda what to do," Elizabeth said.

"You want me to go?"

"You've already done so much."

Tommy's heart sank. "How will you get around? What about Granny?"

She waved her phone. "We can get rides." A sliver of afternoon sun shone through a window and lit up Elizabeth from behind. Her hair was aglow with reddish highlights. Their faces were inches apart. She pushed a lock of hair behind her ear.

In the corner, more activity at the information desk. A third person in a security uniform joined them. Elizabeth turned to follow his gaze. "What a lot of trouble for a little old lady," she said.

Granny sat on the bench with a map of the museum spread out on her walker seat, strategizing their heist, no doubt.

"Could be something else," Tommy said, but the museum team had them under careful scrutiny.

"Granny's dealt with worse." Elizabeth leaned up to kiss him, barely touching her lips to his. Her words said one thing but her eyes said something else. "We're going to be fine. Call me when you get home."

The parking garage was a fifteen-minute walk. He'd be home before midnight and trade cars with Linda in the morning. Tomorrow he would be back at the office, unraveling all the mess that he'd made. And when Linda asked if he'd taken good care of her family...

"There is no way I'm leaving you two," Tommy said.

"But—"

"Nope," he said. "Not until we figure this out."

By *this* he meant everything.

There was a popping sound with a splash. A water bottle rolled on the floor under Granny's feet and the water *glugged* out before Elizabeth got to it and set it upright. She found a couple of flimsy diner napkins and did what she could to mop up the spill.

One of the security guards headed for them while the others watched from the information desk.

"Here we go," Tommy said.

The guard was an older woman, outwardly friendly but with an undercurrent of no compromise, like a school principal. "You folks having a problem?" she asked, her expression stern but her voice light, as if making friendly conversation.

"Not at all," Elizabeth said. "Can we get a towel?"

"Someone will call maintenance." She indicated Granny. "Does the senior need assistance?"

Tommy took a protective side-step toward Granny.

"I can speak for myself," Granny said, staring up at the guard with a glare that would stop a thunderstorm. "I'm staying until those people let me see my dance dress."

The guard turned her body to nod at the information desk. "Museum staff tell me they've addressed your inquiries."

"Did you come over here to kick a ninety-two-year-old woman out of your museum?" Elizabeth asked.

"We're concerned for her health. We could call an ambulance if you'd like."

"I don't need your help," Granny said.

"You're welcome to sit here, if that's what you'd like." She walked back to the information desk.

Tommy swallowed back a hot flash of anger. Sure, they had a job to do, but the lack of understanding, the lack of respect was infuriating.

The exchange had invigorated Granny. "You think they'll throw me out?"

Elizabeth managed a half-smile. "If they try, I am afraid for them."

"Been arrested before. If it happens, make sure I have my medicine," Granny said.

"I don't want to miss this," Tommy said. He found Elizabeth's hand. "I gotta call Linda."

"But you're coming back," she said, hanging on to him.

"Always," he said.

TOMMY WENT outside to find a place to make his call. The museum was on a small rise and surrounded by a huge park with green grass and tall, leafy trees. A landscaping truck was parked on an access road, and two men with leaf blowers moved along the path blowing the leaves back and forth with no apparent goal in mind. A golf-cart with SECURITY painted on the side was parked nearby. The occupants were probably inside keeping the world safe from Granny.

He'd resisted the inevitable long enough. He pulled out his phone and pushed Linda's contact. She answered right away.

"Are you on your way back?"

"Almost?"

Linda made an unhappy sound. "You're not on your way back."

Tommy cleared his throat.

Linda repeated the unhappy sound. He could picture her, one hand covering her face, sagging shoulders, the appearance of being too tired to be as angry as she should.

"What is going on with you? You're handling the insurance tomorrow, right? You promised—your words. I have no time and less patience. I need to count on you, why can't I count on you?"

He admired how quickly the words came out, as if she'd rehearsed them. He had a long history of avoiding duties, performing the minimum while relying on Ester and Rayanne to fill in when it was all he could do to get through the day.

"Have you ever been able to count on me?"

"Oh, Tommy." Linda managed to convey a lot of emotion in those three syllables.

"I need to stay," he said.

"Trust me when I tell you that fleeing your problems never works. It creates even more problems and then you get insomnia and your digestion goes to hell and your memory gets fuzzy. It's a cycle of bad."

Tommy waited for her to finish. Down on the access road, a tour bus, the tall kind with tinted windows and a shiny white paint job, pulled up. Bright blue script announced *Valley Motor Coach Adventures*. He'd always wanted to drive one of those, not as a job, but for fun. It would be like riding a dinosaur maneuvering one of those through the streets.

"Enough about me," Linda said. "What happened with the museum?"

"Granny won't leave," he said and caught her up on what had happened, including the run-in with security.

Linda laughed at that. "She has no fear of authority."

"As we've seen," Tommy said. "Dr. Murray is working on it, but she can't promise anything. How do we convince Granny to go home?"

"You can't make Aunt Dotty to do anything," Linda said.

The bus's pneumatic door floated open and a tall, thin man in a navy-blue suit popped out and dropped a little footstool at the base. A young woman in a navy-blue pantsuit hopped down to join him. The passengers began to exit. Most were seniors but younger than Granny. Only a few used canes. They carried notebooks and had travel bags slung across their chests. They gathered next to the bus.

"We can't leave her here," Tommy said.

"No, you can't," Linda said.

"You can forgive me?" Tommy said.

"I wouldn't go that far," Linda said, but her voice had lost its gloomy edge.

When the group was complete, the young woman lifted a bright purple flag and walked toward the museum, the group trailing after her. The man returned to the bus.

"What do we do?" Tommy asked.

"No one wants to disappoint an elder, especially not that one. Maybe you're trying to solve the wrong problem."

"I don't know what you mean."

"Maybe what you should be doing is getting the museum to show you her regalia."

The tall man exited the bus again, this time with a folded camping chair. He set it up under a tree and pulled out a newspaper.

"We tried that," Tommy said. "Is there some official tribal person who could call and tell them to show it to us?"

"The Tribe has a cultural resources program but I'm sure it takes more than a phone call. You could always make a scene."

Tommy groaned. "A protest?"

"Nothing like a chanting crowd with signs to grab attention. You could get some journalists and TV cameras there and have a terrific time." He could hear the smile in her voice.

"I've designed my life to do the opposite of make a scene. Even talking about it makes me feel sick."

Linda said, "You asked me for ideas. That's what I've got."

Not the solution he hoped for. The tall man set the newspaper on his chest and closed his eyes. A nap in the park, under a shady tree, with his arms around Elizabeth. That's what he wanted to be doing.

"What are you going to do if I don't come back?"

"Ever?" Linda said. "You have my car."

"You're getting your car back. I meant if I'm delayed. Granny said she would wait until the museum lets her see it. Do you have to fire me?"

Linda let out a long, loud breath of air. "When was the last time you took a day off from work?"

"Never. What would I do with a day off?"

"You could do any number of things. Many adults find fun activities to do in their spare time."

"Like you? Go to meetings, conferences, and planning retreats, or take classes to learn about boring paperwork?"

Linda laughed. "I should know better than to scold someone on my staff about leisure time. What do you have tomorrow?"

"A couple of appointments for elders. Basketball we could cancel," Tommy said.

"I'll ask Ester and Theo about the appointments. You'll need to square off the debt to them. Anything else?"

"Meet the insurance adjuster at the impound lot."

Linda made a hissing sound followed by a *thump* that was probably something thrown across the room. "You're lucky you're cute," she said. "You owe me big time forever."

"Already do," he said.

"What about your cousin? Are you dealing with that?"

"No. My uncle keeps calling me."

"Alright. It's not my business. You have my sympathies. I have the famous green car of the Warm Springs Reservation, which is about as fun to drive as it sounds. But it runs, and I can get by until you're sorted out."

"Why do you look out for me?" Tommy asked. "I don't add that much to the organization."

"Yes, you do. Besides, you're family now, and I'm making sure you turn out okay."

Tommy wanted to laugh, but the words went right to his heart. The UIC was more like a family than the family he was born into.

He flashed on the memory of his older sisters in the kitchen with a giant jug of cheap vodka and another jug of store-brand soda. When they watched him, he drank the same thing they did, tall plastic cups of vodka mixed with soda. They had a karaoke machine, and the three of them would slur through one pop song after the other until they passed out.

Linda was the big sister who saved him.

"I am okay," he said, trying to keep the emotion out of his voice.

"If you were with anyone else, I would throw a fit, but I don't know if I would have ended up where I am now without Aunt Dotty.

Besides, helping elders, and preserving culture and tradition, is the heart of what I'm trying to do here. Have you lost faith in me yet?"

"Not even close," he said.

"You have to deal with your family eventually."

"I know."

The senior group had reached the museum entrance. The purple flag disappeared around the corner. A dark rectangle, like a billfold, lay on the sidewalk near the bus. He headed down there so he could give it to the tall man, maybe ask some questions about the bus.

"I gotta go. Thanks, Linda."

*E*lizabeth couldn't believe it, but Tommy managed to convince Granny to leave the museum.

"I have a plan," he told her, "but everyone needs to rest before the final battle." They negotiated something out of hearing and Tommy said, "I promise I'll bring you back." Granny took his arm and let him lead her out of there.

"What did Linda say?" Elizabeth asked.

"We're trying to fix the wrong thing," he said without further explanation.

Granny insisted she wasn't hungry, so they brought her back to the motel, where she fell asleep in front of a game show. She put on a good show but this trip was wearing her down.

Tommy brought in a battered laptop he'd found in Linda's car and he pounded on the keyboard, assuring her he would explain once he had his thoughts organized.

Elizabeth changed into her pajamas and sat next to him on the bed, one eye on the TV and the other trying to eyeball the computer screen.

"Tomorrow we have to go to a copy place," he said.

"For what?"

"Not sure if it will work and don't want to get your hopes up," he said.

"What hope?" she asked.

"Exactly. If it works out, there will be a time for you and Granny to step up and do your thing," he added.

"What's our thing?"

"Cultural lecturing," he said.

"Granny lives for that. She doesn't even need to prepare."

His hands paused and then he was at it again. He was fast for a hunt-and-peck typist. His eyes flicked from the display to the keyboard, his expression absorbed. She wanted those eyes on her, those ridiculous eyes incapable of hiding anything.

He glanced over at her. "Are you watching me type?"

She nodded. "You're cute when you're clerical."

"I'm not sure how to respond to that," Tommy said, returning to his work.

"It's hot," she whispered.

"Now you're messing with me," he said, trying not to smile. "Let me finish this. Then I'm all yours."

"I like the sound of that." Elizabeth flipped through the channels and found a crime show that kept her attention until Tommy shut the laptop. He went to the bathroom to change. Every time he crossed the room, she twitched with desire.

When he returned, he tossed his balled-up clothes to the floor. "I need clothes for this plan."

"What do you have in mind?"

"I want to look professional."

"I can do that," she said, constructing an outfit in her mind. "Jacket-and-tie professional, or nice slacks and shirt?"

"No tie." He folded the sheets back with exaggerated casualness.

Elizabeth turned off the bedside lamp, and they slid under the covers. She scooted next to him.

"Nothing crazy," he said, putting his arm around her as they settled in.

"You think my clothes are crazy?"

"You like to stand out. I like to blend in."

"We can work on it." Elizabeth rubbed one hand over his chest and was rewarded with his quick intake of breath. "You feel good. You work out?"

Tommy cleared his throat. "I have one of those exercise apps on my phone that rates my progress as I go. I run it five days a week whether I do the workout or not."

She snickered. "You put it on but don't do it?"

"Gotta keep the app happy." His hands remained disappointingly to themselves.

She reached under his shirt to stroke his skin. One finger paused to circle a nipple, and his breath caught again. "This okay?"

"Couldn't stop you if I tried," he said, his voice sounding funny in his throat.

"What else do you do?"

"Basketball." He rolled to his side, so he faced her, their faces inches apart.

"Are you any good?"

"If someone's picking teams, I'm never picked first but never last either." He dropped his hand to her waist and pulled her closer and left his hand there, caressing her hip.

"Picked second?" She brushed her hand over him, keeping her touch above the waist.

"Third or fourth." He moved his hand up to cup her breast, brushing his thumb across the nipple. He grinned when she shuddered. "I'm good but not great."

She lined her lips up with his. "I played, too." She kissed him, gently, as if testing it out.

When she pulled back, he asked, "When were you picked?"

"First." She kissed him again, harder. His hand stayed locked on her breast like something he wasn't about to give up.

When she stopped, he said, "Of course you were."

"It was only third string," she said. "Enough about basketball. I didn't get to do you yesterday." Her fingers dropped to stroke him through his sweats.

He grabbed her hand. The sound he made was something between a gulp and a gasp.

"We can't do that with your Granny in the room," he managed to say.

She tugged her hand loose and brushed her fingers along his forehead before tangling them in his hair. "Not in a parked car. Not with my Granny in the room. So many hang-ups." She kissed a trail toward his ear and ran her tongue around the rim. "She can't hear. She sleeps solid. I once invited a whole mess of cousins to her house after a party. We made bacon and pancakes, watched one of those movies with loud music and fast cars, cleaned it all up, and sent them home. The next morning she got up and asked me what time I got home."

She found his mouth again and kissed him harder, her tongue sweeping against his. They went at it like that for a while, no sounds but the smack of frantic kissing mixed with their ragged breathing. His hand reached down to squeeze her ass before rolling her onto her back and settling his body between her legs. She ran her hands over his shoulders and along the dip of his spine. The sensations compiled into a dreamy bliss. She considered asking him to finish her off, like in the car before, when he exhaled in her ear and suggested, "Bathroom?"

She twitched in his arms, the desire unbearable.

"Yes." The word came out as one long, relieved sigh. She untangled herself from him and got out and darted into the bathroom. She expected him right behind her, but she had to wait, her feet dancing on the cold floor while her body ached for him.

He jumped inside and closed the door.

She flicked the light switch and they both squinted in the burst of blinding white light. Elizabeth caught a glimpse of herself in the mirror, bedhead and wild-eyed. She grabbed at his shirt.

"Could we take this off?"

Tommy glanced at the door before pulling his shirt over his head.

"You're beautiful," she said, running her fingers over him, finally able to see what she'd been touching in the dark.

"I'm not sure this light does much for my complexion," he said.

She couldn't tear her eyes away from him and not just the bulge in his sweats. His body was amazing. He wasn't huge, but muscular—like a martial artist or a rock climber.

"No one is looking at your complexion," she said.

TOMMY COULDN'T GET ENOUGH of her greedy hands, as if she was afraid of missing something, and she made quiet murmurs of approval along the way. Elizabeth pushed him against the counter and leaned into him, kissing a soft spot under his chin and trailing more kisses down his neck. The sensation of being touched was a wonder after a long dry spell. In the past, there were many drunken hookups, but in sobriety, he'd had a tougher time knowing how to act around women.

"You're crazy sexy," she said, her eyes shiny, her hair tumbling around her face. Her hands hesitated. His back was to the mirror and she stared at their reflection. Her fingers ran up his back and slowed to trace over one shoulder blade.

"Are those scars?" she whispered.

He couldn't help flinching. He grabbed her chin and looked into her eyes. "It's a sad story and a boner killer. Some other time."

A kind-hearted smile touched her lips but her eyes were wicked. "No boner killers here." She dropped to her knees. "This okay?"

Tommy managed a nod. She took her time pulling his pants down and carefully inspecting what she found, before using her mouth. The sight of her going down on him was electrifying. She caught his eye and winked, and a puff of air hissed from his lips. He wasn't sure what to do with his hands and finally settled on putting them on the counter to hold himself up.

He grunted quietly with his teeth ground together, every sound amplified in the tiny room. Elizabeth's hands kept busy, too, and every few seconds his belly clenched.

When he pulled her back up, she said, "Quiet one, aren't you?"

"There's an elder sleeping about three feet from here," he said.

She gave him a giddy smile. "I told you she can't hear us." She stroked his belly with hot hands. "Should I try something else?"

He held her face a few inches from his. "Slow down a little."

"Like this?" She jumped up on the counter and turned him around and pulled him toward her. She slammed her mouth over his and wrapped her legs around his waist, her hips rubbing against him.

He groaned. "You're about three steps ahead of me. Let me catch up."

She reached for him again and studied his reaction. "You're not that far behind."

He fretted about matching her enthusiasm. "Hang on a sec." He turned on the shower. "Low-tech soundproofing."

She nibbled at his lips and kissed the corner of his mouth. "That better?"

He responded by leaning her back, pulling up her shirt. He worked his way to her breast and slid his tongue over one nipple until she whimpered. Then he transferred his attention to the other side.

He moved his mouth aside long enough to ask, "Is this okay?"

"It's barely enough," she squeaked.

He fisted his hands into her shirt and yanked it over her head. He lifted her off the counter long enough to tug her panties off, and she let out a little yelp.

"Your butt cold?"

"Who cares?" she said, giving him a look of pure lust.

The sound of the shower hummed in the background while the throbbing inside of him grew unbearable. "Where—?"

She slid the condoms over.

"I haven't done this in a while," he said, tearing open the package.

"I can help you put on a condom," she said, feigning misunderstanding.

"I got that part." He pressed his forehead to hers. "I like you. A lot." It felt like the wrong kind of honesty in the moment they were having, but his chest ached to be as close as that.

"Show me," she said.

He rolled on the condom and grabbed her ass with both hands. He pulled her to the edge of the counter and, in one swift motion, filled her up. He wasn't sure whether the animal sounds came from him or from her.

Her eyes were half-closed and she coaxed his tongue into her mouth while their hips searched for the right rhythm. Once they found it, her head dropped back. She shivered in his arms, every hitch of her breath a delight to his ear. Sweat accumulated in the place where their bellies met. In the mirror, Elizabeth's body jolted with each stroke. Every adjustment he made brought a new reaction, a giggle, a yelp, a hot sigh.

His senses jumbled into a white-hot daze. He barely heard Elizabeth repeating his name while she spasmed in his arms. He pounded into her, growling when he lost control. His legs were shaky when he came back to himself. He hung on to her to keep himself upright.

"You okay?" he asked when he could speak again.

"Wow," she whispered, falling against him, one hand running through his hair, her lips on his shoulder.

"That a good wow?"

"That's the best wow," she said. "We should do that thing where we vow no matter where we end up, we'll meet once a year at this snooze lodge and do it on this bathroom ledge."

"I like the part about seeing you," he said. "I think we could do better than snooze lodge."

"Perhaps," she said, a half-smile on her lips. Even in the harsh light, her skin glowed and her smile was radiant. "Now I'm starving."

"For?"

She laughed. "I just had you. Food. I need food."

"I'm hungry, too."

"For?"

"You, only you."

She grabbed his face and kissed him hard. He enjoyed the feel of them touching skin on skin too much to give it up, but she slid off the counter and pulled him into the shower.

20

---

*T*ommy drove in a daze, his mind filled with the sensation of Elizabeth's body rubbing against his, the smell of her skin, and the honey-sweet taste of her mouth. He wanted to say something but couldn't find words for all the things he was feeling.

"A food truck?" Elizabeth said when he stopped.

Tommy coaxed her out of the car. "The best tamales in the city." He expected her to be more open-minded after the last hour. Every cell in his body was buzzing with electric joy. "We can find a greasy diner if you prefer."

She tucked a hand into his pocket and followed him. "We can try your thing."

He hoped her doubts were assuaged when they found the truck with a line six-people deep. She held his hand while they waited.

"What did Linda say, about you staying?" she asked.

"She wants her car back." They arrived at the front of the line and ordered. "We're lucky. On the weekends they sell out early," he told her. They took their food and leaned against the car, a bottle of bright red hibiscus soda on the hood between them. He'd been so wrapped up in his work drama, he'd never asked about hers.

"What did the casino say?"

"Everybody cares about Granny, so I'm okay for a day. But we need to convince her to go home." She mimicked what he did, popping open a container of green sauce and pouring it into the red-checked food tray.

"What's your job going to be?" he asked.

"Marketing and promotions. It sounds fancy but it's a beginner job. Whatever they need."

"Did you always want to work there?"

She made a sound between a groan and a sigh, and refocused her attention on the tamale, pulling back the husk and probing with an index finger before looking back at him.

"No. I always knew I would be coming home so I could be near Granny and Leo, but I didn't know what I would do." She took a careful bite and made a low moaning sound that he felt in his groin. Green sauce dripped down her hand, and she caught it with her tongue. "This is amazing."

"Glad you like it," he said, already half finished with his. "Did you ever think about things you want to do?"

She gave a half-hearted shrug. "I don't know. I never thought about the future like that. I always knew I'd be limited to jobs I could do on the rez. Then the driving problem happened. I'll be okay at the casino."

"Any classes you liked?"

"What, you're a career counselor now?" she said, a hint of irritation in her voice.

"Trying to get to know you," he said.

She twisted her lips into a silly smile. "I like history, especially tribal history. One time I asked Linda about the kind of thing she does and what she studied. I could look at tribal government jobs if the casino doesn't work out." She finished chewing another big bite. "You cook any food like this?"

He shook his head.

"What sort of things do you make?"

He gave her a curious look.

"I thought you said you collect cookbooks."

He laughed. "Surprised you remember that. I was interested when I was younger but everyone made fun of me, so I lost interest."

"Those people are jerks. Cooking is always useful. I don't like to do it, but I like when other people do it. I could eat more."

"Good. I'm getting back in line," he said.

When he returned, she said, "You were right about the food truck. I would never have tried something like this. I like the funny drink, too."

"You more of a patty melt kind of girl?"

She shook her head. "No. I need to try more things. None of this at home."

"Lots of things to try where I live," Tommy said.

"I know." Elizabeth paused. "Tell me your most embarrassing sex story."

"You mean like the time I had my hand up the dress of this insanely hot chick in the back seat of my boss's car? Almost got caught by the cops."

"Nice try but that doesn't count," Elizabeth said.

"I want to impress you. Why would I tell you an embarrassing story?" Tommy nudged her in the side.

"I'm already impressed. Do you want to hear mine?"

"You wouldn't have brought it up if it wasn't worth hearing," Tommy said.

"In college, I got invited to this formal dance party thing, like a prom only in college. It was at this kinda nice hotel. Everyone was partying, as you do, and me and my date got frisky and went into the breakfast room, which was closed at that hour. We thought we'd go at it against the window."

He tried to stay interested in a story where she went at it with some other guy.

"We couldn't see outside, so we thought it was a private moment. What we didn't understand was that people could see in. Perfectly. Someone from the party spotted us and put out the word, so we had an audience plus anyone who looked out their hotel window at the right time. I'm sure there's a clip of it online somewhere although I don't know if I want to see it."

"Reliving the embarrassment?"

Elizabeth laughed. "No. I think I would be judging it too much. Did it look sexy? When you're doing it, that's the last thing you want to be thinking about but if people are watching, shouldn't it look good?"

"I wouldn't want anyone watching," Tommy said. He finished his tamale and took a long pull from the bottle. He leaned over and kissed a spot under her ear, and her eyes slid shut, and she shuddered.

"No fair distracting me until you tell me yours," she said.

Tommy resurrected a series of humiliating sex memories that generally involved being too drunk to perform usually combined with being too drunk to stop trying. There had also been times when he was too drunk to stay awake or the times he'd woken up with a person he never intended to fool around with. But that wasn't the kind of story she wanted to hear even if he was inclined to share.

"I don't know. I've been pantsed. Locked out of any number of houses or apartments."

"I've fondled your parts. You can do better," she said.

"How about this? There was this girl I liked, and she was galaxies out of my league, but somehow we managed to be at the same party."

"This is on the rez?"

"Yeah. I admired her from across the room, while I worked through a half-rack of crap beer, guzzling one after the other. I finally decided I was going to make out with her. I had enough courage, I was ready. I go gliding over, all casual, and sidle up and hold her arm and kiss her shoulder. This goes on for a while. I'm thrilled at my success. Eventually—who knows, minutes? hours? later—one of my friends whacks me across the head. Turns out I have been enthusiastically nuzzling the shoulder of a winter coat hanging over a coat rack."

Elizabeth burst out laughing. "You did not."

"Why would I make that up?" Tommy said. "I'm not sure if I started out nuzzling the girl and in my inebriated state, she was able to offload me to the coat or if I'd been doing the coat the whole time.

Brought my best moves to winter wear. My friends all gave me a ton of shit about it. For years."

Elizabeth said, "I want to laugh, but that's so sad. Cute but sad."

"*That's* what I'm known for," he said.

WHEN IT WAS time to go, Elizabeth went to the driver's side.

"You want to drive?" Tommy asked.

"I don't know, maybe?"

The night was quiet. The only sounds were a faint hum from the food truck and the grind of vehicles on the freeway overpass nearby.

He opened the car door for her, but she didn't get in. She stared at the steering wheel like it was on fire. "I was thinking I could drive Leo's truck and maybe visit you. Now I'm afraid." The notion was impossible. If she couldn't drive at home, how could she drive anywhere?

"What happened?" Tommy asked.

"What makes you think something happened?" She gave him a sour look.

"A few minutes ago you said so." When she stayed quiet he added, "You know all my business."

"Like the scars?"

He shook his head. "Not talking about that. Forget it. We'll go."

"I'll tell you," Elizabeth said. "When I was in college, something did happen." Her shoulders went tight and her voice fell, like she'd run out of breath to say the words. Her hands fluttered, first wringing together then flopping on her hips, searching for pockets and then smoothing down her sides. Tommy grabbed one and threaded his fingers through hers and held it to his heart.

"I was with three of my friends, and we were coming back from the movies." The fear returned and a tremor started in her legs.

He squeezed her hand. "Take your time."

"It doesn't even sound like such a big deal. A random dude road raged on us. I don't even know what I did but he came alongside and swerved and I jerked the wheel and lost control. We went into a ditch and rolled over."

She stopped, shuddered, then tried to laugh it off, afraid of what he would think. "When I talk about it, it's like it's happening again. Loud crunching and scraping." She wiped her eyes.

"The guy stopped and hiked into the ditch like he's going to check to see if we're okay but instead he starts going off, completely unhinged. He screamed, calling us names. Stupid bitches. Dumb whores. Telling us to die.

"One of my friends had a broken arm and she was sobbing for help. He did nothing. After he finished raging, he hiked back up to the highway and left. It took forever for the EMTs to get there."

Tommy pulled her into his arms and she rested her head on his shoulder.

"The whole thing was crazy and upsetting, and now I'm afraid to drive."

Tommy kept his arms around her. "Terrible things happen and it's hard to get over."

"I want to get over it, but every time I think about it I get panicked and shaky. There's always someone to drive us at home so I keep putting it off."

"I get it," he said, one hand stroking comfortingly down her back. "There'll be another time."

"No, there won't," she said, a few tears leaking out.

"Try sitting in the driver's seat. If you don't want to, we'll stop there."

"I can do that part." Elizabeth unwrapped herself from him and plopped herself into the seat. She took the keys when he offered but held them in her lap.

"It's late. The road won't be busy. I'll be right beside you, talking you through it." He went around and got in next to her. Already his presence was comforting, his voice low and gentle.

The second she inserted the key, her heart accelerated. Her hands went cold and she dropped them back to her lap while she huffed several furious breaths. She sat back in the seat and tears of frustration sprang to her eyes. This was the point where George would chide her, as if getting over the fear was a simple task that she could be mocked into doing. "The roads haven't changed, you have," George had told her. "Just make yourself do it."

She put her hands on the wheel, imagining what it would feel like to be in motion. Tommy stayed silent, gazing patiently ahead, his whole body at ease.

She was close, but she couldn't quite bring herself to do it.

"You might need more time. We don't have to do this tonight," he said.

"I want to while I'm with you." She started the car and her heart kicked up again.

"You want to adjust the seat—"

"I know how to fix the seat," she snapped.

"Sorry."

"What should I do?" she asked.

"Take a second to figure out where you're going. How are you getting out of the parking lot? Take your time."

"I don't know where I'm going," she said through gritted teeth. The trembling moved into her legs, too.

"Do you feel comfortable driving around this parking lot?"

"I guess." She put the car in drive and drove a slow lap around the parking lot. She did another lap, faster this time, and stopped at the exit.

"Can you tell me specifically what you're afraid of?" He took one of her cold hands and rubbed it in his warm ones.

She couldn't think of how to put it into words. "It's like I get overwhelmed when there are so many cars and giant trucks, and everyone is in a big hurry, zooming around, looming up from behind and whipping from lane to lane. They all know where they want to go. I feel like I need to hurry and get out of their way or they'll be mad." She pulled her hand back and put it on the wheel.

"It's like that sometimes," he agreed.

"Now you're going to tell me that I shouldn't worry so much about what they're thinking. I have as much right to be there as they do. They aren't thinking about me, they've got their own problems."

"So, you can read minds. We don't have to do this."

"No, I trust you. I want to. I just don't want to."

She put her hands back on the wheel and slowly pulled out on the main street and stopped at a red light. In the rearview mirror, a car pulled up behind her.

"There's someone behind me," she said in a small voice.

He checked over his shoulder. "Not uncommon."

"Don't make me laugh," she said, a smile threatening to come. She readjusted her hands on the wheel. The light turned green, and she pressed the accelerator.

"The onramp is up there. You can make a right from this lane. No sweat."

"No sweat," she repeated.

"Once you get on, you can stay in the slow lane and exit at the next exit. One easy test."

"What's something you're afraid of?" she asked.

"Enough about me already," Tommy said.

"I'm driving, aren't I?"

"You know, the usual," he said.

She turned on to the onramp, probably too slowly but Tommy didn't say so. Once she was on the freeway, the anxiety mixed with a hint of elation. The terror remained but she was doing it.

"I can do more than one offramp," she said. "Now tell me what you're afraid of."

"I'm afraid of disappointing Linda," he said.

"What *activities* frighten you?"

"I don't like to swim in the ocean."

She took a moment to process that. "You're kidding. I love to swim in the ocean. What are you afraid of, sharks?"

"No." He laughed.

She hit freeway-speed, keeping up with the other cars around her. The traffic was light. Her confidence grew. She hit the turn signal and glanced over her shoulder to change lanes.

"I don't like the waves or the cold or the water sloshing around all unpredictable and knocking you over and dragging you back. Riptides."

"Some of that is the fun part," she said, plotting out where to take him when they got home. "I can't wait to gently expose you to the sea. Get your feet wet, so to speak."

"I don't know when that's going to be," he said.

They passed another exit but she wanted to keep going, not exactly enjoying the experience but exhilarated at her progress. "I'm doing good, huh?" She came up behind an ancient VW van and stepped on the brake.

"You're doing great. Better than I'm going to be at swimming. You going to pass this guy?"

"Getting to it," she said, using the turn indicator, moving into the passing lane and accelerating past.

"You're a natural," Tommy said.

"How far are we from the motel?" she asked.

"At least ten minutes. You want to stay behind the wheel?"

"Yeah." She flicked a quick glance at him, to see if he had a death grip on the door handle, but he was the same easy-going guy. He was back in his dingy sweatpants and T-shirt. She couldn't wait to get him dressed up. Sure, he could work the rumpled sweats and stretchy T-shirt, but cleaned up he was going to be all hottie.

"What are you thinking about?" he asked.

She gave him an evil grin.

"One thing at a time, lady," he said, pretending not to laugh.

"I'm good at multi-tasking," she said.

"Confidence has come quickly, my daring driver," he said.

A cab came up behind her, and she moved to the other lane. "Speaking of coming quickly..." she said.

"I always knew someday my manly hip swivel would command some special lady's full attention."

She laughed. "The ladies will line up once I'm gone."

He went silent.

"Will you tell me about those scars?" she said.

"Nope," he said with finality.

She waited another minute before asking, "From when you were a kid?"

He tried to laugh it off. "Sad childhood story. New topic."

A trio of cars came up the freeway entrance. She swallowed while they merged around her. "What do you think all these people are doing in the middle of the night? Like, the truck drivers or pizza delivery I get, but what about everyone else?"

"People with jobs with off schedules, like bartenders or security. Some people like to be out late. I did back in the day, although it was never for a good cause."

"George and I talked about that when I was going for a job at the casino. If I wanted to get more on the hospitality side, I would have started with more weekends."

"Who's George?" Tommy said.

She shouldn't have brought up his name, but he was in the back of her mind. He'd texted a number of times and then tried to phone when she didn't respond. She'd finally texted to tell him that she and Granny were doing fine and she'd see him when they got home. "A friend from home. I've known him forever." She should explain more but to say what? Reassure Tommy that the thing with George was long over? Try to find some lighthearted way to describe the unexpected range of feelings she had developed in such a short time? She couldn't bear the idea of saying goodbye and she pushed it out of her mind, focusing instead on the time they had left.

"Can you talk me back to the motel?" she asked.

"Follow the exit signs that say City Center. It's on the main drag. I'll mention it when we get close." His voice had gone flat.

Thinking about the two of them in the future was silly. She knew that when she'd talked him into taking them on this failure of a mission.

21

---

*L*inda had driven rez cars before and the green car measured up with the worst. A patchwork of exterior duct tape kept both bumpers on and the interior smelled like moldy campfire. The engine dropped into a deep rumble punctuated with gasps like the car was on the verge of dying every time she stopped at a light. She would have left it at the house and taken the bus if she didn't have two meetings, a dentist appointment, and a giant box to drop off at the shipper.

She couldn't get the image of Arnie's house out of her head: tidy as she would have predicted, but not a sign of Katie anywhere. Not even an extra toothbrush in the bathroom, which she was ashamed to have snooped around but she was in Arnie's house, how could she not? Then Arnie's mom charging over, followed by that bizarre exchange about her staying the night as if she might have forgotten that he'd always treated her like a sister.

But those words to his mom: *"She didn't come with me this weekend."*

She promised herself she wouldn't dwell on the idea but it kept sneaking in, Katie on the rez with him and his family.

The minute she'd gotten home she'd left a message for Virgil. Time to pour on a little gasoline and see if they could get a fire going.

The morning's first order of business was dealing with the insurance adjuster for the bus. Tommy's greatest talent was getting out of aggravating tasks. If he were doing anything besides helping Aunt Dotty, she would be plotting a grievous punishment for him.

The impound yard was in a part of town she rarely visited. The insurance adjuster had sent an address and her phone gave her reassuring instructions as she navigated past strip malls and older apartment buildings into a mix of warehouses and commercial sites.

The sky was a solid block of low gray clouds that had looked ominous all morning. It finally broke and a light drizzle splashed across the windshield. Linda reached for the lever for the wipers, only it wasn't there, because Tommy had her car and she was in the automotive equivalent of a racehorse with a broken leg.

She took her eyes off the road long enough to scan the dashboard, touching various knobs and buttons until she found the right one. The wipers *whooshed* back and forth so rapidly she was afraid they would fly off. She attempted to adjust the speed control, but this was it. One speed: lunatic. The defrost button was apparently decoration only because the rear window was still a foggy haze. All her hard work and smart financial sense and she was still the one driving a rez car.

She arrived at the impound lot and waited at the front gate. The Drivemaster was easy to spot through the chain-link fence. Angie had done a number on it. The right side was a series of dents and scrapes culminating in the front with a smash of broken plastic and hanging bumper. Nothing Arnie couldn't fix with a little duct tape.

The insurance adjuster was late. The rain picked up, and she went back to the car to grab her raincoat, forgetting that it was another item she conveniently stored in her car. The only things stored in the green car were a set of chains, a sledgehammer, and a scary blanket that looked like it had been used while committing a crime. For some reason the person she was annoyed with was Arnie. A gust of wind drove big cold drops straight to her skin. She tried to duck back into the car but the driver's side door was stuck. She yanked on it with growing fury then got the keys out, thinking it needed to be unlocked.

The showers turned out to be true spring rain, the kind of rain that went from pleasant mist to refreshing shower to firehose blast. The cold rain dumped down on her while she struggled with the door. She slapped the window with an open palm. When the driver's door failed, she tried the passenger side, then worked her way around the vehicle. None of the doors would open. Her hair stuck to her neck and the rain dripped into her eyes. Her hands ached in the cold and there was no dry place to put them.

Someone ran toward her with an umbrella. She hoped it was the insurance guy or any human being who could get the car door open so she could drive away. She could go to Mexico and open a little margarita stand and live on the beach.

The person with the umbrella was an older man with a beard and a smile of patient weariness, like a school teacher. He held the umbrella over her, but with the whipping wind it didn't help much.

"You need help?" he asked.

"You insurance?"

"Afraid not," he said. He handed her the umbrella and tried the door.

"It's unlocked. It's stuck." Linda showed him the keys.

He tried again, putting his weight into it. "It is stuck," he agreed. "You want to wait in there?" He pointed across the street to a two-story red brick building with white framed windows flanked with tall leafy trees.

They dashed across the street. Linda followed him up the stairs and wiped her feet on the mat before entering through a giant oak door.

The man said, "Hang on a sec and I'll bring you a towel."

She found herself in a cozy reception area with couches and coffee tables, like a college study center. Two women about her age sat on one couch, reading. They gave her a smile of commiseration as she stood there, dripping on the floor.

"I'm Arlo," the man said when he returned with the towel. "You new to town, or suffering a misfortune?"

"I'm Linda. The second one," she said. "What gave it away?"

"Most locals wouldn't be caught without some rain protection at this time of year."

"Someone ran off with my car. That's a loaner." She mopped up the worst of the water but couldn't do much about her wet clothes. "I know who has it," she added. "He's suffering a misfortune himself, but I would be happy to kill him right now."

Arlo found her a place to sit and brought her a cup of hot tea. The warm cup felt great in her hands.

"Perhaps you'd like to join one of our classes," Arlo said.

"You teach classes for killing people?"

"This is a meditation center," he said, sitting down across from her.

Linda took a more careful look around the room. The muted color scheme, the huge canvasses in gilded frames depicting peaceful outdoor scenes, the quiet so thick she could feel it in the back of her throat. "The frantic buzz in my head does feel threatened. What do you do here?"

"We host retreats and practice sessions. We sell books and CDs, too, although everything is changing with so much happening online." He was still studying her expectantly.

"I'm not the meditation type," Linda said.

"No one is," Arlo agreed. "You said you're waiting for insurance?"

"That banged-up short bus out there belongs to the Crooked Rock Urban Indian Center. My employee—the same one who ran off with my car, his cousin took it for a joyride."

Arlo cracked up. "Maybe your employee would like to take a class. You're welcome to wait here as long as you like."

"I should be out of your hair shortly," Linda said.

Arlo floated off to do whatever calm, unhurried people did at a job that consisted of helping people relax. That could be her, peaceful and soft-spoken, deflecting panic with the power of breath and posture.

Her spine grew straighter as she serenely contemplated her problem. There had to be a way to avoid bringing Arnie into this, having to ask him for help, forcing him to drop what he was doing and run over to fix things for her once again. She twisted the phone in her hands. The girls were at meetings. Tommy was gone. Virgil would have been happy to assist but he was working out of town. She'd blown through the automobile roadside service's annual maximum during the flat-tire incident. The options were to pay them or call Arnie.

She searched her purse for the auto service card, envisioning how this would proceed. The roadside assistant would drive up, and they would find a rez car, a car that probably had no recognizable parts or systems. She put the card away and called Arnie.

"Your car—" she said.

"Did you wreck it?"

"No, I didn't wreck it."

"Damn," Arnie said. "I would have considered it a favor."

"I can't get in. The door is stuck."

"That happens. You try all of them?"

"It's raining. It isn't funny."

"Sorry, Lulu, er, Linda. I thought you were getting your car back."

"Tommy's still helping Auntie." She didn't have the energy to explain.

"A few sharp kicks to the door, right underneath the handle, will do the trick."

Inspired by her surroundings, Linda waited the space of three complete inhales and exhales. She finally said, "You're serious."

"It's the green car. That's what it does."

"I guess that explains all the funny dents. I was worried I did that."

"Nope. I can be there in an hour," Arnie said. "Or I can get Henry to help. Or should I not be offering to help? Do you want to call your roadside people?"

"The card for the roadside service is in my car," she lied.

"It's okay if I help? Say the word."

She could picture him standing outside some meeting, looking at his feet and admiring his smirk in the tops of his shiny shoes, relishing this moment with her asking for help. Again.

"I'll text you the address. Insurance guy drove up." She ended the call and took her time folding the wet towel and preparing to go back outside.

Arlo returned, waving a giant plastic garbage bag. "Better than nothing."

She took it from him, trying to decide whether she wanted to put it on. Outside, the trees trembled in the wind. "Do you have anything I can belt it with?"

"I'm sure there's a piece of rope around here somewhere," Arlo said. He held up a pamphlet. "In case you want to visit sometime."

2 2

Something lurched in Elizabeth's chest every time Tommy doted on Granny. He brought her old-fashioned doughnuts and a big cup of coffee and set her up at the table in the motel. Once he reiterated his promise that he would take her to the museum, she agreed to relax in the room while they ran their errand.

On their way to the car, he offered the keys.

"You were right," she agreed while pushing the keys away. "Once I was doing it, it wasn't so bad, and I will practice again but not now."

"Wouldn't hurt to try again while you're comfortable with it," Tommy said.

She wished she could drink up his calm attitude about the whole mess. She considered it, but a big truck rumbled by and the street was much busier than the night before. She said, "I promise I'll try again."

"You're the boss," he said.

They found a copy shop for Tommy's plan and then went to the thrift shop advertised as the best in the city.

Inside, Elizabeth took a quick lap before guiding him to a long rack stuffed with slacks.

"Tell me what it is you're wanting," she said.

"I need to look nice," Tommy said.

"Nice, as in formal wedding nice?"

"No, nice like not jeans or athletic wear," he said.

She couldn't help smiling at that. "Athletic wear?"

"People call it that," Tommy said. "Linda would say I need to look professional."

Elizabeth held up a pair of black pants.

He glanced at them, then said, "Sure, if I wanted to go door-to-door selling magazine subscriptions."

"Be open-minded. For me." She took his arm and guided him to another rack, part of her brain still reliving the memory of his hands all over her. She took a calming breath. "The secret to thrifting is patience." She attacked another jammed rack. The first few items were worthless. She thrust a possibility into his hands.

He held up the hanger. "Are these skinny jeans?"

"They aren't jeans," Elizabeth said. Now that he held them up, she wasn't sure about the color. Dark brown sometimes looked like a mistake.

"Pants? Skinny pants? I can't wear this."

She took them back. "I didn't want brown anyway." She handed him two more pairs. "Before you go in, let me find some shirts. Do you see the changing room?"

"There's a sign in the corner," he said, his voice resigned. "What kind of shirt are you making me wear?"

"It's not going to have the name of a sports team." She guided him to a rack with shirts and then ran her hands over his chest and across his shoulders.

"Excuse me, ma'am," he said.

"That's how I verify your size," she said.

The white button-downs were dingy, the best one had a stain on the collar, but she found a light blue one to get them started. She paused over a collection of sweaters.

"What about this?" He used his elbow to point at a light gray Henley.

"That's practically a T-shirt. You said professional." She pulled something else off the rack.

"Is that a sweater vest, because I'm not wearing a sweater vest," Tommy said when he spotted what was in her hand.

"Some might call it that. I call it cashmere. Feel how soft it is. You will look terrific in it," she said, urging him to take it.

"Someone else will look terrific in it."

"Fine," she said, but she didn't put it back.

The changing rooms were nothing but tiny nooks with flimsy curtains to hide the occupant. She studied them carefully.

"I know what you're thinking," Tommy said. "Jeez, you can't keep your hands off me."

"Nope, I can't," Elizabeth agreed.

"Do you like to do it in a normal place, like a bed?"

"Yes. Do you see one?"

"Not right this second." He paused, then gave her a quick kiss on the lips before ducking behind the curtain.

Elizabeth couldn't help smiling.

As soon as he came out, she wanted to rip the clothes back off him. "You look incredible. What do you think?"

Tommy fingered the fabric. "I'm not sure about this."

"It looks amazing."

"I feel uncomfortable," he said.

"Meaning the fit? Or like you're not accustomed to looking so ridiculously sexy?"

Tommy checked out the pants again. "The second one, I guess. What is this?"

"Pinstripes. Men's dress trousers for the professional. Total contemporary native. All the guys on the rez will be wearing it next season." She hooked a finger through one of his belt loops and considered how to complete the outfit.

"I don't think that will happen," Tommy said.

"I wonder if we can find a jacket," she said.

"Now you're out of control," Tommy said. "Plus, my shoes look stupid. A nice pair of athletic—"

"Stop," Elizabeth said. "You said you wanted to look nice and you put yourself in my capable hands."

Tommy gave her a pained look. "Something something *capable hands?*"

"Later," Elizabeth said. "Try on the other stuff. I'm going to dig around for shoes and a jacket. You might like some of those other things."

"I won't," he said.

"I drove on the freeway and changed lanes. Try on the clothes," she said.

"No matter what I do or where I go in this world, there's always an Ind'n woman ordering me around."

Her heart stuttered again. The heavy feeling in her chest was more than she was accustomed to. She pulled him closer and pressed her forehead to his. "What are we going to do?"

TOMMY KNEW she wasn't talking about the museum. "You said you could visit."

"And you visit me?" Her voice had lost its confidence.

"As much as I can. But how long can we make that go on? You want to live in the city? Linda and Arnie love finding young Ind'ns jobs." He imagined showing her around, and trying new restaurants, and going on day hikes. "I bet there are great thrift shops where I live."

The playfulness was gone and a sad seriousness in its place. "I can't leave Granny. Would you ever live somewhere else?"

During any number of drives, he'd considered going someplace else. Running or relocating, the difference was slim, but he couldn't abandon his own family responsibilities. "What about Angie?"

"What about Angie?" Elizabeth said, something extra in her voice.

His body tightened up, and he pulled away. "It's different for you and your family?"

Elizabeth chose her words carefully. "She is an addict, right now, in the middle of it, manipulating and lying. You need to take care of yourself without a sick person derailing you."

"Do I look derailed to you?" he said.

She expelled a sharp breath. "How can you not see it?"

Cold, sharp anger flashed through him. Whatever truth might be in that statement, he wasn't going to talk about it. He shook his head. "Not from you," he said.

"Sorry, it's your life," she said, but it was too late.

"It's your life, too," he said. "The whole world is in love with Dorothy Scott, but it's you putting everything on hold to take care of her."

"I am not putting everything on hold." Her eyes gleamed with anger.

At this rate, the day would be ruined. He took her hands and held on when she tried to pull back. "Let's not do this. There's so little time. Let's stick together for Granny. We'll sort us out later."

"How? How will we sort us out?"

"Maybe we won't," he said. "Maybe we say goodbye. If not now, then sometime. I haven't figured it out yet."

He let go and returned to the changing room, sweeping the curtain behind him. But not before glimpsing the sadness in her eyes. He sorted through the rest of the clothes she picked for him, his heart so heavy he felt sick. His phone vibrated and he took a peek.

Angie.

Maybe she was derailing him. Or perhaps he was helping her. His finger hovered over the ignore button. They were family. She was trying. He accepted the call.

"Where are you?" Angie said, her voice shaky.

"Helping an elder. Where are you?"

"I was in jail but Dad bailed me out. We got a lawyer like you said. I'm at the apartment. Are you coming home soon?"

Tommy closed his eyes. She was back at his place, again, and waiting for him, like nothing had changed. "I hope so. Are you okay?"

"I'm not drinking. I'm going to be good this time. I promise." Her tone was sincere, contrite. The accident was the wake-up call she'd needed.

"Good. I'll be home late tonight or early tomorrow. I'm supposed to work."

"Okay. Sorry, Tommy. When you get here, I'll apologize to your boss. I'm going to talk to some people about a job. I'm going to do it right this time."

"Good to hear, Ange," Tommy said with a breath of relief.

When he came out, Elizabeth stood in front of a mirror wearing a sequined gown like a movie star would wear to a premiere. She dropped a hand to her hip and shifted her body so that the smooth bronze line of her leg showed. With a tilt of her head, she swept her hair back, and he caught a glimpse of the back of her neck where he'd kissed her the night before. His heart kicked up a notch.

"You're amazing," he said. "You getting that?"

Elizabeth stood back as if waiting for the punch line. "You're not going to tell me it's too much or make a cutting remark about a fancy gown and the rez?"

Tommy shook his head. "Why would I do that?"

Elizabeth put her arms around his neck and kissed him. "This is the best weekend I've ever had. If I wasn't so worried about Granny, I would never want it to end."

"Me either," he said, and hugged her back like he would never let her go.

When Arnie arrived at the impound lot, he spotted the green car but no Linda. Heavy rain battered the windshield.

A text arrived: *Across the street.*

He searched until he spotted her, waving from the front of a two-story brick building that looked like a funeral home. He drove across the street and went inside.

"Insurance has been and gone. I'm waiting out the cloudburst here," Linda said. She wasn't kidding about getting stuck in the rain. Her hair was damp, and she was wearing a plastic garbage bag, which was oddly adorable.

"What did he say?" he asked.

"He muttered a bunch of stuff that sounded helpful but wasn't informative. We have a rez bus now."

"We want our clients to feel at home," Arnie said. "You okay?"

She looked down at herself and then offered a grim smile. "No worse than usual. My rain jacket is in my car. These past few days I've learned that I keep many critical items in my car."

"Noncritical items, too," Arnie said.

"Don't start," she said, but she gave him a goofy grin, almost like old times. "I need to finish my tea and thank Arlo."

"Arlo? How long have you been here?" he said.

Inside, the place was like a study hall with tall bookcases and heavy rectangular tables surrounded by chairs. It had a library's heavy air and smelled like wood polish and flower arrangements. Library or funeral home—you'd never raise your voice in this room. She picked up a teacup and her bag and motioned him across a wide hall, their footsteps tapping along the shiny wood floor. They passed a set of double doors, and through the windows there was an expanse of grass and some playground equipment, dripping in the wet weather.

"What is this place?" he whispered.

"A meditation center," Linda said, sounding thrilled.

"A cult?"

"No. People who practice being calm." Her eyes were shiny as she looked around.

"You interested?"

"Kinda," she said.

Linda needed something, but he wasn't sure this was it. She introduced him to a man with a beard and a palpable serenity. "I'm taking off," she told him. "Thanks, Arlo."

Children's laughter rang down the hallway.

"We share some of our space with a daycare center," Arlo explained. "Do you want a tour?"

They couldn't possibly look like good recruits. "Sorry, have to get going." Arnie tried to sound regretful. He looked at Linda. "I can get you in the car and then take off, if you want to hang out here."

"I don't have time, either," Linda said, as if suddenly remembering her own agenda. Linda thanked the guy, and they took the rig back to the impound lot.

He said, "I was surprised you called me, after what happened last time."

When they were in college, she was always tracking him down to show him an editorial she'd written for the school paper or to ask him to help brainstorm ideas to get more students involved in native issues. Back then he liked being the one she looked to for help.

The rain drummed against the windshield. Linda smoothed the front of the plastic bag she wore. "Not my car. I wasn't sure if you wanted it driven into the river."

"Not with you in it," he said, the words sounding loud in the enclosed space. A funny spark of tension stretched out between them.

"Of course not, who else can run your organization in such fine fashion?" she said. The tension disappeared.

"True words. You did a great job out on the rez, by the way. They're talking about forming a tribal consortium for urban issues. You should tell them your idea for a city liaison."

"You like that idea?" She turned to look at him, like she was peering into his head. He always felt like he was one step behind her, scrambling to catch up.

"It's a brilliant idea," he said.

She gave him a grateful look. "City says they have a site for us to look at. You have time in the next week or two?"

"Of course," Arnie said. "Staff coming?"

"Nope. I don't want to get anyone's hopes up. Or destroy them either." She gave the green car a grim look, a look he'd given it many times himself. "Shall we get this over with?"

"Why don't you wait in here?" he said, pulling on his rain jacket.

"Why bother?" she said. He found her a baseball cap with a casino logo on it, and they got out. It took him several attempts before he managed to get the door open, mud marking the driver's side door by the time he finished.

He kicked a low tire. "What is it with you and tires?" He walked around the car to inspect the others.

"Maybe I'll get another flat and we could argue again." Between the cap and the garbage bag, she looked smaller, more like the girl he went to college with, and his heart went tight at the memory.

"There's a gas station a mile or two down the road. We can put air in the tire, and you can keep an eye on it. How's your gas?"

"Kissing empty. Would you expect any less? Thanks for the offer but I need to get back."

"It'll take five minutes. Save me from making another trip." He winked at her.

They drove to the gas station and finished up with the green car. He topped the truck off, too.

"Oops," he said when he put the credit card away. "Accidentally used my government credit card. Again. I have to remember to clear that up when I get back to the rez or I'm in big trouble. Send me the info for the city appointment?"

"I will," Linda said. An overhang protected them from the rain. She still wore the plastic bag. She ran her fingers through her damp hair. "Thanks again. I think Rayanne has a hair dryer at the office. I'm going to go put myself back together."

They stood there for an endless pause, the awkward silence of people who weren't sure how to talk to each other. He was about to invite her to coffee when her phone rang. She glanced at the ID and her mouth curved into a smile. A hot pang of envy shot through him when he guessed who that smile was for.

"Thanks," she mouthed and squeezed his forearm before she got into the car. Inside, she fought with the seatbelt before managing to hook it, the phone still glued to her ear.

She wasn't paying attention when he said goodbye.

"You look good," Granny said, admiring Tommy's new clothes. The compliment made him more self-conscious. The longer he thought about it, the more flawed the plan became. Any plan that relied on him standing in front of a group and speaking was bound to go wrong.

The museum entry chamber was crammed when they arrived. Several groups of school children filled one half, their voices echoing throughout the room. The kids ran back and forth, taking photos, shoes slapping against the floor. A group of foreign tourists waited near the entry to the exhibit halls.

Elizabeth said, "Are we supposed to seize control over one of these groups?"

"I've got a group on the way," he said. "We'll take them back. I'll do some talking, and then you and Granny will dazzle them with your own story-telling."

The students had taken over all the benches, so Granny sat on the walker seat.

"Talking in front of people and playing the machines are Granny's two favorite things," Elizabeth said.

"I like other things," Granny said. "I like hiking around the woods and the beach, and eating French fries, and being around you kids."

"Good life Granny," Elizabeth said. She fiddled with Tommy's shirt sleeves, rolling them up his forearms and checking that the sides were even. "I like this shirt the best. Looks sexy."

"Sexy is not what we need here," he said, the light and familiar touch stirring him up.

Elizabeth shook her head. "I don't understand that remark. You could use a haircut."

"What? And let you succeed where not only Linda, but also Rayanne, and even Ester have failed? This is my haircut."

"How about a ponytail then? You've got enough to pull back."

"I've tried. It never looks right."

"I can help you," Elizabeth said.

"What about when you aren't around?" Tommy asked.

She ran her fingers through his hair, smoothing it back and gathering it together. "We're going to sort us out later, we decided."

He'd successfully talked Elizabeth out of the jacket, but she'd found him a pair of dress shoes that he had to admit weren't terrible, but they gave him an awkward gait like he was tromping around in snowshoes.

"I'm not sure about these," he said.

"New shoes—well, new to you—always feel weird," she said.

"I don't think I've ever worn dress socks," he said.

"I don't believe you," Elizabeth said, adjusting his collar, taking her time sliding her finger along his neck as if the act were more complicated than it was.

He took her hand so she would stop distracting him. "Thanks for the outfit," he said.

"Didn't your mom make you wear nice outfits for events?" she asked.

"What's an event?"

"Weddings. Graduation. High school dance?"

His mom would have had to buy him a nice outfit if she wanted to make him wear one. His mom barely remembered to buy him clothes at all. Linda was the one who got him a nice outfit under the guise of giving him a graduation gift when he came to work for her.

"My mom didn't make me wear things," he said.

Elizabeth wore another outfit from that magical bottomless backpack. Today it was a turquoise sundress with a beaded belt and long beaded earrings. Her wavy hair was loose and every time she looked at him, his chest went tight, a mix of desire and uncertainty.

Everything she said about Angie spooled through his head on repeat. She thought Angie dragged him down, but Elizabeth didn't know his family. Angie needed family support, and their family wasn't built for that. He was it. Everyone needed someone.

He would never have made it without Linda. He was lucky he met her since he originally planned to ditch the Native Student Association mentoring workshop. She was assigned to answer his questions about school, help him with financial aid, and encourage him to participate in school activities. She'd done more than that, sticking by him when he fell off the wagon, insisting he was perfect for a job that she must have invented just for him.

She never gave up on him, always doing little things like giving him gift cards or bringing him cold medicine when he was sick. Her over-achiever frazzle was welcome after the years of a family who sat around getting loaded and yelling at each other and who made fun of him when he tried to do anything responsible. That's one of the reasons he'd spent so much time playing basketball. The adults who hung out around the community center were more predictable.

He wasn't about to abandon Angie if he was the only one to help her.

The woman with the purple flag came into the museum followed by a group of seniors. Tommy mustered up a cheery wave, like he imagined a camp counselor would do, welcoming them to their informative tour. He wasn't sure how this next part was going to work out.

"Too bad Rayanne isn't here," he said under his breath. "She's got Coyote in her blood. I, on the other hand, hate this."

"No one knows but you." Elizabeth's hands lingered over him, brushing the fabric on his shoulders, the careless display of affection soothing. "Remember, you look amazing."

He wished he had her confidence. He'd written a statement, memorized it, and now it was folded up in his pocket. He touched his pocket again to be sure.

"Who are these youngsters?" Granny asked, looking over the group as they approached. She looked brighter, re-energized by the upcoming hijinks.

His stomached creaked and his palms grew sweaty. He wiped his hands on his pants and jammed them in his pockets as he studied the group.

"Here we go," he said under his breath before addressing them. "Welcome, everyone!"

He'd summoned his memories of Linda and Rayanne doing talks about the center and what they wanted to achieve, why their work was necessary. He wished he'd paid better attention.

The only advice he could remember for speaking to a group was enthusiasm, which he would have to manufacture, and to take his time and not talk too fast.

"Glad you could make it," he said, giving the tour leader a thumbs-up. He urged the group to move in closer. "I'm Tommy Weaver, Klamath Tribes."

Seniors were so different from kids; they paid close attention. Most of the men wore baseball caps, and most of the women had bags slung diagonally over their shoulder. Everyone wore glasses. Some of them held notepads with pens ready.

"Nice to have you here," Tommy said, flooded with doubt the minute their eyes were on him. Too late to give up now. "This is Elizabeth Lewis, and this amazing lady is the great activist and tribal leader, Dorothy Scott, both Yurok citizens. Let's get going."

Granny went first, setting the pace across the entry, moving at top speed with the wheeled walker.

"She likes to compete with other elders," Elizabeth whispered.

"She's the only one in a hurry," Tommy said, with a fresh wave of nerves. Getting into the exhibition hall was the first test. He led the group to the entry and mustered his best confident smile.

The attendant stuck her arm out to block their path. "Which group is this?" she asked.

"Senior learning," Granny said, nudging the lady's arm out of her way.

"Hang on," the attendant said. She lifted her radio and said, "Group entry?"

A sheen of sweat broke out on Tommy's back. There was no backup plan. The attendant was searching for instructions from someone across the room. Tommy forced himself to face forward and hold his face in a mask of confident expectation.

Granny cleared her throat. "This place don't like me much."

The attendant smiled apologetically. "Why don't you go ahead," she said, waving them through.

Wow, Elizabeth mouthed.

Tommy guided the seniors into the exhibition. "The focus of this talk is tribal citizens and ceremonial objects."

WHEN ELIZABETH WATCHED Tommy lead the group into the exhibit, it was like seeing a different person. It was more than the clothes. He moved like a man made of confidence, chatting with the seniors, asking them questions, like you'd expect from someone who drove elders around every day.

He went into the main hall and brought the group to the ceremonial regalia on display. There were a few moments of throat clearing and a long awkward pause before Granny said, "You gonna talk?"

"I am," he said, glancing around the group with a nervous laugh. He indicated the exhibit. "For a lot of people, an exhibit like this is the closest they get to Indian people. When they see this, they see Indian people as something exotic, or something in history."

Once he began, the words sounded natural and he lost the

panicked look in his eyes. Whatever preparation he had done, it worked.

He continued, "People forget that we are still here, we still practice our culture. And for today when I say we, I'm generalizing for the three of us here. I don't speak for all Indian Country. As tribes, we use our natural resources and we take care of our citizens. On the rez, we have our own law and order, our own social services. I'm an urban Indian, and I work with an organization that provides services and community to urban Indians."

He faltered, and she spotted why. A security guard, someone they hadn't seen before, came over and stood at the edge of the group. This guy was big, but his body was relaxed, and he had a half-smile on his face, more like a teddy bear than a bouncer.

"A lot of what we do is preserve what we have and try to get back what we have lost. That means lands or hunting rights. And that means our sacred objects." Tommy pointed to the display. "In Western culture, you might see these as fancy historical clothing, but to us, it's much more. These items have a purpose, and they need special care." He turned and gestured at Granny. "This is Dorothy Scott, an honored elder of the Yurok Tribe and she is going to talk to you about this display."

Granny began her talk, pointing out each item. Elizabeth passed around copies of the archive photo of Granny in her ceremonial dress. Elizabeth had listened to Granny and Leo advocate for tribal people her entire life. Granny was an excellent speaker and knew how to read her audience. Just a day earlier she'd seemed so old, but today she looked strong. Fierce.

Elizabeth could tick off in her head the topics Granny would cover. How the Ind'n kids were taken to boarding school to assimilate into white culture. About all the culture that was lost since conquest.

The security guard from the day before, the lady who probably hadn't laughed in a decade, joined the teddy-bear guy. They exchanged a few words, disagreement apparent. They both moved back but didn't leave the room.

Elizabeth sidled up to Tommy, sliding her hand into his and giving him a squeeze, more to reassure herself than him. "Are you catching this?"

He nodded. "Everything is going according to plan. Maybe."

Granny explained the role of the items in the display. "The duty is to care for the ceremonial things and bring them out for everyone. They have a purpose to the People. Here in a museum they're just stuck in the drawer."

One of the men pointed to the display dress. "And that's the same outfit like this one in the picture?"

"Different dress. Same person. That's me in the picture," Granny said.

There was a general murmuring and rattling of paper as everyone checked the photo more closely.

"Do you still have this dance regalia in your family?" a lady with red-framed glasses asked.

"No," Granny said. "It's locked up in a box somewhere in the back of this place."

"She's going to get these seniors all worked up," Elizabeth said.

Tommy made a quiet whistling sound between his teeth. "That's the idea."

"If the things belonged to you, how did they end up in the museum?" Glasses lady asked.

"When the times change, we had to get money somehow. Families sold their ceremonial things. Not always with permission. Now they keep them here, so you can look at them."

"Is there a way we can see it?" someone called.

"That's what I want to know," Granny said.

There was more rumbling among the group. Elizabeth didn't hear what Granny said next. The security lady waved an arm toward the barrier of the display until the security man moved toward it.

"They're coming to kick us out," she whispered to Tommy. Her heart thumped harder in her chest.

She dragged Tommy to meet him before he interrupted the talk. The man's name tag said Joseph.

"Problem?" Tommy asked.

Joseph shook his head. "Sorry, I've been asked to keep an eye out."

"You mean this dangerous elder?"

He shrugged.

"Who's keeping an eye on you?" Elizabeth asked.

He smiled. "You never know."

Tommy said, "We don't mind taking this up a notch. Is Dr. Murray in the building?"

"I'll call for her," Joseph said.

Elizabeth lost track of what Granny was saying, but the seniors had pulled in closer. The lady with the red eyeglasses turned around and waved at Joseph. "Is it true you won't let her see her family's ceremony outfits?"

"I don't let people see things," Joseph said, holding his hands up in protest. He laughed and said, "I keep people from getting out of line." To Elizabeth, he said, "Your Grandma is getting them worked up. We're on the verge of our first senior riot."

"She's done it before," Elizabeth said.

"You come up here," Granny called. She beckoned with one hand until Elizabeth joined her. "This is my great-granddaughter. She finished college and now she's the new generation advocating for our people."

The words shot straight to her heart. She always thought of herself as the person caring for Granny while Granny did her thing. But she could see a part for her in all this, too.

Dr. Murray came into the room with another museum official and they looked around the group in confusion. She spotted Elizabeth with Granny.

Elizabeth said in a loud voice, "The museum has this ceremonial dress for an inventory project. Granny's been hoping to see it for the first time since this picture was taken. Have you got it for us, Dr. Murray?"

Dr. Murray closed her eyes and pressed the back of her hand to her forehead.

"Could you bring it out for all of us?" Red eyeglasses lady asked.

Granny winked at Tommy.

Dr. Murray said, "You've succeeded in getting them to change their priorities. Someone is working on retrieving it. I was coming to bring you back."

"Why can't you bring it out here, so everyone can see?" Granny said.

"I'll see what we can do," Dr. Murray said.

ommy was the last one in. They ended up in a museum classroom. A bank of windows along one wall let in the sunshine, making the space bright and welcoming. Another wall had built-in bookshelves overloaded with books and plastic boxes with large-print labels that said things like Mammals, or Rocks. Tommy took a quick lap around the room. A set of drawings from a previous class was displayed. The kids had drawn creatures they'd observed outside, which looked like squirrels and dogs and, in one case, a ladybug.

One of the seniors studied the drawings with him.

"You think they'll let us draw bugs?" he asked.

At the front of the room, Elizabeth stayed with Granny, the two of them with their heads together. They had the same smile, pointed chin, and sly look in their eyes.

After all this, he still wasn't convinced they would bring Granny her dress. Maybe they'd bring whatever they had, hoping the elder wouldn't recognize the slight at her advanced age.

Dr. Murray came in with a plastic box and called the group to gather around the table. Some of them stood on their tiptoes to get a peek. Dr. Murray put on a pair of plastic gloves and took out a basket the color of dried grass with a faded design of triangles.

Granny gave her a dark look.

Dr. Murray laughed. "I've got a team getting the ceremonial regalia. This is a big place. Lots of research goes on here. The work we do is for good, I promise." Dr. Murry stopped to catch her breath. "While we're waiting, perhaps you'd like to talk about this."

This time, she didn't even offer gloves. She held it out. Granny studied it for a moment. "For storage. Keep acorns or pine nuts in a basket like this."

Elizabeth didn't touch the basket, but she pointed to the contrasting brown and pale-yellow design. "Where did these come from?"

"I was hoping someone would ask me that," Granny said, the two of them sharing a look.

He could watch Elizabeth all day. The force of his feelings, both frightening and invigorating, stirred up something that he wasn't sure he knew how to handle. She looked up long enough to give him a secret smile before returning her attention to Granny, prompting her with another question, like they'd rehearsed it. Elizabeth's head tipped down to listen, her loving gaze making his heart hurt. Whatever happened after this, they had to make sure that everything that Granny worked for kept moving forward.

Granny described the different materials used for weaving and reminded them that contemporary Indians gather what they need from the forest and along the river to make baskets today.

Tommy's phone vibrated in his pocket and he checked. Angie phoning again. Not ready for that yet. He hit the ignore button.

Elizabeth drifted back to the corner to join him and whispered, "She's good, huh?"

"You, too. You're a good team." His gaze traveled over her face, his eyes resting on all the places his lips had touched the night before. She leaned into him. "I know what you're thinking." She was warm and solid next to him. "I can't believe we did this." Her eyes were shiny when she grabbed his arm. Everything about the moment felt right:

being with Elizabeth, helping an elder and showing the visitors a living heirloom. Linda would be proud.

"We leaving after this?" she asked.

"If they ever bring that dang dress out," Tommy said. "This might be a trick, too."

"I don't think so. Will you stay tonight? Go home in the morning? I could show you around the rez, and we could have a little more time." Her gaze locked on his, her intentions clear.

A flush of desire and affection washed over him just as quickly as the brisk reality. "I promised to be back tomorrow. I can leave late and drive all night."

"If you insist," she said. "I can make late work."

A series of images went through his head, their bodies coming together, Elizabeth's hands stroking his chest, her mouth finding every sensitive spot.

He cleared his throat.

She gave him a sideways smile.

Granny handed the basket back and made an impatient sound. Another staff member came in with a big flat box. The seniors moved back so they could slide it on the table. Dr. Murray opened the box and pushed it over to Granny. Her face lit up as she lifted it out of the box.

She slid the faded yellow buckskin off the table and shook it out with a snap. The beads and shells on the heavy leather fringe clacked together.

Dr. Murray's eyes widened, and she fumbled for words.

"Our people make things sturdy," Granny said. She grabbed the red-eyeglasses lady and tied the dress on her and showed her how to move so that the shells jangled together. "This makes the music," Granny told them.

Granny's pure joy was worth it. Maybe Linda could help him learn something about tribal cultural items. The idea was completely foreign and impossible, but he wanted to try.

With some help, Granny put the dress back on the table. "Nice to see it again. I want to take this home. Get it back to the dance, so it remembers itself."

Elizabeth exhaled. She was so close he felt her breath on his cheek. She said, "I should have known that was how this would go."

Tommy thought Granny was making a joke. "She's serious?"

"She didn't want to see it; she wants it back."

"They're not going to let us take that home," Tommy said.

At first, Tommy thought Elizabeth was angry, but she laughed to herself. "I guess we're not done here yet."

THAT LOOK in Granny's eyes...Elizabeth had seen it before. Next thing, she would have some crazy idea about sitting around the museum until they agreed to give the dress back to her.

"Is it possible to get it back?" one of the seniors asked. "Or could they borrow it?"

"Are visitors allowed at the ceremony? Would we be able to see it?" another asked.

Dr. Murray took off her glasses and pinched her nose before taking a deep breath. "Unfortunately, we don't have a procedure for loaning these ancient artifacts to outside organizations."

"Our relations. These are our relations," Granny clarified helpfully.

"How did this go into a collection in the first place?" someone asked.

Dr. Murray said, "Items come from different sources. There were collectors long ago, who gathered items from different tribes. The museum gets donations or purchases items. When you ask about returning, there is a process called repatriation."

"You have to give our things back," Granny said.

"It's more complicated than that, but yes, repatriation is a process for returning certain items. There's a research process before anything is returned."

Tommy took out his phone. "Linda said we're supposed to take detailed notes." He smiled at her. "Have you heard anything I should note?"

"All of it," Elizabeth said.

"Let's get it started," Granny said.

"Hold on," Dr. Murray said, her patience flagging. "The process is initiated by a Tribe, and the museum would research the item being claimed and work with the Tribe's research team. If the item meets certain criteria, it would go back to the Tribe. This museum has returned tribal items before."

Elizabeth's mind raced. She didn't know they could get things back. She could help Granny with the research. There were probably other items they didn't even know that they could bring back.

Tommy had a serious look on his face as he typed into his phone. "If the Tribe got it back, you could wear it."

Elizabeth suppressed a laugh. "I'm not a maiden."

"Oh," he said, and after a moment he added, "I suppose that's my fault."

"We have lots of girls in the family. Someone could wear it." They would have to find someone at the Tribe who could teach her. Or find her a class. They'd probably have to come back here and find a way to bring Tommy. He helped make this happen. She didn't want to make another trip without him.

Dr. Murray steered the discussion back to the ceremonial dress and the materials used. She let Granny explain how the ceremony unfolded and the different roles of the women and men dancers. They wrapped up with a few more questions before the tour leader and her purple flag headed out the door.

One of the seniors squeezed Elizabeth's arm. "You two help her get that stuff back," she said.

Tommy had his eyes on her. She liked his hair better without the ponytail, but she'd tell him that later. His lips were pressed together, and she wanted to feel them on her neck again.

He said, "You're like her. You're not going to give up."

Her heart stuttered. She'd only known him a handful of days, only woken up next to him twice. But she never wanted to wake up without him again.

"They're putting it away," he said.

"I want another look." Elizabeth tore herself away from him so she could study the dress close up. It smelled like dusty leather, and home. The shellwork patterns were complex, and she couldn't imagine how long it would have taken to braid all that beargrass. Granny had tried to teach her a handful of times, but Elizabeth was easily frustrated, happy to gather the materials and process them but not as patient with the weaving. She examined the tangle of fringe, afraid to touch it.

"Go ahead," Granny said.

Elizabeth wiped her fingers on her dress before she ran them over the shells. "So old."

"You understand we're doing our job," Dr. Murray said. "If we handed back items to every person who came in and asked, we wouldn't have much of a collection. Some items are in the museum legitimately. I'll initiate a research request for this obj—, your relation. When the Tribe makes a repatriation request, we'll be ready.

"The item is scheduled to be here for one year, and then it goes back to the historical research center. Honestly, I'm not convinced this item is eligible for repatriation." She held the side of the box with gloved hands.

"We can convince you," Granny said cheerfully, putting it away herself, her hands lovingly smoothing over the deer hide and arranging it in the box. "It wants to come home with us," she added.

"What do you remember about it?" Elizabeth asked.

"Heavy. Back then we didn't do so many traditional dances. It was a little bit scary if we was going to get into trouble."

"Who had the dress?"

"One of my uncles. I don't remember." Granny shook her head. "I'm eighty-two years old."

"You're ninety-two, Granny."

"Oh. Creeps up on you," she said. "What next?"

Dr. Murray said, "It starts with your Tribe. Have someone contact us formally and we'll get the process going. We will talk again."

"How long does it take?" Elizabeth asked, trying to remember the ceremony schedule in her head. Summer was coming. Maybe they could bring it out soon.

"Years," Dr. Murray said.

"Years?" she repeated, her eyes flashing to the elder, gazing into the box like she was looking at a newborn baby, her crooked index finger tapping pieces of abalone together. "Does it always take years?"

"Not everything gets returned," Dr. Murray said, not unkindly.

"She has her job, we got ours," Granny said.

"I'm going to learn how to do this," Elizabeth said as they fitted the top back onto the box.

"Good. This one too," she said, looking at Tommy.

"If I can. I'm not good at paperwork," Tommy said.

"You can learn," Granny said. She gripped the side of the table with both hands.

"We're headed out. You get to sleep at home tonight," Elizabeth told her.

Granny nodded. "I'm proud of you two. You see how to do things now."

ommy was surprised by how quickly the ride back went by. There was still light in the sky when they reached the reservation. Elizabeth insisted he see the ocean before he left, so they dropped Granny off and headed out.

"You call this a road?" Tommy said when she directed him to turn off onto a bumpy stretch of grass.

"Don't you see the tire tracks? Park by those rocks and pop the trunk."

Tommy obeyed. She hopped out of the car and dug around in the back until she had an armload of blankets and towels and said, "Follow me."

The sun was low, and a cool breeze stirred the trees, not what he recognized as swimming weather.

"We're really doing this?" The thought of immersing in any cold water—much less ocean chop—brought goosebumps to places he didn't know could goosebump.

"We are," she said with a crafty smile. "Our rez is along the river and where the river meets the ocean. We don't have time to go out to the beach, but this spot is good, too."

The trail snaked through the trees before plunging down, rocks and tree branches helping him stay on his feet. At the bottom of the trail, the ground was a river bar composed of coarse sand and smooth rocks in a range of sizes: softball, bowling balls, basketballs. The water stretched out shimmering gray and gently lapped at the shoreline.

He was relieved he wouldn't have to slosh around in crashing waves. Elizabeth moved easily, hopping from rock to rock, leading away from the trail. She threw the blankets and towels in a sheltered spot. She stared into the distance, dark eyes glazed over, the smallest frown on her face.

The desire to kiss her was overwhelming.

As if reading his mind, she turned and took his hand. "You ready?"

"Which thing?" he asked.

She offered a sly smile and indicated he should kick off his shoes.

"Am I going to drive home in wet underwear?" he asked as she tugged him toward the water's edge.

Elizabeth shook her head. She pulled his shirt over his head and threw it on the rocks. He stopped her hands when they tugged at his waistband.

"Do not fear, no one will bother us," she said.

The spot was not secluded. There was a wide expanse of water, steep mountains covered with trees with a road just out of sight, and not one but two boats far out on the water.

"But—"

"Exhilarating, isn't it?" She yanked her dress over her head. Her bra and panties weren't far behind. She glowed, even in the fading light, her smile radiant. He studied her carefully to bank the memory.

Tomorrow he would be back at the center, repairing the damage with Linda, dodging prying questions from Rayanne and Ester, dealing with Angie, and the bus, and elders, and basketball. Once he was gone, there was no guarantee he would ever see this again.

He'd be back to it: work, sleep, and staying sober. Would he wake up in ten or twenty years and realize that nothing had changed? Would this be the moment he returned to, his best chance to move things to a different course but he let it go?

"Do you want to run away?" he asked.

"If I thought it would work, I would insist," she said. "Stop stalling and take off your pants."

She tip-toed to the edge of the water and took three graceful strides before diving under. Her head burst back out of the water. "Strip for me, baby," she yelled.

Tommy took another quick look around. The boats were in the distance. He stripped his pants off and made his way to the water's edge and froze when he was ankle deep. He'd been in cold water before, but this was frigid.

"Someone looks cold," Elizabeth said.

"This was your idea," he reminded her. He stumbled into the water, lost his footing and splashed under, the cold water shocking the words out of him. He surfaced and kicked toward her with heavy limbs.

Elizabeth swam over, wrapped her legs around his waist, threw her arms around his neck, and stuck her tongue in his mouth. She stopped long enough to ask, "You want to try to do it like this?"

"I don't think that's possible," he said.

She giggled in his ear. "You're swimming in the wild. It's not so terrible, is it?"

"I'm too cold to be properly frightened," Tommy said.

"Granny would be proud. 'Cold water makes good for your healthy' she would say."

"Worked for her," he said through chattering teeth.

"You getting used to it?"

"Not even close."

Elizabeth kissed him again and then turned his head to face the sunset, a hint of orange above the dark line of the horizon. "Drink in this beauty for thirty seconds, and we'll get out."

His eyes remained on her, her wet lashes stuck together, her hair slicked back. She hung on to him, moving with the rise and fall of the water.

"Would you come back with me?"

"You are the only one who has ever made me think about it," she said, "but I can't. Come on, I'll warm you up."

~

ELIZABETH DRIED herself off with a towel and then turned her attention to Tommy, rubbing him down until she got the response she wanted.

"Are we ever going to do it in a bed?" Tommy asked, sweeping the towel around them, their cold, bare skin pressed together. She kissed along the crease in his neck, warming that spot with her lips.

"Stay tonight."

The sky had faded to purple, the night perfect for a bonfire if they planned to stay out and watch the stars. She rubbed against him, the friction helping to heat them up.

Tommy's voice was hoarse. "Come up for a visit."

His hands kept the towel secure, so hers were free to wander. She kept them moving, stroking his back, squeezing his butt, and skimming over his belly. "Take me for a quick drive in Leo's truck when get back to Granny's. After you go, I'll practice getting used to it." She bit his earlobe and smiled when he shuddered.

He let go long enough for them to spread out the blankets and bundle into them.

She stretched out on her side, and he swiftly circled his arm around her waist and closed the space between them.

"The best part about doing it outside is letting everything flap about in the open air," she said.

"The best part of doing it outside is that I'm with you," he said, his breath warm and delicious against her mouth. "I'm not worried about flapping. I'm worried about wind chill."

He clamped his mouth over hers and kissed her frantically, first on the lips, teasing her tongue, and then to a sensitive spot under her ear, pausing to whisper her name. One of his hands slid down her thigh to tickle the inside of her leg.

She tangled her fingers in his hair and pulled his face up, his eyes ablaze with lust and raw adoration. No one had ever looked at her like that.

Tommy rolled onto his back. "You get on top. I don't want my woman getting sand ground into her ass."

She would have hated the sound of 'my woman' from anyone else, but she loved hearing him claim her. As they reconfigured, the blanket fell open, and the chilly air washed over them again.

"Wind chill," she muttered.

Tommy arranged the blanket over her again, then his hands moved to her breasts, rolling the hard nipples between his fingers.

She gasped and momentarily lost track of what she was doing, her body melting into his. He rocked his pelvis to bring her back. After a brief search, she found a condom and slid onto him.

From the back of his throat came a quiet, happy sound. He pulled her to him, kissing her deeply, his hands moving possessively, skimming down her back and tracing up her thighs before resting on the curves of her ass. She took the lead with a slow, steady rhythm, the chill forgotten as heat spread through her.

He kept his eyes open, never leaving hers, between kisses whispering, "I love your eyes, I love your mouth, I love your hair."

Night had fallen. They were a single spark in the darkness, nothing but the two of them and the sound of the water lapping along the river bar.

She moved more quickly, and his hips shifted in response. Their bodies fit together, comfortable and exactly right. His fingers dug into the curve of her hips, pulling her closer, and she let a high-pitched moan escape. He didn't try to quiet her this time. The tremor inside her grew, heat and bright light rising together in wave after dizzying wave until she collapsed onto him, flushed and trembling, their breath ragged in her ear. His thighs shook underneath her, and he gasped several times.

She stayed on him a few moments longer, heavy and sated, happy to hear his heaving breath and feel his heartbeat under her. She slid off, and they wrapped themselves around each other, facing the same questions they'd been dodging for the past few days.

"Would you move?" she asked.

He stroked her back. The desire to hear him say yes made her ache.

"Is that hypothetical or an invitation?"

"Invitation. I'm asking you right now," she said, her head filled with ideas. "I have a friend you could stay with until you get settled. Maybe you could work at the school or whatever you do for Linda. She could do a recommendation."

He brushed his lips over hers, slow and lazy like they had more time than they did. "I'm not sure anyone would give me a job."

"Linda did."

"Linda is doing a public service," he said.

"You're not that bad."

He said, "I would move for you. You're the most amazing thing that's ever happened to me. But I can't do it now, and I can't ask you to wait."

"Waiting would be my choice," she said.

"I HAVE SAND IN UNCOMFORTABLE PLACES," Tommy said, trying not to hurry back to Granny's. He still had a long drive ahead of him. Elizabeth rested her hand on his thigh.

She squeezed. "The drawback of beach noodling."

"Not complaining," he said. "We still have time for a quick lap in Leo's truck?"

"Yes. I want to drive around once while you're here, so I can imagine your confidence every time I do it myself." A waver crept into her voice. He dropped his hand to hers and wove his fingers into hers.

She showed him where to turn into Granny's and he pulled up next to a bright red truck. Elizabeth made an unhappy sound at the back of her throat.

"Someone you were expecting?" he asked.

"I should have," she muttered.

Before he killed the engine, the front door opened and a big native guy with a not-especially-friendly face came out.

"George, what are you doing here?" she said, her voice flat.

"Checking in on you two. I wasn't sure what to think when you didn't go to work." The guy wrapped her into a big hug, twirling her around before setting her down. "You must be Tommy. I'm George." There was no mistaking the territorial claim in his voice.

"Nice to meet you," Tommy said out of habit. There was nothing nice about it.

"How did you find out we're home?" Elizabeth asked.

"Small town. Granny said you had a big adventure. I can't wait to hear about it." He remained at Elizabeth's side, more than just old-friend familiar. Tommy couldn't read Elizabeth. She was half-annoyed, half-uncertain, like there was something she needed to say but didn't want to do it.

George said, "I hear you work with Linda?" What he meant was, *You'll be moving on soon.*

"Yeah," Tommy said, feeling strangely inadequate.

Elizabeth said, "He helped us a lot."

"Oh, really?" George said, pretending to be conversational but there was hostility in it.

"Drove us around. He's the one who got the museum to show Granny her dance dress," Elizabeth said.

Even out under the open sky, the world felt too small. He was trapped between the car and George, with Granny's funny house looming over them.

"Next time I can drive you," George said.

Elizabeth appeared to be trying to convey a series of complex emotions via her eyes. Whatever was going on here, she wasn't able to explain it, or she didn't want to.

He could save her the trouble.

When they were talking about the future and it was the two them, a future where they ended up together was possible, but now he had an equally complex series of thoughts of his own.

The distance was something they couldn't avoid right now. And seeing her here, where she belonged, where she wanted to be, he could feel the distance growing.

It would feel like hell now, but they would get over it. If they ended it right, it would be a fond memory of something that could have been, not something that they could never get right after it should have been over.

George either knew too much or too little, but he was more than happy to hurry Tommy's exit along. "Thanks for watching out for them," he said. "I guess you're headed back." It was a statement, not a question.

Tommy glanced down the driveway that would take him away from her, all the problems waiting for him at home looming back into view.

"Yeah," he said, the word sticking at the back of his throat. He swallowed and tried again. "I need to get the car back. If I leave now, I'll be home by morning."

Elizabeth's face was stricken, her eyes shiny, her mouth open in a distressed *no* as she shook her head.

George came forward to shake his hand. "Thanks again. Great to meet you."

"Don't rush him off. He has to say goodbye to Granny," Elizabeth said.

As if on cue, Granny appeared at the door. "Get in here, you," she said to no one in particular.

Tommy waved at her. Now that he knew he was leaving, he couldn't get out of there fast enough. "Thanks, Auntie." He opened the car door. "Thanks for everything," he said, not sure what he meant.

Elizabeth came around and hissed quietly, "He's just a friend. Don't go." The look in her eyes was terrible—grief, a hint of tears.

He took a moment to collect his thoughts. "I'm not any good at this kind of thing."

"Which kind of thing?" Elizabeth said.

He flicked a wrist at her and then himself. "Knowing what to say." He could feel Granny and George's eyes on them.

Elizabeth insisted, "I have plenty to say if you wait a minute. Please, we—"

Tommy grabbed her hands in his. "Listen. You...this weekend is the best thing that's happened to me in my whole life. My life is a mess, and you have everything here."

"You said you'd drive with me in Leo's truck."

"I can drive with you, Lizzie," George said.

Her head whipped around. Through clenched teeth, she said, "Let me talk to him." She pulled Tommy away from them.

Out of the corner of his eye, Granny tried to urge George inside, but he ignored her.

Elizabeth said, "Don't rush off. Not goodbye like this."

His heart was breaking in a way he couldn't have imagined before this moment. He wrapped his arms around her and hugged her like she was that last thing keeping him tied to the earth. She slowly hugged him back, hiccupping quietly in his ear.

"We're not going to talk to each other anymore?" she said.

"I'll call you when I get home," he said.

He could feel the sob she was holding back.

"Bye, Elizabeth," Tommy said before he got in the car and drove away.

2 7

_T_ommy sat at what Ester jokingly referred to as the quiet bar at Frenzy's. The dance club had a massive bar in the front room and this smaller one tucked in the back. When the club's sound system was at full power, the back bar was only marginally quieter than anywhere else in the place.

In the early hour, the club was almost dead, although a few folks seeking to skip the cover had arrived. The music pounded from the speakers while flashing colored lights weaved back and forth over the almost empty dance floor. A man dressed in a sharp black suit with a red rose pinned to the jacket spun back and forth alone, his steps quick and light and from another era. The salt-and-pepper hair suggested he was old enough to be a grandfather.

"That's Hector, isn't he adorable?" Ester said from the seat next to him. "He comes in at opening and drinks one martini, then dances for about a half hour. Then he leaves. I danced with him once, and he made me look like I was wearing clown shoes."

Tommy figured there was a sad story behind Mr. Dance Alone.

Ester's boyfriend, Theo, came over to the bar and took the coffee the bartender, Fran, offered.

"How's your bus?" he asked.

"Body damage only," Tommy said, feeling like he was talking about something else. "Cody is helping me fix it. Well, he's fixing it. It will be filled with elders again in no time."

Theo nodded. "Sucks, what happened, but lucky it wasn't worse." Again, Tommy felt like they were talking about something else. Theo gave Ester a quick squeeze and went to work the front door. If he was curious about Tommy's disappearance the previous weekend, he didn't mention it.

Fran set identical tall frosty glasses in front of each of them.

Tommy raised an eyebrow at her.

"A little chemistry project," she said. "I like a challenge. Muddled mint and berries with ginger-ale—the fancy crafted kind that uses real ginger—and this blend of magical flavors I call fruit nectar, with a splash of club soda."

"How can I refuse?" Tommy took a careful sip while Fran waited. He nodded and gave her a thumbs-up. Ester made a happy sound.

Fran gave him a guarded look of pity before she smiled and retreated. He was tired of everyone's careful kindness.

It felt like he'd been gone a lifetime while he'd been off with Granny and Elizabeth, but now he was back and nothing had changed. He'd swapped cars with Linda so that he drove the infamous Warm Springs green car, which didn't run any worse than any other vehicle he'd driven. Arnie said he could keep it as long as he wanted, which was simultaneously reassuring and demoralizing.

"I'm surprised you came out tonight," Ester said.

"Why? I love going out." Tommy offered a fake smile.

"Are you going to dance with me later?" she asked.

"You already know the answer to that," he said. "I'm going to be out of here in less than an hour."

"You can always change your mind," she said.

"I'll try to remember that," he said.

"So," she said, "do you want to talk about anything?"

"Like what?" After everything that happened that weekend, the punctuation mark that hit him in the gut every time he thought of it was George and how politely he'd made his disdain known. The guy was half a head taller and probably had sixty pounds on him, and the bearing of full-on Ind'n bad boy, like the guys at home who had picked on him when he lived on the rez.

Elizabeth's response: "George, what are you doing here?"

He replayed that over and over in his head, trying to read into the tone or gain something from the way the words dropped out. He couldn't be sure whether she was surprised, pleased, or maybe expected it and regretted not filling him in.

Then George's response: "Checking in on you two." He had his place there, next to Granny and Elizabeth, no question.

He shouldn't have been surprised, but he'd let his heart open a crack and expectations followed. He zipped it all back in as best he could and took another sip of his drink.

"Nothing interesting happened when you ran away?" Ester asked.

"I didn't run away. I helped Linda's family. You come here every weekend?"

Ester made an unhappy sound. "Kinda. I come here with Theo, and when they call, I deliver pasta dinners for that restaurant across the street."

"You're driving?" He flashed on the image of Elizabeth, hands gripping the wheel. If George hung around, she would always have a ride.

"I hate it but if Theo is working, I might as well, too. A little extra money to go toward paying down my loans."

"And then what?"

Ester played with her straw. "Not making any major decisions until I find out about my filmmaking workshop and we know what's going on with the center."

The future of the center had been iffy for so long, he'd stopped worrying about it. If it fell apart, he would need a resume and interview skills and something to show for himself.

"You think the center is finished?"

Ester shrugged. "I think we need to keep our options open. Rayanne is lined up with her elder meal program. If the center falls apart, she would spin off on her own and, knowing her, figure out another way to serve urban Ind'ns."

"I'll deal with it when I have to," Tommy said.

Hector was still on the dance floor. A bachelorette party had come in and gathered around while he spun a woman in a little black dress and tiara with white flashing lights.

Ester nudged his arm. "What happened?" She said it in the most tender, sisterly voice. She said it like a person who genuinely cared what happened to him. And there was a part of him that did want to talk, but when he tried to figure out where to start, he couldn't.

He laughed the question off. "What didn't happen?"

"I worry about you," she said.

"I hear that a lot."

"Are you still talking to her?"

He'd told her he'd call, but then he didn't. He put it off and now it felt too late and he had no excuse to give. "Maybe you guys could set me up with a haircut," he said.

Hector held the woman in a dancer's embrace, his smile dignified while she giggled and tried to follow.

Ester made a theatrically confused face. "Sure. Why now?"

He could imagine the conversation later: Ester, Linda, and Rayanne, trying to figure out what happened by unpacking his question about a haircut.

"I don't know, something should be different." He put his empty glass on the bar. "Should we tip Fran?"

Ester polished off her drink, too. "She'll give it back if you try."

Hector finished the dance and gave a small bow to the group before heading to the door.

"Do you think a person can help people with things that he's bad at?" he said.

Ester didn't hide her confusion. "What are we talking about?"

"Being a counselor, or teacher, or something."

"Are you interested in that?"

"I don't know. Thinking about how I could do more but no idea what skills I have."

Ester's phone vibrated. She slid off the bar stool and waved to

Fran. She grabbed his wrist and headed for the door. "You could be good at lots of things. I like the idea. We'll investigate."

When they got to the door, Theo looked him over. "You're leaving?" he said, feigning surprise.

"I need to keep an eye on my cousin," Tommy said, "but thanks for inviting me. It was nice to get out of the house."

Theo nodded. Tommy waited while Ester and Theo said goodbye. The way they looked at each other made him ache for Elizabeth. He shifted his gaze to the ground as if something interesting could be found there.

He walked Ester to the restaurant. Before she went inside, she asked, "Do you still have your magic rock?"

"Hate to break it to you, but there's no such thing as a magic rock."

"There should be," she said.

ELIZABETH CARRIED the box down a long hallway in stocking feet. She'd slipped the heels off when she'd arrived. The gown was stiff and itchy, but the weight of it felt glamorous and she liked the way her bare leg popped out of the long slit in the side. One of the straps refused to stay up and she found herself repeatedly yanking it back over her shoulder. She'd thought about and discarded the idea of sending a picture of herself in it to Tommy.

She stopped at the narrow room where they kept the copier, the shredder, and a long narrow table that might have been useful in another location but in here served as a place to deposit broken monitors, lost and found, extra extension cords, or any item with no obvious home. She made room and set the box down, and began removing clips and then shredding the pile of job applications. The little room was always hot and smelled like coffee and whatever people were microwaving in the lunchroom.

Somewhere a door opened and slammed shut. The business part of the casino was as locked down as the money-handling parts. If you wanted a door to stay open, you had to prop it open, and that wasn't allowed.

The shredder made a high-pitched metallic gnashing sound that ramped up to another octave. She reduced the number of pages she fed in. A week ago at this time, she'd been coaxing Tommy into the back seat of Linda's car. She smiled at the memory of the thoughtful way his hands had lost their timidity, and his hand covering her mouth, afraid her enthusiasm might draw unwanted attention. The sense of his body against hers, and her arms hooked around him, hanging on.

He never called.

She didn't call, either.

She couldn't forget the stunned look of betrayal on Tommy's face when George had come out of the house, being George, all familiar and protective. It was supposed to be a bittersweet goodbye with promise, and instead, it was like they'd chased him off. She should have tried harder to get him to stay.

The sadness cut through her icy and sharp, but she stuffed it down.

She heard her name. "Back here," she called, unable to hide her annoyance. George's familiar figure sauntered down the hall.

"You're not supposed to be back here." She flipped through the rest of the box, now grateful for the excuse to be stuck there for a little longer.

"Applying for a job in security," he said.

"Everything is closed back here."

"Damn," George said, taking his time to admire her, "what's with the outfit?"

"Super Salmon Wheel promotion. Kora's taking some promotional photos." She yanked the strap back over her shoulder.

"You're supposed to wear that?"

"Why not? It's fun. I like dressing up."

"I suppose. Why are you back here?"

"Putting in some hours to make up for the day I missed," she said. "Grunt work no one ever has time for." George reached for the box, but she slapped his hand away. "Why are you back here?"

George pretended to be hurt. "Looking for you."

"Better not get me in trouble." The dress had felt gloriously sexy moments earlier but now she felt overexposed. She didn't want to be like this with George. The time with Tommy had clarified the confusing jumble of feelings about George. He was not where she wanted to end up.

"Steak dinner night," he said.

"Enjoy," she said.

"You coming?"

"I'm working."

A disappointed look crossed George's face. "How late?"

While the week with Tommy had removed her further from George, the moment of George seeing her with Tommy had woken up something in him. He barely left her alone. He picked her up for work and dropped her off at night. He brought over pizza—for Granny, he said, but spent the entire evening with them. He hung around the house like he didn't want to leave. Now here he was, tracking her down to take her to steak dinner.

"I'm not sure," she said. "It's my first time doing it."

"I don't mind waiting," he said.

"I do. I'm beat," Elizabeth said, dreading the conversation they needed to have. She picked up the box and shook it as if shredding paperwork was a monumentally draining task. "First week of work and then all that exhausting stuff over the weekend."

"It's just dinner," George said. He stood there a long time, looking like he was about to say something she didn't want to hear. She fed paper into the machine, the high-pitched whine turning into the sound of screaming in her head. Before he'd arrived, she wanted to be done. Now she was afraid of running out of paper before she could get him to leave.

George said, "We should make plans to do something like we used to. Remember?"

Her heart went cold. Before she met Tommy, she might have signed on for this. He was a good guy. She knew his family. The only reason they hadn't worked before was they were too young. But they weren't right for each other, they were familiar to each other. No words would come. She didn't want to give him hope. She didn't want to reject him.

The shredder made a grinding squeal. She unplugged it and opened it up, but before she could clear the teeth, George was doing it. "Watch out," he said. When a guy you liked watched out for your safety, it was cute; when a guy you didn't like did it, it was annoying. He put the machine back together and plugged it back in. She fed more pages into the shredder.

"I need to start driving myself," is what finally came out.

George nodded as if trying to follow the conversation, his face carefully neutral. "Leo's truck? I can drive with you if you want."

"No," she said, realizing this was another excuse for him to spend time with her, for her to be beholden to him. "I can figure it out."

She fed the last few sheets of paper in and watched as the teeth ground them up and sucked them into the bin.

"Sorry," she said. "I like you as a friend but nothing more."

"It's not like that," he said quickly, but dejection radiated off of him and maybe a bit of anger. Relying on him for rides had been a mistake, and she regretted it now.

She waved the empty box. "I'm going to put this away and then go out for the promotion. You sticking around?"

"Why? You need a ride?" he said sourly.

Kora's big voice boomed down the hallway. "Wheel time!"

"Kora's taking me home." She wished she knew what to say.

Kora gave a shocked look when they walked out together.

Elizabeth eased the shoulder strap back up again. Kora gave her a stealthy eyebrow wiggle. "You two need a minute?"

Great, let the rumors begin.

George's face curved into a sneaky half-smile. "We're done." He went back into the casino, the jangle of the machines floating in and then muting again when the door slammed shut.

"You two again?" Kora asked.

Elizabeth shook her head. "I like Tommy."

"That guy from the trip?"

"Yeah."

"Doesn't he live up north? When are you going to see him?"

It was too much to explain.

"I don't know. Let's get this over with."

They met the manager out on the casino floor. He explained the procedures while guiding her through the mob of patrons, most of them seniors. A low wooden platform supported a giant spinning wheel, its highest point reaching her forehead. A tribal artist had painted a spiral of salmon starting at the center of the wheel so when it spun they gradually grew larger and then leapt off.

"Take your time," Kora said, moving in to snap photos.

A giant fishbowl rested on a wooden stand. She climbed a step stool and sank her arm as far as she could reach and stirred around before grabbing a ticket. She pulled it out and gave it to the casino manager with a dramatic flourish. She smiled at the crowd while she casually pulled her dress strap up and left her hand on her shoulder to keep it there.

A gray-haired lady shrieked and jumped up and made her way to the platform. Both she and the casino manager checked that the numbers matched before Elizabeth led her to the wheel. The lady grabbed the wheel and gave it a spin.

Most of the prizes were modest. Free meal coupons, discount coupons for rooms, and the gift shop. There was a hundred-dollar cash prize. Then, there was the salmon. If you caught the salmon, you could go to the bigger drawing where the top prize was five thousand dollars. The wheel spun and spun. The salmon grew bigger and bigger before leaping off the wheel. The wheel turned for so long, Elizabeth thought something was wrong. Kora approached the platform and winked while she took photos. The wheel finally slowed, and the final prizes clicked by, teasing a stop before finally settling. The lady had won a steak dinner. You'd think it was ten steak dinners by her reaction.

The casino manager gave the woman her coupon and the three of them posed for a photo before Elizabeth returned to the bowl to draw the next ticket.

2 8

L inda stood next to Arnie. "Are they serious with this?"

"Maybe?" Arnie replied, his voice uncertain.

They were in a quasi-industrial part of town, on a block that could be best characterized as gray. The lot was a slab of cracked and crumbling asphalt, pocked with gaping holes. Even the chain-link fence looked like it didn't want to be there, sagging between the poles.

"Is that a barn?" A single building sat in one corner of the lot. It had a funny shape like a log sliced lengthwise and set flat-side down. It was mottled gray, and the windows that weren't boarded up were opaque with dust.

"I believe that is called a Quonset hut," Arnie said. "We had one on the rez, but it was demolished because of an environmental hazard."

"Someone thought this was a good place for an urban Indian center? I'm not even sure how to categorize my outrage. Are they racist, ignorant, or plain old mean?"

"Let's hear what they have to say," Arnie said, playing the reasonable one.

"At least it's not raining," she said, stepping over a spray of broken glass.

The city had sent young people, maybe fifteen minutes out of college, fresh-faced and smiling like they couldn't wait to help. The city didn't even have the decency to send someone they'd already met.

"You here about the property?" The young man introduced himself as Jess. He was as clean-cut as they come, somehow earnest and phony at the same time.

"I don't know how to answer that question," Linda replied. The air had a whiff of an industrial scent, like burning tires or a chemical process that made the air thick, every inhale feeling unfiltered. The loud blast of a train engine sounded from somewhere close by.

The young woman, Clare, shared his enthusiasm. She shook both their hands and flashed a smile at Arnie. "You're buying?"

"You weren't briefed at all?" Arnie said, not hiding his irritation.

Neither of them flinched. Linda admired their confidence, as if the city's position was superior and they were thrilled to be entrusted to continue this mean-spirited game.

Clare waved a file folder in the air. "Interested in city surplus."

"We are an urban Indian organization that has been in the process of buying a property from the city for over a year now." Linda gestured at the building, feeling as if they'd been punched in the face. "This is an insult."

Jess held up both hands. "If this doesn't work, maybe there's a site that's a better fit."

They walked to the door of the Quonset hut. Linda dreaded going inside, picturing spiders pouring from the ceiling and an undiscovered body in a corner. Jess had a handful of keys that he tried and retried until he found the one that fit. He had to kick the door to get it to open. Stale air drifted out, smelling like sawdust and old trash. Better than expected.

"The materials say it's been weatherized," Jess said, sweeping his hand back and inviting her to enter.

She peeked in first. For some reason it made her think of a roller-skating rink. The floor was swept concrete and, other than a half dozen folding chairs on the floor, the place was empty. She stepped inside.

"What does an urban Indian organization do?" Clare asked. Linda wanted to scream but in the back of her mind she could hear Margie and Aunt Dottie and every other native woman leader before her explaining that describing the work and talking about the mission kept Indian people from being invisible.

"We provide services to Natives who live in the city. Things like help with medical care. Host cultural gatherings. Teach classes. This—whatever this is—is inappropriate."

Clare's face remained frozen with happy confidence. "Now you have an idea of what's out there." As if by wasting their time with inappropriate sites, the city was doing them a favor.

Jess urged them to follow him around inside the building as if there was something they were missing. "You could tear this down. I think the property itself is where the interest would be. It's a good size. Decent location. You could put whatever you wanted here."

"If we had the funding to do whatever we wanted, we wouldn't be stuck having this conversation," Linda said. Arnie touched her lower back, guiding or shushing, she couldn't be certain. She kept her mouth shut while they dutifully walked across the empty space, the idea of conducting activities or even inviting tribal people to come out and look around growing more remote. They could try to cozy it up but it would always look like a place no one else wanted.

Now was the time to storm off, make phone calls, and bring Audra in with lawyerly threats.

Instead, Arnie said, "Interesting." He sounded like he meant it. She held back a steamy retort. He touched her back again. "Why don't you and I take a lap around the lot? Keep an open mind."

Linda had known him long enough to recognize what he was doing. She followed him outside and they walked to the fence line and started around the perimeter. For a half-second, she imagined this was an entirely different kind of outing, like they were out to enjoy the day. This was how it was when she was with him, always aware of him, more than just a colleague or an old friend. He was someone who could make her feel self-conscious and giddy as a school girl.

There was a clear view of the freeway from where they walked. A big rig thundered by, its compression brakes stuttering. There was nothing but blocky buildings and concrete as far as the eye could see.

"This is worthless," she said, "but there's something here you want me to see. What is it?"

"Several of the tribes are getting together to talk about the consortium for urban issues," he said.

Great, another meeting. "They want us there?"

"You, for sure," he said. "If the Chief Building deal is truly unsalvageable, you want to tell them you're looking at alternatives and doing everything you can to make it work."

He was right. No one wanted to hear her rant about how unfair everything was. She took another careful look around the property.

"There's plenty of parking," she said.

"THAT'S A START," Arnie said. He felt like he should say something more but wasn't sure what. Since he'd joined the organization, their entire relationship was a series of strange meetings and disagreements. High highs and low lows.

"You going to be at that consortium meeting, too?" she asked.

"I'll do my best," he said.

The wind gusted up and she bundled her sweater more tightly around her. "Is it supposed to rain?"

"Not until tonight," he said. Across the parking lot, Jess and Clare had gotten back in their car. "Think they're plotting out our next grim destination?"

"I bet they think they're doing great work here today. They'll go to happy hour after work and tell their friends how interesting it is working with Native Americans." Linda pushed her hair out of her face.

Once again, he was confused by this strange pull, the attraction that would not fade. Even when she made him angry, he always wanted to come back to her. She caught him staring.

"How's Tommy doing?" he asked.

"Who knows? He gets through the day exactly like he used to, but he looks...I don't know, abandoned. He's so secretive and he doesn't want to talk."

"Sometimes people need to find their own way," Arnie said.

"People need a support system. That's the whole reason we do this. It's like he has a system but rejects it."

Arnie put his hand on her elbow and they stopped. Any reason to touch her, to stand close. All those days finding excuses to work at her office to keep her close by.

From where they stood, they could survey the entire lot. The structure had a small footprint. The kids were right, the lot was good-sized if they had the resources to develop it, but there was no getting around the terrible location.

"This place is ass," he said.

Linda threw her head back and laughed. She leaned into him. "Finally. I was afraid you were trying to talk me into this."

A giant cup, the kind that you'd fill with pop at the convenience market, tumbled across the blacktop and rolled around in front of them. She picked it up. "Leave every place better than when you showed up. Is that how the saying goes?" Her hair whipped in her face again and she shook it back, offering up a pure smile that he felt in ways that he should not.

The smartest thing to do would be to resign from the board. Leave her alone and focus on his own relationships and work problems.

But he couldn't imagine not seeing her. She took one more look around the lot before holding up the cup. "I'm going to chuck this. Let's get out of here." She frowned and pointed. Not far from where they stood, there was an overflowing dumpster and what appeared to be a small camp constructed with tarps and camp chairs. A cooler box sat in the middle of a pile of filthy sleeping bags.

"If those are homeless Natives, I can't be responsible for what I'll do next," she said.

"We can't fix everything today," he said.

"I know," she said, a frown passing over her face.

"Before we go, let's take a minute and name the things we've learned from this site," he said.

"The building is too small, and the location is terrible. Where do you think the closest bus stop is? We need a structure that we can use now and, assuming we grow like I'm planning, then we can talk about adding on buildings."

Arnie couldn't help smiling. "I like when you talk about the future."

"You know I'm a fool about giving up." They exchanged a heartfelt smile for one long moment.

He used his chin to point to where Jess and Clare waited. "We going to see other sites?"

"I'll talk to them about setting something up." She walked over to the dumpster and took a careful look around, but the campsite was empty. She threw the cup away and they headed back to the car. "I started the job description as a joke, but maybe you could help me finish."

An uneasy feeling tickled in Arnie's belly. "Job?"

"The tribal liaison idea we talked about. The city needs it. This process with them has been troubled from the start. The person could advise on diversity and urban Indian issues plus work with the tribal governments in the area. Sure, no one has asked me, but I'll feel better if I try."

"Would you want that job?" he asked.

"No, but if I did I would tell you. Remember, no more secrets. I want *this* job," she said. "We're going to be successful. We'll figure it out."

"You sound sure," he said.

"I am sure. You are too. We're going to do great at that meeting."

29

*E*verything would be fine as soon as he got Elizabeth out of his head. A week went by and then another but the ache for her did not fade. Each day duplicated the day before. He went to work. He took elders to the health clinic in the repaired-but-not-quite-the-same Drivemaster. He organized basketball games for kids. The mornings remained cool and gloomy but in the afternoons the clouds burned off and he took the kids to play basketball outside, too. He kept an eye on Angie. Everything fell back into place like Elizabeth had never happened.

He came home and threw his keys and his phone on the counter, his nerves jangling for no obvious reason.

There was a bunch of Angie's laundry strewn over the couch, and he threw it in the empty basket and put it back in her room. She did everything she promised while she waited for her court date. She'd been sullen and resentful at first but once they got back into their old routine, glimpses of the good-humored cousin he remembered returned. She was in high spirits, attending meetings during the day while he was at work. She found a job at a coffee shop and worked the night shift, coming home after he'd gone to bed. She even tried to throw in some money for rent, but he insisted she save it for the future.

He flipped on the TV and shuffled through the channels, failing to muster interest in anything for more than thirty seconds. Elizabeth's voice kept playing in his head, "…but what's your long-term plan?" He couldn't come up with one.

He snapped off the TV. His eyes settled on the shelf of cookbooks, the source of endless teasing and mocking from family and friends. Elizabeth had said, "Cooking is always useful."

He eyed the titles, searching for a book with something easy that he could make with what he had on hand. He had little equipment, few skills, and a bare pantry. The first book he grabbed was all about grilling. He tried a different one but didn't think he was up for Italian specialty.

He pulled two more off, and something *thunked* at the back of the shelf. He reached behind the books, thinking one of them had fallen back. Instead, he pulled out a half-empty bottle of vodka. Not the cheap stuff, either.

He stared at it for at least thirty seconds, his breath even, his mind racing. This was the place he would have hidden a bottle if he lived with a person who never took books off the shelf.

He picked it up with two fingers and carried it to the kitchen counter. When they were drinking together, he and Angie called it crazy juice. They would drink it out of the bottle, passing it back and forth quickly, laughing at stupid jokes.

With a heavy sense of dread, he went back and checked the other shelves. He found another bottle of vodka, this one empty, and an unopened bottle of gin. He set those on the counter with quaking hands.

He understood, but his head kept making excuses. Maybe all these had been there a while and she'd forgotten about them. He'd hidden booze when he was drinking, although he'd hidden it from other drinkers. He'd never forgotten a bottle.

He was too dumbfounded to be angry. He'd been so confident in her; it hadn't even occurred to him to check. For one strange, conflicted moment he considered returning them to where he found them.

He opened the vodka first and poured it down the sink, registering that even after all this time, how wrong it felt to throw booze away. A part of him thought he should be keeping it in case he knew someone who could use it. After a brief hesitation, he cracked the seal on the gin and poured that out, too. The buzzy medicinal scent was the smell of hangovers.

He left the empty bottles on the counter. He went into her room, the privacy breach feeling wrong but unavoidable. She'd cut open the box spring, and he found two more bottles in the ragged hole. There was a pint in her nightstand, this one not even hidden because she knew no one was checking.

He lined those up on the kitchen counter. He knew before he checked, back in his room, the cash he hid in the flashlight—his 'travel someday' money—was gone. He swore to himself. He emptied all the bottles but one. After what felt like an endless consideration, he hid the bottle in his room in a duffel bag that held camping gear. He put all the empty bottles under the sink and waited for her to come home.

He was asleep on the couch when she came in. She did not look pleased to see that he was out of his room.

"You work late?" He'd never seen her getting home from work before. She wore jeans, a T-shirt, and a hoodie.

She put her purse on the counter and opened the refrigerator. "I always get home at this time. Why are you up?"

Tommy got up and followed her to the kitchen. He grabbed her arm and turned her around. He didn't have to get close to smell it on her.

"You're drinking at work?"

She pulled her arm away and brought her hand to her mouth, shaking her head, trying to stifle laughter.

"You don't have a job, do you?" he said, wanting to kick himself for being so stupid.

"I applied but unfortunately did not meet their needs at this time. They will keep my application on file in case something suitable comes up in the future." She went back to the fridge and brought out a takeout container and checked the contents. "You ever eat anything besides Pad Thai?" She got a fork and ate it cold.

"You can't be drinking," Tommy said.

Angie stabbed at the food. "They aren't going to know. You didn't, and you live with me."

"*You* live with *me*," he snapped.

Angie glanced at the ceiling as if summoning epic patience. "It's not that big of a deal. Some medical professionals say you don't have to completely give up drinking. Any person can drink in moderation. You should try it."

"I don't want to try it," he said. His mind flashed on the hidden bottle.

"Fine," she said with a dismissive wave. "Stay out of my business." She returned to her food.

Tommy picked up her purse and searched for her wallet.

"Give me that." Angie tried to grab it, but he shoved her away with his shoulder.

"Is any of my money left?" She had a hundred dollars in twenties folded in her wallet. He put it in his pocket.

She jerked the purse out of his hands. "That's mine."

"Where did you get it?"

"None of your business," she said, slapping his arm. "Give me my money." She slapped him again, harder, and then moved to his face. He shoved her away and she flopped to the floor.

"You hit me," she said, her voice rising in pitch and the tears starting. "I can't believe you hit me. You could get in trouble."

It was the middle of the night and they were fighting like trashy drunks.

"Be my guest," he said. "Call the cops."

Angie stopped crying and glared at him. She stood up, her face flushed. She opened the cabinet under the sink and when she saw the empty bottles, she kicked the cabinet door.

Tommy put his hands up in defeat. "I'm leaving. We'll talk tomorrow."

A few weeks earlier, he could have taken a long drive on a back road and that would have soothed him, but the green car wheezed like every mile was its last and driving made him think of Elizabeth and all the miserable days ahead to get through. He drove to campus and got into the Drivemaster. There was an extra sweatshirt in there, and he put it on and stretched out on the bench seat in the back. He pulled up Elizabeth's contact and texted: *Is it too late to talk to you?* Before he could change his mind, he sent it.

∼

ELIZABETH DIDN'T SEE the text until after her morning shower.

Is it too late to talk to you?

She flipped through a series of emotions: elation, anger, sadness. Why now? She set the phone aside.

She put on makeup and slid into the sequined gown. She put on a pair of long dentalium earrings that almost brushed her shoulders.

Granny made an exasperated face when she came into the living room. "Why you wearing that?"

"Noon promotion and Kora wants more promotional shots for advertising. Good thing I went for the glamour look. My first idea was to dress up like a salmon."

Normally Granny would have smiled at the idea but she focused her glare on the blank television screen.

"You want me to fix a program for you?"

Granny didn't respond.

Elizabeth thought about mentioning the text but changed her mind. She put on the coffee. "Cereal?"

Granny made an unhappy sound at the back of her throat and rearranged herself on her easy chair.

"What is up with you?" Elizabeth said.

"Lotta trouble to go to college and then dress like a gameshow hostess."

Elizabeth slammed the box of instant oatmeal and a bowl on the kitchen table. There was a folder sitting there with Granny's name on it. She flipped it open.

"You talked to the Tribe about getting your ceremonial dress back?"

Granny lifted her chin, her look said: *None of your business.*

"I thought we were going to do that together," Elizabeth said, uncertain whether she was hurt or angry.

Granny waved the comment away. "You don't want to worry about that."

"After dragging you around on a multipart road trip and steam-rolling the museum into letting you see it? I want to learn how the process works."

Granny pointed at her dress before picking up a newspaper from the little table next to her chair and taking her time unfolding it. "You work at the casino. Let other people worry about cultural things."

Elizabeth stared at her, stunned. "I spent my entire life hearing about cultural things. Why would you leave me out now?"

Granny peeked around the newspaper. "Thought you was busy."

"Busy with what? It's my family, too." Elizabeth shuffled through the papers in the file, trying to understand what the process entailed. Something about interviews and research. "Do we need to go back?"

Granny threw the paper down and her expression shifted from day to night. She was weary or disgusted or resigned. Like she'd given up. She sighed. "Why are you still here?"

"What do you mean?"

Granny waved her hands in the air. "Why are you here? Wearing that thing. I don't know."

"It's for work." She pushed a spangled strap up, the sequined dress feeling ridiculous under Granny's scrutiny.

"We need our young people looking after our things," Granny said, growing more agitated. "Working for us. Keeping what we have."

"That's what I'm doing. You don't have to explain it. I understand."

"That's right. You understand. You." Granny pointed a crooked finger at her. "We need you to explain it to *them*." Granny's arm swept across the room, meaning the world.

"That's what we talked about. I can take you back. The museum, Dr. Murray's research center. I'm here for you."

Granny sank back in her seat as if exhausted. "Me and Leo always wanted you to go away. To do something before you settled back here. We thought you could do more things."

"What's wrong with here? You settled here."

"I got knocked up when I was a teenager," Granny said. "I didn't have any choices. You can do anything."

"I am doing things," Elizabeth said, not sure what she meant.

"What are you afraid of?"

Elizabeth's chest tightened, and a rush of confusing feelings moved through her. She tried to sort through everything that was happening, but it was hard to think in a sparkly dress. She'd hated being so far from home. She'd hated being away from family and Granny and Leo. She'd been gone when Leo died and it felt terrible.

"I'm not afraid," Elizabeth said, but she felt fear in her entire body while she said it.

Granny was still in her chair, giving her the stink-eye. Her hands flopped down on the chair arms and her cane, the one Tommy had given her, fell to the carpet. Elizabeth went over and put it back in Granny's reach. She knelt next to Granny's chair.

The tears were forming, but she held them back. "I'm afraid something will happen to you if I go away, like losing Leo and there was nothing I could do."

"There's nothing you can do when you're here. Then I'm gone, and you're stuck in a job you don't like, and you gave up that boy for nothing."

"You liked him, too?" she asked even though she already knew the answer.

"I see you moping around here. George turned out okay, but he's not the one for you."

Elizabeth's heart surged with possibility.

"The rez is always going to be here," Granny said. "Learn some stuff, you can always come back."

"What about you?"

"I got too many people looking after me. I need some peace and quiet." Granny patted the armrest.

"What will I do up there?"

"We need our people inside those museums," Granny said.

Elizabeth imagined the path before her, the opportunities unfolding. All of the time she'd spent with Granny and Leo, listening to them. Listening to all the boring old-people talk. Tuning them out when she'd heard the stories enough times. All of that had a purpose.

"If you don't leave on your own, I'm going to kick you out," Granny said.

"You're not going to kick me out," Elizabeth said.

"You don't know what I can do."

"Can I take the truck?"

"It's always been yours. He wanted you to have it. Old, but he said it would run forever."

The tangle of emotions intensified. The thought of leaving hurt her heart, but being away from Tommy was painful, too.

"Get out of here," Granny said.

"I'm going, but I'll be back," Elizabeth said.

"I know," Granny said.

TOMMY AWOKE to the sound of voices and, in his muddled state, thought it was Elizabeth. The sense of relief almost brought tears to his eyes and he trembled at the thought of pulling her into his arms. But as the grogginess wore off, the scent of fake pine air freshener with notes of hot dogs and sweaty athletes reminded him of where he was.

He unfolded himself from the cramped seat and looked out into the campus parking lot, busy with people going to class. Elizabeth was at home. They were supposed to be forgetting each other.

All the drama of the night before came flooding back. He'd failed again. Angie was out of control. He needed to call his uncle but when he checked his phone, the battery was dead. Given the number of people traipsing across campus, he was most likely late for work.

He went to the men's room and tidied himself up as best he could and made his way to the office.

Rayanne and Ester crowded in front of a computer monitor. Ester's face was wide open with joy while she talked to someone on her cell. Rayanne waved with greater than normal enthusiasm. "Get over here. Ester got accepted into her film workshop."

"That's great," he said, trying to inject some energy into his voice. He was afraid to hug her, anxious about bringing attention to his disheveled state. Too late. Ester flicked her eyes over him and he didn't miss her look of dismay.

"She found out this second," Rayanne said. "She's telling Theo. The workshop put samples of the other people who got in. We're checking them out."

As soon as Ester got off the phone, she skipped over and threw her arms around him in an elated hug.

"You okay?" she whispered.

"I'm great," he lied.

When she let go, she covered her eyes with her hands. "I don't know how we're going to make this work."

"We've been preparing for this since you applied," Rayanne reminded her.

Tommy got a cup of coffee and sat at the monitor with them, watching the film clips.

"Everyone is so much more interesting than me," Ester said.

"I believe that is called imposter syndrome, and you are not an imposter," Rayanne said.

"I'll get over it," Ester said. She opened a paper bag and handed Tommy something wrapped in foil. "You look like you need this more than I do."

"I don't need your food, Ester," Tommy said.

She slung an arm over his shoulder. "I think you do."

"Ester, you said you were starving," Rayanne said.

"Now I'm too nervous. It's a breakfast burrito. Theo made it. If you don't eat it, I'll throw it away."

Tommy got up and found a plastic knife and sawed the thing in half. "Share."

"Fine," Ester said. "What's going on?"

"Nothing. Didn't sleep well last night," Tommy said. The burrito was lukewarm and delicious. It took all his power not to gulp it down.

"You look like hell," Rayanne said.

"Get off my back." The words were quiet but the tone savage. It surprised all three of them. He bit back an apology. "Linda coming in?"

Rayanne blinked a couple of times and he braced for her retort but instead she said, "She and Arnie have to go do their thing at the new tribal consortium that's forming for urban issues. When all else fails, start a new committee."

"This is good for us. I think the center is going to be okay," Ester said. "The city already showed them an alternate site."

"That Linda said was a post-apocalyptic wasteland," Rayanne said.

"You know how dramatic she is," Ester said.

Tommy showed her his phone. "You have a charger for this?"

Ester took it from him. "Doubt it. I'll check when I'm done eating."

The coffee had no effect and he couldn't stop worrying about Angie. If he went home, he could shower, put on clean clothes, get his phone charger, and check on her.

That unopened bottle was still in the house.

"There's one thing on your calendar this morning," Rayanne said to him. "Are you going to be in this afternoon? When Linda's here, we need to strategize for Ester's absence."

"Stop saying that, it makes me nervous," Ester said. She dug through a box under her desk. "No charger, my friend. Sorry."

Tommy checked the calendar. "I'm driving some folks to the Native veterans' center. I'll be back after lunch."

"Great," Rayanne said. "We'll get everything organized then."

30

*W*hen Virgil had told Linda to meet him at his office before the tribal consortium meeting, it seemed like a good idea. Now that she was sitting there, she realized it was a mistake.

"This is a terrible layout," Virgil said as if reading her mind. The attorneys had individual offices, but they were partitioned with glass panels. From where she sat, she could see each person who came through the front door, and all the tribal leaders in the conference room waiting for the meeting to start. In one office, an attorney finished a sandwich. In another, a woman slumped over her desk, her hand propping her head up.

If Linda could see them, they could see her, too. For reasons she couldn't clarify, she didn't want Arnie to see her there.

Linda rehearsed what she wanted to say to Virgil and how to say it. She'd given it a lot of thought. She wanted to take this thing to the next level. Make more time for each other. Coordinate their schedules. She was never going to fall for a man that she couldn't spend time with.

But Virgil wouldn't stop talking. "This pile here," he said, indicating a stack of expanding files, "is from the last two weeks of the hydro case. These here"—he waved at a stack of books and file folders —"are the research for the timber issue. That stack on the floor is fisheries litigation. And those are the fun projects." He rattled the stuff off with fidgety charm.

She wasn't sure how to start. Maybe she should propose a dinner date. Maybe just invite him over for dinner. Wasn't that code for "Let's start doing it"? The shelves of law books and stiff-backed chairs gave the air of a discussion more serious than it had to be.

Virgil rattled on, stringing together more sentences than he had the entire time she'd known him. His hands tidied up piles of paper and adjusted his computer keyboard. He mentioned framing his law school degree, his tenure with the firm, the associates who would be dividing up his work when he left.

Out of the corner of her eye, she saw Arnie come through the door and pause at the reception desk. She imagined he spotted her and she felt her cheeks flush. She let her hair fall into her face.

Virgil sat across from her. His hands never stopped moving, one minute searching through a desk drawer, the next lining up pens on his desk, then darting up to rake through his hair.

The words finally sank in. "Did I hear you say you're moving to Colorado?"

He nodded and grabbed the empty coffee cup in front of him and looked inside, took a sip of nothing and set it back in front of him. He gave her a nervous smile. "It's a great opportunity."

She glanced up long enough to see Arnie slip into the meeting room. He wore a light gray suit with a dark gray tie. She liked his darker suits better. He worked his way around the room, shaking hands. He said something that made them all break into laughter.

She returned her attention to Virgil.

"I know how crazy it sounds." He had the cup again and turned it around in his hands. "I'm telling you regardless of what happens between us. There's a position in an established urban Indian center. Not director, now, but they want to groom the person for that. Given your challenges here, I wanted to mention it."

She could feel each breath with her entire body, her heartbeat in her ears. It was as if a trapdoor had sprung open and she teetered on the edge, not sure whether she should stay in the room or let herself fall into whatever was waiting below.

"That's a lot to process," she said.

Virgil was moving to another state. The news left her feeling...what?

All the feelings she'd been cultivating scattered into a confused mess. Her eyes flicked back to the door, wishing she could sneak out and pretend this never happened.

"I know," he agreed. "I should have mentioned it sooner, but I wasn't sure I would get the job."

"I can see that," she said. She could feel Arnie's eyes on her and tried to imagine what he saw. Virgil, alert and earnest, and what did she look like right now? Stunned? Reeling? He wouldn't care.

"I won't be leaving until fall. I'd like to spend time together," he said, hopeful. "Lots of time to talk about this."

A move would be a fresh start. A new community. Different opportunities. "Yeah," she said, not sure what she was agreeing to. She gulped a few breaths because she still had a meeting to get through. "We'll talk more."

It figured the first thing he saw when he walked into the law firm was Linda hunched over in private conversation with Virgil. Arnie tamped down the confusing mix of feelings. The consortium was the most important duty, and he and Linda needed to make their best impression.

He gave her a professional smile when she joined them. He recognized that look; something had just happened. She could always muster a cheerful face, but if something was bothering her, it showed in her eyes.

"You going to start?" she asked when she sat next to him. He detected a tremor in her voice, but she poured herself a glass of water and gave him one of her ambitious *it's showtime* looks.

"It's all yours," he said.

The meeting went as well as they could hope. The tribes identified their priorities and ideas for urban Indian issues, and Linda talked about Crooked Rock's goals and setbacks. The leaders got a little salty about her funding priorities and gave her some grief about the delays with the property purchase, but Arnie jumped in to stick up for her, and by the time the meeting ended, everyone was feeling more positive about the future.

Linda waited for him after the meeting, waving to Virgil as they left the office and got on the elevator to the lobby.

She sighed a big long sigh. "I need to talk to you."

He knew what that meant. Bad news. What was it this time? Was Margie sick again or Tommy's cousin causing more trouble? Maybe Ester was rejected from her film workshop.

"Here? Or go somewhere?"

The elevator doors opened. The office building lobby had a couch and a few chairs. She crossed the floor and sat in a chair but stared out the revolving door without speaking.

"Lulu?"

A flinch. She remained matter-of-fact. "Nothing is decided. I'm not even sure how seriously I'm considering it, but I promised no secrets. I don't want you caught off guard. Virgil is moving to Denver. There might be something for me there."

Few things could have surprised him more. It was like the air disappeared from the room and he forgot how to breathe. He was surprised to find himself feeling panicked, like she was on a boat that pushed away from the dock and he could see her drifting away and there was nothing he could do about it.

In spite of what he told himself, he cared about the UIC measurably less if she wasn't a part of it. He wanted to be angry. She'd never been one to give up or walk away, but no one had made this any easier for her. The disappointment made his heart ache, and he didn't know how to say it.

He cleared his throat and did his best to keep his voice even. "I had no idea you two were that serious."

Linda kept her eyes on her feet. "It just came up. I need to think it through."

"Do you have a timeline?"

"End of summer. That coincides with the one-year deadline you guys gave us at the retreat last fall. There's a lot of ways we could do this." She still wouldn't meet his eye. "I shouldn't have said anything."

"I appreciate it. I don't like surprises." He tried to imagine saying goodbye to her. They'd run into each other at a conference or NATG every couple of years. They would become people who knew each other a long time ago.

"Me either," she said.

His phone vibrated in his pocket. He took it out. Any other time, he would have ignored the call, but he held it up. "I gotta get this. It's Katie," he said, apologetic, as if there was no avoiding it. "Tell me what you decide. If you go, we'll need a succession plan."

"I'll talk with the staff," she said. "If I do."

3 1

$\mathcal{E}$lizabeth hated driving. She hated stopping for gas. She hated the big rigs and the fast-moving sports cars. The whole exercise wasn't any less terrifying except that while she was doing it she was so busy doing it she couldn't worry about it.

What she was worried about was Tommy.

Is it too late to talk to you?

She'd texted. She'd called. No answer. No response. She'd expected to talk to him first and explain her plan. Except she didn't have a plan. The idea was to find him and sit him down and find out what was wrong.

All she knew was she didn't want the highlight of her week to be standing up in a sequined dress, watching people spin a wheel so they could win a steak dinner.

Her phone bleated out the directions to campus. Just like the first trip, there was a mass of cars packed into the intersections, and bike lanes crowded with bikes, while on every corner giant mobs of people waited to cross. Her heart pounded like she was fleeing a swarm of angry wasps. If she could, she would pull over and leave the truck. The desire to be parked and safe and not driving was overwhelming.

She'd forgotten how controlling a vehicle could manifest such a cold, buzzy, physical terror.

"Turn left in two hundred feet to destination," the phone said.

"Left? Two hundred feet?" There was no way to get into the left lane, and there were any number of driveways. How was she supposed to know where two hundred feet was? She inched forward in the lane she was in, hoping she didn't block the intersection if the light changed.

"Arrived at destination," the phone said with unearned joy. "Arrived at destination."

"Thanks for nothing," Elizabeth said. She made a right turn into a parking lot and rolled through the crooked lanes with a million other cars, all trying to find a place to park. She was desperate for this part to be over. There should be a reward for challenging your fear, and that reward should be a parking place.

A car ahead began backing out. She exhaled with relief, her anxiety notching down one tiny increment. A horn blared behind her and her heartbeat ratcheted up again. The guy in her rearview mirror waved impatiently.

How did people live like this?

She pulled into the spot and sagged with relief. Now all she had to do was fight through all the people and cross the huge and confusing campus to find Tommy's office. She got out of the truck and followed one of the pathways snaking off in every direction until she found a campus map. She studied it as if she knew what she was looking for. The UIC wasn't on the map and she didn't know the name of the building.

She looked around the campus, trying to see if anything looked familiar.

A guy on a bike stopped. "You need help?"

"Urban Indian Center?" she said.

"Urban what?" He shook his head.

"How about the longhouse?"

He waved to one path and then turned around and waved to another. "Not sure."

"Thanks anyway," Elizabeth said, turning back to the map. She was on her way to the longhouse when she spotted a familiar figure with a bulging computer bag slung over her shoulder, eyes downcast and an expression of doom on her face.

"Linda!"

"You're back," Linda said, surprised.

Elizabeth threw her arms around her and hung on, still shaky from the drive. "Granny kicked me out."

"You're joking."

"More like a love tap," Elizabeth said. "But not kidding. I need to learn about repatriation."

"You could have called me to ask about that," Linda said.

"Really, I need to see Tommy. Something's wrong, and I'm worried." Elizabeth was relieved to let Linda lead the way.

"We all are," Linda said.

"He texted me late last night that he needed to talk, and he hasn't answered me since."

"Ester sent me a note that said he looked like he slept in a dumpster last night, but he wouldn't say a thing. She emphasized he didn't smell like he'd been drinking."

They crossed back across the busy street. Elizabeth couldn't wait to get to know her way around this place. She said, "I think he's solid with the not drinking. It's the not talking that worries me."

"He's been like that as long as I've known him. I know almost nothing about his personal life. I guess you two did hit it off. He never said a word, but he's been miserable."

"I left the rez for a boy. I drove Leo's truck up by myself. Yes, we hit it off. I'm changing my whole life around for him, if he'll have me."

Linda wore a look of suppressed grief, but she didn't say anything. She pointed to a door that Elizabeth would never have found on her own.

Tommy stood in the middle of the room as if he'd been caught doing something he wasn't supposed to. Ester wasn't kidding. He looked exhausted, circles under his eyes, thinner—if that was possible. His clothing was rumpled, his expression: utter defeat.

Ester and Rayanne looked at her in surprise.

Now that they were in the same room together again, Elizabeth hesitated. What if she'd misread this entire thing?

"Hey," she said, though it came out like a hoarse whisper. "I couldn't get ahold of you."

His eyes squeezed shut. He didn't say anything. One shaky hand worked into his pocket. There was no sound other than the bumblebee buzz of the fluorescent light overhead.

Elizabeth crossed the room and circled her arms around him. After a second, he hugged her back, tentatively at first, but then stronger, as if he was afraid she'd disappear. His entire body shook with misery.

"What's going on?" she whispered.

"We're going to grab coffee," Ester said brightly. "Give you guys a few minutes."

"Don't," Tommy said, choking the words out, his arms still holding tight. "Don't go." He cleared his throat. "I need help."

THERE WERE no words for the burst of relief he felt when she came into the room. Now that she was holding him, and he felt how real she was, she was probably the only thing keeping him on his feet. Every setback and failure stacked up in his mind. She'd come for him, and he was more of a wreck than ever. He'd run away from her on the rez, and after all that, she'd still come to him, warm and soft, smelling like peppermint and the road.

"You want to talk now?" she said.

He had all their attention but didn't know how to start.

Elizabeth released him and guided him to a chair. A painful surge of emotion made his chest tight, and he took a deep breath to keep it from spilling out. She pulled up a chair next to him and held his hand.

"What's going on?" she whispered.

"I slept on the bus."

Ester brought him a cup of water, but when he tried to drink, his throat was too tight.

"Angie," he managed to say.

"What happened?" Linda asked.

"She's drinking," he said, his voice tight. "She hid booze all over the apartment. We got in a big fight. She stole money from me."

Rayanne made a sound of fury.

Linda gave her a look he missed, and Rayanne went quiet again, her chair making a *thump* when she settled back into it.

"I don't want to let everyone down, but..." He couldn't find the right words to explain. "I—I can't do this."

Elizabeth squeezed his hand. "It's someone else's turn."

She looked out of place in the room. She had on another one of her outfits, a lacy green dress, and boots. She'd knotted her hair on top of her head, but it was coming loose.

"You look nice," he said.

Her expression was heartfelt concern, but her eyes were amused.

"I missed you, too," she said.

Rayanne cleared her throat. She shuffled through a stack of paper on her desk. "Forgive me, but I have been keeping tabs on a bed in a rehab place. It's not native run, but they have a recovery track that has native influences."

"She'll never go," Tommy said, already convinced they should give up. He'd brought it up before, when Angie was low and without hope, but every conversation ended with her at his place getting sober with his help.

"Your uncle?" Ester suggested.

"He hasn't been helpful so far," Tommy said. "I can't kick her out."

"I wish you would consider it," Linda said. "I know it's your family, but if you fall apart, the sacrifice isn't worth it."

"What if we take her back to your family on the rez?" Ester said. "Me and Theo could drive her."

"That's such a huge favor," he said.

"We'd do it for you," she said.

"You'd have to tie her up to get her to go back," Tommy said.

"We would do that, too," Ester said, a sneaky smile on her face.

"Give her an ultimatum: rehab, home, or the street," Rayanne said.

Angie loved drama. She would pick the street and she'd stand outside his apartment and sob and tell passersby what a terrible person he was.

"I need to talk to her," he said.

"This is how this is going to go," Linda said. "We will all go to talk to her. She will choose rehab. We will take her there today, no excuses."

Rayanne picked up the phone. "I'll tell them to expect her."

Tommy imagined Angie with her arms crossed over her chest, shaking her head, unmoving. "She won't talk to you. It's better if I talk to her alone."

"We're not doing that," Elizabeth said.

"You're a good man, Tommy, but she knows how to punch your buttons. You need us behind you," Linda said.

Now he had four Ind'n women in his life telling him what to do, and for the first time in weeks, he felt better.

3 2

*A*ngie was on the couch watching TV when they arrived. There was a half-empty bottle of rum on the table, a bottle he hadn't found.

"Now what?" she said. She frowned at his support crew and turned back to the TV.

Tommy went around and shut it off.

Angie gave him a smug smile. "They should know before they take your side." She looked over her shoulder. "He hit me."

"I didn't hit you. You hit me, and I shoved you away."

She waved at Elizabeth and the others as if to say, *see?*

"You can't stay here anymore," he said, his voice sounded uncertain. "We found a place in rehab—"

Angie snorted with laughter.

"Or you can go home."

She shook her head. "I'm getting better."

"You aren't even close to getting better," Tommy said.

She scrunched her face up and sniffled. "I'm trying my best. Everyone isn't like you."

Tommy didn't know how to respond to that.

"Can we talk without them watching?" Angie said, pointing over her shoulder as if the others couldn't hear her.

When Tommy looked at them, all four of them shook their heads together, like they'd rehearsed it.

"No," Tommy said.

Angie picked up the bottle and he went over and grabbed it out of her hands. He held on to it for a moment too long, studying the label with the fancy lettering and a woodcut of an island with a sun shining down. Ester came over when he held it out and she took it to the sink.

"That's mine," Angie said with a whine. But her eyes flicked away. She had more hidden elsewhere.

"Angie? Please?" He couldn't keep his voice from breaking.

Angie tried tears again. "Why are you doing this? We're family."

"That's why," Tommy said. His eyes watered and he could hardly keep it together, but every time he wanted to cave, he saw this wall of Ind'n women there for him.

The tears switched back off. "You're a loser. You can't make me do anything." Angie got up from the couch, but one look at the cold, hard glare from his team and she plopped back down and sat on her restless hands.

"I'm not that bad," she said. "This should be a family thing. Not them. You've always been my favorite, that's why I came to you. I need you."

"Knock it off," Tommy said. He wished he had a chair. His knees were weak, and he was so tired. "You sound like them. You sound just like them. Mean and nasty and jerking me around."

"I'm not jerking you around," Angie said, her voice sharp as a whip.

"Do you remember that night we stole gin out of my mom's truck?" Tommy's heart was racing.

Angie smiled then and she let out a chuckle and held up two fingers. "Two bottles. They were big ones."

"We thought we were so clever. You know what happened when I went home, reeking of gin that belonged to them? They beat me up. All of them. My sisters, too."

His breath was short. He didn't mean to tell this story in front of

Elizabeth or the rest of them, and now he was in the middle of it and trying to figure out how to cut out the worst bits. He let the momentum carry him. He'd never told anyone.

"They kicked me with boots on. They whipped a belt or a rope or something across my back. Then they locked me out of the house. It was freezing. I broke into the garage. I felt so awful, I searched for gasoline, so I could drink that and end all the stupidity."

One of them gasped. If he looked he wouldn't be able to finish.

"That's not true," Angie said, a dumb look on her face.

"Why would I make that up?"

"You should have called me."

He couldn't help laughing. How was drunk Angie going to rescue him from that?

"Mom found me the next morning and freaked out because they'd cut my back open, so there was blood everywhere. I couldn't stop shivering. They brought me into the house and wrapped me up and, just like this, they couldn't stop telling me how sorry they were. They didn't want me to be upset. They didn't want me to cry. They wanted us to be a family. That is not how a family acts."

Angie broke down for real. "I'm not like them."

"If this is how you want to live, fine, but don't pretend that there is anything great about it. You can't live with me anymore. You can go to rehab, or you can go home. You cannot stay here."

Angie shook her head.

"Rayanne? Can one of you tell her?" He still wouldn't meet their eyes.

Linda's voice came, calm and firm. "The rehab is not native run, but they have native-specific programs and counselors. You're not going to get a better offer."

"Shut up," Angie said.

"Don't talk to her like that," Tommy said. "She's been more of a family to me than any of you."

Angie sobbed some more. Tommy stared at his hands. He didn't know how much more he could take.

"You're being selfish because you have a girlfriend," she said, tears still coming.

"You're sick, Angie. You need people who can help you get better."

She covered her face with her hands and kept sobbing.

"Go to rehab. Please."

Angie sighed and took a long shuddering inhale. "I won't go unless you take me."

Tommy could feel himself wavering, but he forced himself to say, "That isn't the deal."

Angie sobbed again. "What if I go look?"

"Close enough," Rayanne said. "I have a list of things you can bring."

There were a few more rounds of eye rolling and bargaining before Rayanne was able to get her into her room to pack.

Tommy sighed. When he finally dared to look up, all of them had tears in their eyes. Elizabeth came over and hugged him hard.

"I'm okay. You guys are taking this harder than I did."

Elizabeth let go long enough for Linda to grab him. "I don't think you're taking it hard enough," she said.

Tommy was uncomfortable with the emotion rising in him. "Don't—"

Linda sighed. "I love you, Tommy. I'm always here for you."

He hadn't cried since he was a kid, so he didn't remember what it was like, but the ache in his heart made him uncomfortable. He let out a long shaky exhale. His eyes were damp when it was Ester's turn. Ester trembled in his arms when she hugged him. "I love you, too," she said.

A sob snuck out, and he hung on to her for a few extra moments before Elizabeth edged her way back in.

There were a few more arguments before they got Angie out. He wavered about going along, but Linda gave him a firm no and told him to stay home and rest. After they'd gone, he looked around the apartment.

"I think everything is going to be okay," he said.

~

ONCE THE TERRIBLE cousin was gone, Elizabeth led Tommy to the couch and curled up with her arms around him. Even in his current state, he smelled like she remembered, like mountains and sunshine. His face looked relaxed for the first time since she'd arrived. She ran her fingers through his hair.

"You got a haircut," she said.

"I thought you'd never notice," he said with a slow smile.

"It's been eventful since I arrived," she said.

"You drove all the way from the rez," he said as if just realizing.

"I had to get here somehow," she said. "It was awful."

He felt warm and heavy in her arms. He gazed at her through half-closed eyes. "I think I'm in love with you."

The words took her by surprise, thrown out there like that, freely given. She lowered her lips to brush over his. "But you're not sure?"

"I've never been in love with anyone before."

He was quiet for a long time, his head tilted back, exhausted and relieved like he'd been rescued in the wilderness after being lost for days. "Thanks for coming. I thought it might be too late."

"I couldn't stop thinking about you," she said.

"I never should have left like that. I regret it every minute." His breath was choppy with emotion.

"It was confusing for everyone. I wasn't prepared to see George and didn't know what to say. He's—"

"I don't want to talk about that guy," Tommy said.

"Me either," Elizabeth said. She adjusted her body again. She felt like she couldn't get close enough.

He fought the exhaustion, his head dropping down and then jerking back up to look at her.

"Why don't you sleep?" she said.

"I don't want to miss you."

"I'm not going anywhere," she said.

There was another quiet pause. Tommy's breathing evened out, his face peaceful. He forced his eyes open again.

Elizabeth said, "I mean it. I'll be here. I fell for you when you brought out your cane collection for Granny. I left the rez and drove just for you. I'm in love with you, too. I'm sticking around, if that's okay."

He settled back into her.

She said, "Everyone was right. I wasn't cut out for that casino job. I don't want to live here forever, though. Someday I want to go back to the rez."

Tommy let out a long sigh of relief. "As long as I'm with you. I want you to be my family."

"I don't know," she said. "You've got quite a team of badass women on your side."

"Yeah, I do. But everything feels right when I'm with you."

"Me, too."

His eyes closed for another minute before popping open again. "Can you do me a favor?" He told her about a bottle he'd hidden.

"I'll get rid of it."

"There might be more."

"Then we'll look for them together." She kissed the top of his head. "Rest now. I'll be here when you wake up."

EPILOGUE

*T*ommy was still fiddling with the tablet when Elizabeth came through the door and tossed her bag on the table. She gave him a full body squeeze accompanied by a kiss that he felt all the way to the bottom of his feet.

"I rushed," she said.

"You're okay. We've got a few minutes."

"Good," she said. She rummaged around in the kitchen and poured a glass of orange juice. She drank half of it in one gulp. "I needed that. How did it go?"

"Angie's doing good. She told me about two more bottles we didn't find."

"And?"

"Glug, glug, glug."

Elizabeth flashed a smile. "I had no doubts."

"She wants to move back here when she gets out of rehab."

Elizabeth's smile lost its wattage. "What did you tell her?"

"No way. I almost offered to help her find a place, but that felt like opening the door."

"She doesn't have a job," Elizabeth said. "She have a plan to earn money?"

"Not our problem," Tommy said. "She's going to talk to her dad. Fingers crossed, he will help."

"Say that again."

"Crossed fingers he will help?"

"The other part."

"Not our problem."

Elizabeth smiled again. "Those words sound amazing from you."

A tinny bell rang.

"That it?" Elizabeth asked.

"The tablet alarm. It's time."

Elizabeth grabbed her phone and joined him in front of the screen. Tommy launched the app that Ester set up for them while Elizabeth called Kora. He propped the tablet up in her lap.

"You guys on?" Elizabeth said, squinting at the screen.

There were adjustments to be made on both sides before Granny's face appeared.

Elizabeth said, "I can see you. I can't hear you. Can you see us?"

"There's a button to click," Tommy said. He tapped it and Granny's creaky voice came through the speaker.

"This damn thing do anything?"

"It works!" Elizabeth squealed. "Does it work for you guys, too? Okay. I'm hanging up. Hi, Granny!"

Elizabeth's joy washed over him. He'd never spent so much time with a person made of sunshine. Granny's expression was equally happy.

"I like this fancy thing," Granny said.

"Me too. The research center loaned us a tablet. We're learning how to write a grant, so we can try for a tribal history project to preserve stories from elders. Even elders who live far away."

Granny had a delighted look on her face. "Good for you."

"You're one of my topics," she said.

Granny faked a bored look.

"We worked with Dr. Murray at the research center and sent all the information to the Tribe. They're going to initiate a formal process to get your dress back but in the meantime we're trying to develop a process for borrowing the dress for a dance. Not sure how soon we can get that to happen."

"It's okay," Granny said. She tapped her heart. "I know it will someday. Now I want to ask that one some questions." She meant Tommy.

"Hey, Granny," he said.

"How's that other one doing with city living?"

Elizabeth's hand snuck around behind him and dug into his waistband—not sexy, just familiar.

"She's doing great. She drove during rush hour on a Friday to get home from a meeting," Tommy said.

"I knew it," Granny said.

"She's homesick. We're coming down to visit..." He looked at Elizabeth.

"Soon," she finished. "I enrolled in a museum training workshop. Turns out being Dorothy Scott's great-granddaughter looks good on your application. My class is an introduction, but if I like it, there are more in-depth classes. I'm going to finish that, and then we'll zoom down for a weekend."

"You gonna get a job?"

"Yeah, there's a casino not far from here," Elizabeth teased.

Granny rewarded them with a terrifying reproachful look.

"She's kidding," Tommy said. "Linda is in the middle of a giant thing with Crooked Rock. Once we get that going, she can do anything she wants."

"I'm going to save our ceremonial objects," Elizabeth said.

"Good," Granny said. "I'm proud of you. Visit me soon."

"I love you, Granny," Elizabeth said.

After they signed off, Elizabeth said, "What are we going to do if Linda can't get the center going?"

"That's not an option. I'm going to figure out how to do more. With Ester gone, I'll have to learn things. I wrote down a bunch of ideas to research. I'm not going to let Linda down. I'm not going to let any of you down."

He put his arms around her, content at last.

THANK YOU FOR READING

The story of the Crooked Rock Urban Indian Center will continue.

Book 4 Crooked Rock Braves is about Linda and Arnie and will wrap up the story events that began in Book 1 Heartbeat Braves.

Estimated release date: Spring 2019.

Join my mailing list to get the news when it's out. Your email will never be shared and you may unsubscribe at any time.

Reviews help readers find books. All reviews are appreciated.

ENDNOTES

Indian Country is a diverse place. Tribal communities, individuals, and organizations are different depending on their history, culture, traditions, geography and leaders—this is true of individual tribes, and is true of urban Indian communities. There is no typical organization that serves urban Indians.

I've created Crooked Rock as a place to serve my stories. My intentions are always respectful and based on my experience and observations as an Indian, and in the course of my work in Indian Country.

I've presented an over-simplified explanation for how cultural objects are returned to Tribes. You can learn more about the repatriation process from the National Museum of the American Indian. (http://nmai.si.edu/explore/collections/repatriation/)

You might be wondering about the cover. Are those native people? Unfortunately, no. The cover is made from standard stock photos. The selection of stock photos of indigenous people is skimpy, and sadly, my numerous attempts to set up a photo session of my own failed.

ACKNOWLEDGMENTS

As always, a huge thanks to my early readers Kira Walsh, Marguerite Croft, and Hannah Parker. Your time and comments are always helpful and appreciated. More thanks to editor Lorelei Logsdon (www.loreleilogsdon.com) and cover artist Holly Heisey (www.holly-heiseydesign.com). And a huge grateful hug to my ever-patient husband Bob Hughes.

ABOUT THE AUTHOR

Pamela Sanderson is a citizen of the Karuk Tribe and lives in the Pacific Northwest. She is employed as a legal assistant working on behalf of Indian tribes and tribal organizations. When she isn't working or writing, she enjoys baking, gardening and following Major League Soccer.

ALSO BY PAMELA SANDERSON

Crooked Rock Urban Indian Center

Book 1: Heartbeat Braves

Book 2: Lovesick Braves

Book 3: Sweetheart Braves

Book 4: Crooked Rock Braves (anticipated 2019)

Stand Alone:

Season of Us